THE
CONSULS
OF THE
VICARIATE

A MAGES OF BLOODMYR NOVEL : BOOK II

BY BRIAN KITTRELL

The Consuls of the Vicariate is registered with the United States ISBN Agency using the following designation:

ISBN-13: 978-0-9829495-3-5

First Edition

The work is published by:

Late Nite Books
P.O. Box 321
Brandon, MS 39042

email: publisher@latenitebooks.com

United States of America

Cover design by Brian Kittrell with some artwork/art elements (commonly known as "brushes") used from Obsidian Dawn (http://www.obsidiandawn.com). It is with great appreciation and admiration that I was allowed to use these assets for creating part of this cover. Rights for reuse granted specifically by Obsidian Dawn (or their representative) in the form of licensing terms found on DeviantArt at
http://www.redheadstock.deviantart.com/journal/12379986.

Next in the Series:

THE IMMORTALS

OF

MYRDWYER

Book III

DEDICATION

This book is dedicated to

Elizabeth S. Kittrell

my dear wife

Who always endures with hope,

❧ CONNECT WITH THE AUTHOR ☙

You can easily reach author Brian Kittrell by the various methods described below.

On Twitter:
> *@Brian_Kittrell*
> *http://www.twitter.com/Brian_Kittrell*

On Facebook:
> *http://www.facebook.com/author.BrianKittrell*

On the Web:
> *http://www.latenitebooks.com*

On YouTube (author interviews, discussions, and more):
> *http://www.youtube.com/user/LateNiteBooksDotCom*

Through eMail:
> *brian@latenitebooks.com*

Through the Mail:
> *Late Nite Books*
> *Attn: Brian Kittrell, author*
> *P.O. Box 321*
> *Brandon, MS 39042*

❧ TABLE OF CONTENTS ❧

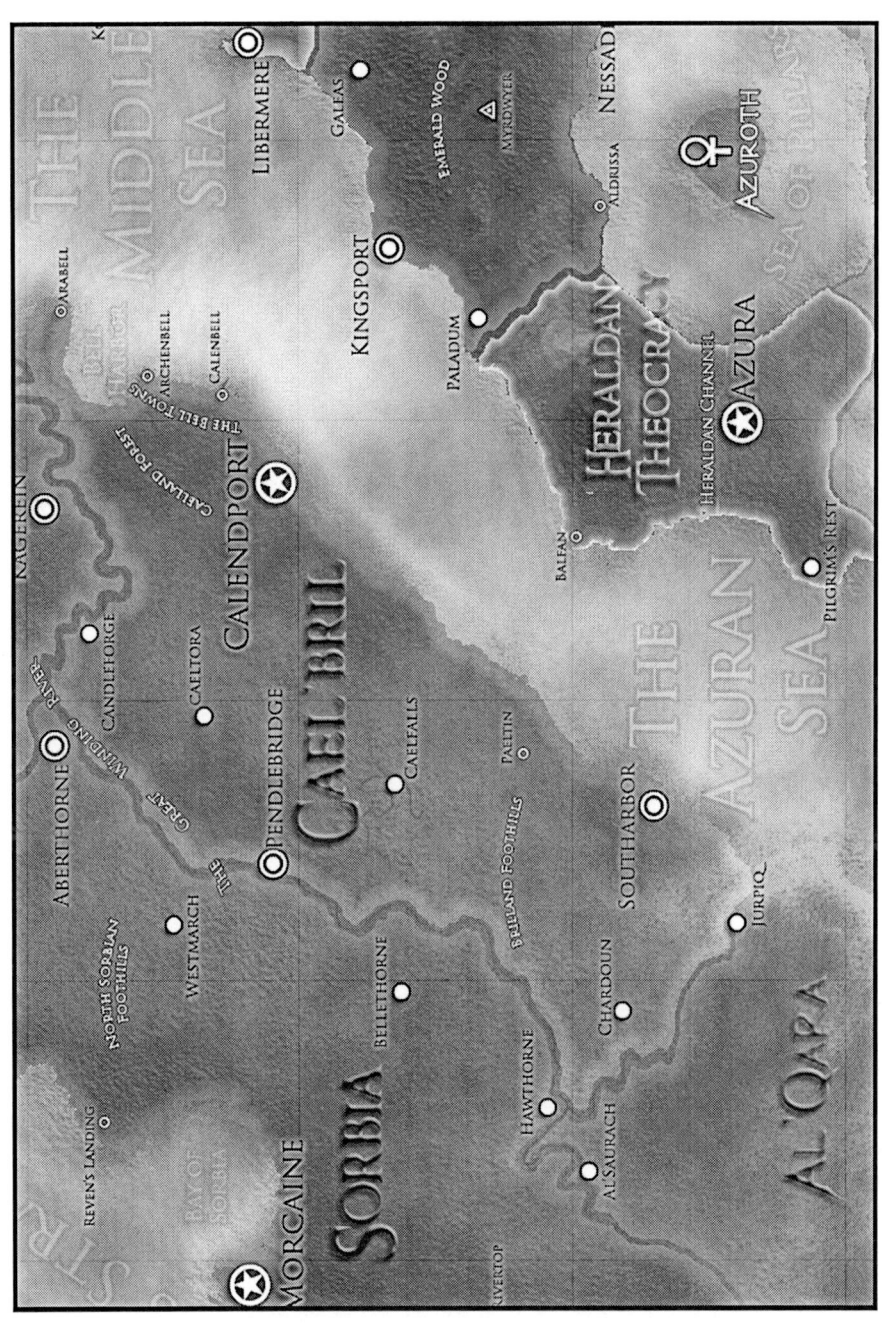

THE CONSULS OF THE VICARIATE

FIRST EDITION

THE CONSULS OF THE VICARIATE

PROLOGUE

War rages across the Bloodmyr Isles after a sneak attack by Heraldan forces against the Morcaine Mage Academy of Sorbia. Duke Hadrian Fenric, a skilled Sorbian general and the king's brother, makes preparations to invade the Heraldan Theocracy. On opposite ends of the archipelago, Falacoran and Sorbian ships blockade enemy ports, trade routes, and supply lines. Meanwhile, Grand Vicar Tristan IV, willing to do anything to bring the faithful nations under one banner, draws the reigns taut and vies for more power over the Heraldan world.

Sorbia stands alone against a coalition constituted by the Heraldan Theocracy and the kingdoms of Falacore, Lasoron, and Albiad, but one would be a fool to doubt the Sorbians' pride, strength, or resolve. Reeling like a beast against the slash of a sword, King Xavier II of Sorbia orders his armies and ships to show his enemies that his orange and black colors will fly forever over the Midlands.

The rest of the world can only wait for the outcome of the conflict, a fight that is sure to change the course of history. If the Sorbians succeed, the Heraldan church and the Holy Land would face complete destruction, but if the Heraldans win, Tristan IV would see to it that both the Sorbians and their precious sorcerers are wiped out of existence. Magic, freedom, and sacred traditions hang in the balance, and to the victor go the spoils.

ᗒ Chapter One ᗕ

Resolving to Act

A simple five-candle chandelier dangled from the ceiling. With the sunlight and the candle flames, the room was illuminated just enough for Laedron to see without straining. The Shimmering Dawn crest hung above the door, and Laedron remembered the first time he'd seen it at the Westmarch keep. *Westmarch,* he mused. *That was once the biggest city I'd ever visited, and now I find myself deep in the enemy's homeland, far away from my old oak and gentle shores.*

Marac and Brice, his old friends, sat gathered with Jurgen, Piers, and Caleb, his new allies, all of them prepared to discuss their next move. He glanced at Valyrie at his side, then he turned to Piers when he heard the scraping of wood against stone.

"Let us determine our next course of action. What, pray tell, is your plan, Sorcerer?" Piers asked.

Though the title instilled an awkward feeling, Laedron felt a measure of validation in being addressed in such a way. "We've been on the road for quite some time now. I would first like to hear of the situation at present."

"Situation?" Piers asked.

"Yes, the war and its participants. New happenings."

Piers nodded. "Falacore has naturally sided with the church, for their ties run long and deep. We've heard troubling news from our agents in Albiad and Lasoron. Their inability to join in the war is good for us, but the fact they cannot is interesting."

"Lasoron and Albiad? Remind me of where those are."

"The Lasoronians inhabit the lands northeast of here, just beyond the Sea of Pillars. The nation isn't much unlike Cael'Bril—vast grasslands and forests, gentle rivers, and the occasional fortress citadel. Albiad, on the other hand, is a hilly country with mountains throughout its interior. Both of them share the same problem, though—the Almatheren."

"The swamplands, right?"

"Indeed. Even strong and able adventurers go there never to return. The Almatheren Swamp is a place where the dead walk."

Laedron's jaw dropped. "The dead walk?"

"Surely you've heard the stories of Vrolosh and the Great War. Well, I can say to you that it didn't end with him. The taint of Necromancy remains on the swamplands and devours those who wander there."

"I don't understand. The Lasoronians and Albiadines are sending their armies into the swamps?" Laedron asked.

Piers took a swig from his cup. "No, not quite. From what our agents tell us, they have been keeping their armies in Darkwatch and Southwatch. The dead are emerging from the wetlands."

"But why?"

"It happens every once in a while, when too many fools have lost their lives in that dreadful place. Overpopulation, that sort of thing. But Lasoron and Albiad must be more than a little concerned to hold their armies back at a time like this. Even the Grand Vicar, who happens to be a Lasoronian, cannot convince them to send aid." Piers paused. "Enough of that, though. There are more pressing matters at hand. What did you have in mind for us?"

"We intend to replace Tristan IV with the priest Jurgen."

"Difficult, to say the least." Piers scratched the long scar besmirching his forehead. "Have you any thoughts as to making that a reality?"

Jurgen leaned forward and cleared his throat. "I still have connections in the consulship, and as I've paid my penance, I am allowed to return to the chamber."

"What do you mean by that?" Laedron asked. "For what did you owe penance?"

Jurgen grinned. "When the Drakars came, I questioned their legitimacy to sit on the council, for they had no proper proof of their identity. The day after I levied my concerns to the other consuls, they produced the evidence, but I had my doubts as to its integrity."

"You thought they fabricated the proof?" Marac asked.

"In a way, yes. The other consuls would hear nothing of it, and when the Drakars came to power, I was punished. They exiled me to Balfan and gave me charge of the tiny church where you found me."

Laedron stared at him with curiosity. "What I don't understand is how you came in contact with the Shimmering Dawn, much less became an ally in this war."

"The complexities of a life well-lived, I should say." Jurgen sipped from his cup, then returned it to the table. "I first met Meklan Draive during a mission trip to Sorbia. I was tasked with uplifting the people following an unfortunate series of famines throughout the region, and the Shimmering Dawn was an important Heraldan order in those days.

"We struck up a friendship of sorts right away, and even though the Dawn Knights eventually broke from the church, we continued to exchange correspondence. When I informed Meklan of my being sent away from the consulship, he was quite concerned, and my last letter to him indicated how unhappy I was with the Drakars and how I longed to be free of their persecution. It had become clear to me that I was an obstacle to Andolis and his want for destroying the Circle, but thankfully, my friendship with the Shimmering Dawn was never revealed."

"Did he respond to your last message?" Laedron asked.

"Not in a letter. He sent a young mage and some of his knights." His lips curled into a smile.

"Why did the knights break from the church?"

"The consulship has made many decrees regarding their dislike of spellcraft, and since its inception, the Shimmering Dawn has been known to be supportive of mages. It was not until recently, with the consecration of Tristan IV, that the church finally acted upon its feelings. No, this war has been in the making for quite some time, and the Drakars were the spark that ignited the flame."

"The order is more than just supportive of mages," Marac said. "We have a number within the order itself."

"Forgive me if my meaning wasn't clear." Jurgen turned to Marac. "I meant to infer that fact, but merely returning to this city seems to have brought back my propensity for guarding my tongue."

"Why would you need to be guarded about it? Isn't it common knowledge?" Laedron asked.

"In Sorbia, perhaps, but not this far from your homeland. Regardless, few would care about the distinction in these times. The theocracy is at war with your country in its entirety. I only meant to say that matters of politics require a certain measure of tact."

"Agreed." Laedron nodded. "Have you considered what you will do? Of course, you must return to the consulship, but how?"

"Simple," Jurgen said, taking another swig from his mug. "I walk in and take my seat."

"It's that easy?"

"Yes, but I do require a clerk to accompany me."

Laedron shifted in his seat. "A clerk? Why?"

"To scribe notations and aid me with my duties, of course." Jurgen gestured as if holding a quill to a piece of paper. "Consuls need the services of an assistant whilst in the chamber."

"Where are we to find such a person? We have little money left to hire one."

"Surely one of you can write."

Shaking his head, Laedron glanced at his knights. "We can write, but it's far too dangerous for us. I killed Gustav Drakar, if you have forgotten, and few left the cathedral without seeing my face. Also, any number of people could have witnessed Marac and Brice running from the guard the previous night."

"Then we would require someone the church couldn't possibly recognize." Jurgen fixed his stare on Valyrie. "Or a person they wouldn't deem to be a threat."

During the conversation, Valyrie had done little beyond staring at the table, but she glanced up when the room grew quiet, seeming to feel the eyes falling upon her. "Who? Me? No, I can't."

"Can't you?" Jurgen leaned toward her. "I've known you and your father for quite some time, and I find it hard to believe that you would be unable."

"I can't," she repeated.

"We cannot ask this of her, not at a time like this. She just lost her father," Laedron said, patting her arm. "There must be another way."

"That's not the reason." She rubbed her eyes. "I must send word to my uncle; the inn will need a caretaker. I'll have to watch over it until he can send someone."

"If you prepare a letter, one of my men will carry it to him directly," Piers offered. "I swear it."

"That still leaves the inn empty. It could be a week before my uncle receives notice, then another before he could arrive."

"If you want, my men can secure the inn and post guard until he comes."

Nodding, she crossed her arms. "I'll need to make funeral

arrangements, too. He always said he wanted to be placed in the Sea of Pillars so he could rest near Azura's heart."

Jurgen removed his spectacles and rubbed his nose. "Out of the question. The Arcanists wouldn't allow it."

"What do they have to do it with?" Laedron asked.

"They keep the secret knowledge of navigating the Sea of Pillars, but they are also responsible for the sea itself, keeping the water sacred and holy. No common man's remains may be spread there. Such an act would be likened to throwing paint on a temple."

"Perhaps we can come to a compromise." Laedron tapped his chin. "If I reduced his remains to dust, we could spread them along the banks of the sea. Would that be in keeping with his wishes, Val?"

"Azura teaches that our bodies return to the cycle after the soul has departed." She paused. "Yes, I think he would have liked that."

"You'll serve in the capacity of a clerk, then?" Jurgen asked.

"Yes, I'll do it. For the memory of my father. In exchange, you will serve him one last time by committing him to the sea with Azura's blessing."

"Of course. It's settled, then. I'll make arrangements for housing somewhere near the Vicariate. Valyrie and I shall need a separate place to reside for our task."

Laedron raised an eyebrow. "You won't stay here?"

"It wouldn't be wise to remain here. If anyone followed me, they would locate the order's secret headquarters, and our mission would be jeopardized."

"Very well," Laedron said, despite wanting to be near Valyrie. "You're right."

Valyrie stood. "I want to see my father one last time. Where is he being kept?"

"Downstairs in the private chapel." Piers gestured toward the hall. "Caleb will show you there."

Laedron watched Caleb close the door behind them. "She's lost so much."

"It is unfortunate, and if I could do anything to change the past, I would." Piers folded his hands in his lap. "All I can do now is offer to help her in any way I can."

Brice nodded. "What is this place? If you don't mind my asking."

Laedron turned to him. "We haven't heard a peep out of you until now."

"I didn't want to interrupt," he replied. "I didn't want to upset her any more than she already was."

"It's a good thing you didn't talk, then," Marac said.

Brice smirked. "Really, what is this place?"

"An abandoned church. Our order once occupied a place of honor in the city, but when the schism happened, we were cast out from our fortress," Piers explained. "To remain in the city, we needed an unassuming base of operations, and we found one in this church."

"Schism?" Brice asked.

"When the order separated itself from the church, the situation degraded quickly, and the militia confronted us openly in the streets. That's where I got this scar." Piers pointed at his face.

"We took what money we had and bought this building under an alias."

Caleb returned, and Laedron glanced his way before looking at Piers again. "No one knows you're here?"

"No one outside the order, for our own safety. If the church were to find out, especially now, they would imprison us—or worse. As a result, we've become experts at keeping ourselves hidden over the years."

"You've never been tempted to leave?" Laedron took a drink from a tray Caleb offered. "I would hate having to hide all the time."

"It's crossed our minds, especially when the war began. We came to a decision to remain here, though. What better place to be than under the enemy's nose?" Piers let out a chuckle. "Any work we do for the order here is more important than any we could do elsewhere."

Laedron nodded. "I can't argue with you there."

Piers put his elbows on the table. "So, have you thought about what you will do while Jurgen is away?"

"Away? It's not as if he's going to some distant city."

"Yes, but his task could take some time. In the meantime, we could accomplish a great deal with a sorcerer's aid."

"What sort of thing did you have in mind?"

Smiling, Piers leaned back in his chair. "Tomorrow, after Valyrie's father is laid to rest. We'll talk then."

"All right." Laedron stood. "I'm going to check on her and perform the transformation."

"Caleb, will you see our new friend to the chapel?" Piers

gestured toward the door and received a nod from Caleb.

Laedron made a quick stop by his room to get the appropriate spellbook, then Caleb led him to the bowels of the church. When they stopped at the chapel door, Laedron said, "Sorry about that earlier."

Opening the door, Caleb remained silent, then closed it when Laedron passed through. *I feel bad for punching him, but he really deserved it*, he mused. *Perhaps he'll find a way to forgive me someday.*

Valyrie stood beside an oaken crate. Laedron could only see her back, but he heard her quiet whimpering. The sound of her crying slammed him into a wall of sorrow, but he could do nothing to ease her suffering beyond handling the transformation and the ceremony with care and respect.

"I never knew it would be like this." She dragged her sleeve across her nose. "The few times I thought about losing him, I assumed we'd have plenty of time to resolve our differences."

Taking a deep breath, Laedron stepped closer. "Sometimes things don't turn out the way we want. Regardless of how I may feel, the Fates have never asked me about my wishes."

When she turned around, he could see the pain in her eyes, the whites blistered red from her tears and anguish. Instinctively, he averted his eyes, both to ease his own suffering and so she wouldn't feel as though he were gawking at her pain. The recollection of Ismerelda's death rushed through his mind, the images flashing like a collage hastily painted in blood.

"You seem as if you feel sadness at my father's passing, but you never knew him."

"I only sympathize with you," he replied. "Seeing you now

takes me back to the death of my teacher and how I felt, though it seems long ago."

She turned to the improvised coffin. "Yet you've come to this city despite the dangers."

"I carried on in her memory." He joined her next to the crate. "At first, I sought vengeance against the one who killed her, but now, I see we must go beyond that. To end the war and prevent countless others from dying over a lie, that is a cause worth fighting for."

She nodded. "My father would've liked you, I think."

"Why?"

"It's not because he would have agreed with you; that's for sure. No, I think he might have enjoyed the debate."

"He would've disagreed with what I've said?"

Looking at her father's face, she formed a smile beneath her tears. "I don't think so, but he wouldn't have let you know that. He was the type to argue the unpopular end of any disagreement."

"What about you?" He met her gaze when she turned. "Do you think we're doing the right thing?"

"Yes." She took a deep breath and stared into the coffin. "Goodnight, Father. See you in the morning." She held her hair back, leaned over, and kissed Pembry's forehead.

"Take care of him," she said, turning and walking to the door. "You know, it doesn't seem real. I keep telling myself that he'll come back, that he'll come through the door and give me a big hug, but he won't—he can't. Take care of my da, Lae."

Once Valyrie was gone, Laedron gazed into the wooden box and sighed. *How many more innocents will lie dead by the time we're done? Far too many.* He walked to the dilapidated stone altar, placed his tome upon it, and flipped through the pages. Thankfully, he'd become so skilled at reading Zyvdredi texts that he no longer needed the book Mathias had given him. Though he still had trouble with a few of the less common words, he could derive their meanings without the need of a manual.

He held his scepter above the crate and chanted slowly. Black wisps dripped from the ruby at the tip of the rod down to Pembry's body. The wisps danced and coiled freely through the air like ink dropped into a pool of water. He held it until only ashes remained. He gathered Pembry's ashes into a bronze urn, then moved the crate to the floor. He carefully placed the urn at the center of the stone slab where the coffin had been and took his spell book from the altar. After one last glance at the urn, he returned upstairs.

When he reached the hallway, he noticed the door to Valyrie's room was closed, and he prayed silently for the Creator to watch over her and guide her during her time of mourning. Remembering how he felt when Ismerelda had been killed, he decided to leave Valyrie be. He could only imagine how it must've felt to see her father killed before her very eyes—a feeling which likely would not have been matched even if they had been tortured by Piers and his men.

"Might I have a word?" Brice asked, snapping Laedron out of his thoughts.

Brice led Laedron into his room, then closed the door behind them. "I wanted to ask if you would mind if I trained with Caleb?"

Laedron raised an eyebrow. "Training?"

"Well, I've been thinking about things. I'm not as big as Marac, and I'm not as smart as you—"

"Don't put yourself down."

Brice grinned. "I just want to make the most of my abilities, you see? I helped my parents in the loom, and I've always been handy with a needle. Such work takes nimbleness and precision."

"So… Caleb is a tailor?"

"No, not at all." Brice sighed, seeming frustrated. "I saw him practicing with locks a little while ago, and he showed me some of the basics. I was thinking maybe I could learn from him. Maybe that would be a useful skill to have."

Laedron smiled. "Useful indeed. Very well, but don't forget to practice your swordsmanship, too. We must always be ready for a fight."

Opening the door, Brice bobbed his head. "Thanks."

"Get some rest," Laedron said on his way through the door. "Tomorrow will come sooner than we expect."

Joining Marac in the common room, Laedron took a seat at the table, put down his spell book, and sipped from the cup he had been given earlier. "How do you feel about all this?"

Marac looked up from sharpening his sword. "Dangerous, but isn't everything we do?"

"Perhaps." The glints of candlelight on the blade drew Laedron's eye. "It would seem we will be splitting up for a while. Jurgen and Valyrie, Brice and Caleb, and you and me."

"Brice and who?" Marac was busy sharpening again.

"Piers's man, the one I punched."

"Ah, what's the thimble doing with him?"

Laedron took another sip. "Learning of lock picking."

"At least he'll be making himself useful." Marac held up the sword and inspected the edge. "About time."

"Why are you so hard on him?"

"He's soft." Marac put the weapon on the table and took a swig from a cup. "He hasn't had a hard day's work in his entire life, and it shows."

"Neither have I. Does it show in me, too?"

"It's different with you, Lae. Your ma taught you to be strong and persevere, but Brice's parents had resolved to see him working a loom for the rest of his days."

"No matter. It might take more time, but I'm confident he'll come around."

"That makes one of us," Marac said. "I'm not so convinced."

"Give him time." Laedron stood, grabbed his spell book, and patted Marac on the shoulder. "Apparently, we have plenty of it."

"Lae?" Marac called out before Laedron entered the hall.

"Yes?"

"The wand and the scepter, what purpose do they serve?" Marac glanced at his sword. "Simply tools of the trade?"

"Yes," Laedron said, then paused to consider a more thorough explanation. "To manifest our spells, we require three things—concentration, a focus, and an incantation. The wand, with its intricate carvings, sturdy weight, and rough finish, gives something real to focus upon."

"And priests? They use staffs?"

"Or rings, like Jurgen's." Laedron grinned. He was glad Marac was showing interest in his craft. "Goodnight, my friend."

After entering his room and closing the door, Laedron put the scepter on the nightstand, then placed the tome in his pack. He saw his practice wand poking through the flap on the side. As he traced the intricate carvings running deep along the shaft, he remembered how, during his training, he couldn't reproduce an illusion of his wand. Then, he recalled the powerful image he had conjured from his memories, his happy days with Marac and his sister Laren by the old oak in Reven's Landing. Before going to bed, Laedron knelt and appealed to the Creator for Ismerelda's soul to arrive safely in the heavens.

❧ Chapter Two ❧

A Day of Remembrance

The morning light drove away his nightmares, and Laedron opened his eyes to sunlight dimmed by the foggy stained glass in the narrow window of his room. The hazy yellow image suggested the figure of a holy man of some kind, probably a Heraldan saint whom he neither recognized, nor deemed important. *To think, an entire world littered with such icons. Well, I suppose there are worse ways to waste glass. At least it's pretty to look at.* He snatched the scepter from the table, then headed to the common room.

Caleb was busy stirring a cauldron suspended from an iron hook in the fireplace. The scent of a fine stew drifted into Laedron's nostrils, exciting his empty belly. He wouldn't have thought of eating anything the day before; his near miss upon the executioner's table and his sympathy for Valyrie's situation had been enough to ward off any hunger pangs. Sitting at the table, he eyed the clean bowl in front of his chair and waited as patiently as he could.

"Morning," Jurgen said.

Laedron noticed Jurgen wore his ceremonial robes. "Morning. Do you think you're a bit overdressed?"

"The dead deserve utmost respect, regardless of their station." Jurgen poured some wine into his cup. "Sleep well?"

"Everything was fine until I woke up."

"I know the feeling." Jurgen watched Caleb ladle some stew into his bowl. "Thank you."

"Do you have any preparations to make for the ceremony?"

"A few, but it's well in hand." Jurgen carefully sipped from his spoon. "We'll make it to the seaside before noon, I would imagine."

"Is it so far?" Laedron started on his stew as soon as it landed in the bowl.

"A few miles from the city. Not to worry, though. I know a private place."

Laedron heard a door close down the hall, then Valyrie joined them and took a seat. No sooner than she had picked a chair, Brice wiped his mouth and followed Caleb out of the room.

"Where's he going?" Marac asked.

Jurgen shrugged. "They mentioned something about practicing, but they went quiet when they noticed me."

"Ah, well, I hope the little fool doesn't get himself in any trouble." Marac crossed his arms. "I suppose we'll end up having to rescue him."

"I seem to remember rescuing *you*, Marac Reven." Laedron paused as Marac's head drooped with guilt. "And I'd do it again.

Without reservation."

Marac returned Laedron's smile. "Point taken. Sorry."

Having eaten the large bits with the spoon, Laedron lifted the bowl and drank the broth, then wiped his mouth with a scrap of linen. He glanced at Valyrie and felt some guilt for eating so freely while she had barely touched her meal. "Are you feeling well?"

Of course she's not, fool. She just lost her father. Unable to withdraw the question, he waited for her to respond.

"As well as I can, I suppose." Her eyes remained locked on the chunks of meat floating along in the bowl.

"Jurgen said we can have the ceremony around noon. Would that be acceptable?"

She dipped her head. "When do we leave?"

"Not long now." Jurgen brushed breadcrumbs from his otherwise pristine robes. "In fact, let us be on our way. You'd better cowl yourself, Sorcerer."

"I'll get my things," Valyrie said, standing.

"All right." Laedron stood. "I'll get the urn, too."

"No need." Jurgen pointed at a dimly lit corner of the room, and Laedron saw the urn sitting on a table. "I've already done that."

Jurgen opened the door. Laedron followed, but turned to Marac before leaving. "Aren't you coming?"

"No," Marac said, leaning forward. "I leave it to you, friend."

Laedron nodded. "We'll be back soon."

Valyrie wore a black shawl, and Laedron complimented its quality before closing the door behind them. Pulling the hood over his head, he looked at the building which, up to that point, he had never seen from the outside. The structure had every feature of an aged, abandoned church he could imagine. The otherwise plain and dilapidated exterior set off the dirty stained glass windows running the length of each wall and the base of the dome. *Gray and tan stones to match the silver and gold themes? Perhaps.*

Following Jurgen, he caught himself before stumbling on the platform holding a fountain resembling a dull golden cup. *Looks like I've found the golden chalice, Meklan. Almost bathed in it, too.*

Jurgen led them through the shady parts of town, apparently unconcerned with or unafraid of the sordid persons walking the lanes. *They would never interfere with a priest, right?* Laedron thought, eying them. *Perhaps clergymen are off limits in this place.* For once, he was thankful to be in the company of a holy man.

Laedron saw—and in some cases, smelled—people from all walks of life and nations of origin, but most were clearly Heraldan or of some Midlander descent. He reckoned that the xenophobia and religious intolerance of the population caused the lack of foreigners. *It's a good thing I'm a Midlander. Easier to fit in if I look similar to the locals.*

The priest seemed to find his way to the eastern road with ease, as if he'd walked the route a hundred times before, and Laedron followed him along the dusty road and into the hilly landscape beyond. Only an odd tree graced the roadside, each obviously planted by the inhabitants of that country; the trees towered above the highway in a straight line into the distance, and each stood a precise increment away from the cobblestones. With the sun peaking in the sky, Jurgen stepped off the roadway, through the first meadow of tall grass Laedron had seen, and down an embankment. Laedron helped Valyrie descend the steep hill to the waterside.

On the sandy banks of the Sea of Pillars, a lacquered bench carved entirely from a single piece of wood sat beneath a drooping willow tree, its long branches swaying with the breeze. That breeze, thick with saltwater, gave Laedron some relief from the heat of the day, and he removed his hood, deciding that no one would see his face in that secluded nook of the shore. They stood isolated from the rest of the world with only the sound of the waves washing onto the banks and the occasional chirping of the indigenous birds to remind him of the larger world outside the alcove.

Jurgen stared across the sea into the distance, then turned toward Valyrie. He raised the urn above his head. "This gift we return to Azura and the Creator in the heavens. This man, Arthur Pembry, we commit to your sea."

Arthur. The mere mention of her father's name drove the true feeling of loss through his heart. The emotion was not unlike the one he felt the times anyone had said *Wardrick* in his presence. With his head still tilted downward, he shifted his eyes to Valyrie. A sparkling tear found its way down her face.

Jurgen spoke some words in Heraldict, then paused and smiled benevolently. "To live in the hearts of those we leave behind is not to die. To live in the grace of Azura is to truly live forever." He opened the lid of the bronze vessel, then from his robes, produced an engraved silver scattering spade. Standing with his feet and robes in the surf, he tossed the scoops of ashes into the sea.

"Thank you, Jurgen," Valyrie said. "My father would have liked that."

"An honor." He patted her on the shoulder, then turned to Laedron. "I'll wait for you by the road."

Watching Jurgen climb the embankment, Laedron rubbed his hands together, trying to find the right words to say.

She gazed sorrowfully at him. "You don't believe in any of this, do you?"

He sighed. "Some of it."

"What do you mean?"

"Sorcerers, for the most part, believe in the Creator. We believe in the heavens and the hells, but not Azura—at least not in the same way the Heraldans do." He walked to her side.

"For the most part?"

"Some don't believe in any of it, and there are others who accept Syril as their master."

"Syril?"

Laedron could feel her hate of the dark god seething through her words. "Yes. Those hungry for power and the ultimate knowledge of magic tend to, but I've never heard of anyone having their prayers answered by him. Except Vrolosh, perhaps."

"And what are your desires, Mage?" She turned to face him. "You speak of that supreme power as if you wouldn't mind its taste."

He grinned. "Many paths lead to the heights of spectacular magic. Devoting oneself to Syril is but one, and to worship him is quite an undesirable activity to me."

"Then how?"

"When my teacher was killed, I took possession of her spell books. Everything I need to complete my learning is in those books." He drew the scepter from his boot, and her eyes immediately locked onto the large ruby. "I find magic easier by use of her rod, too."

"I've never seen a ruby that big before, not even on the finger of a Grand Vicar."

"Or the hand of a king, I'd say." Laedron hid the scepter again. "Not that I've ever encountered a king."

"You two coming?" Jurgen asked, poking his head through the limbs and bushes. "We wouldn't want to be on the roads after dark."

Laedron offered his arm to Valyrie, and she slipped her hand around his elbow, so he could help her up the incline. Once they reached the road, Jurgen led them west, but he walked slower than he had on the trip there. Not wanting to be recognized by any passersby, Laedron replaced the hood to obscure his face.

Laedron moved to his side. "Feeling all right?"

"Yes," Jurgen replied in a haggard voice. "I was a few years younger the last time I walked this road."

Laedron reached for the rod. "Want me to—"

"No, that will be quite all right, young man. No need to take any chances. You never know who might be watching."

"Out here?" Laedron glanced at the trees and open fields around them.

"Especially out here, my boy. Never think you're completely alone in this country lest you make the same mistakes I did."

"What *did* you do, exactly? To get banished the way you were,

I mean?"

Jurgen stepped to the side of the road and stopped beneath a shade tree. He eyed the trees before looking at Laedron. "Oh, it doesn't matter now. Old news."

"I'd like to know."

"The Drakars were brought to the consulship, and we were told they were missionaries who had recently come from Darkwatch."

"Darkwatch?"

"A small village far to the east of here. It lies on the eastern coast of Lasoron, and it remains a bastion against the defilers of the Almatheren Swamp."

"What happened then?"

"Well, I didn't believe them, and I certainly didn't think we should be raising unknowns to the status of a consul, regardless of their deeds. I wasn't alone." Jurgen leaned against the tree. "We tried to block the exemplification, but we failed."

"And when Andolis became Grand Vicar, he expelled you from the consulship?"

"Precisely. They sent me to live in Balfan and run the church there, and I had precise instructions not to meddle in affairs above my head any longer."

Laedron grinned. "You don't follow instructions very well, do you?"

"No, not very well at all," Jurgen said, smiling.

"Will it be dangerous for us?" Valyrie asked.

"Don't you worry, my dear." Jurgen patted her arm. "If there's any danger, I'll be their target. Not you."

26

"And you're willing to take such risks?"

"I'm an old man. I've lived a full life, and I've done nothing but serve Azura the best I could. I have nothing to fear in this life or the next."

"You're a brave man." Valyrie gave Jurgen a hug. "I wish I were as brave as you."

"Nonsense. Your father was courageous. I'm just an old fool trying to put right what once was wrongly done."

"Either way, I respect what you're doing," she said, pulling away from him. "If what Lae says is true, the Drakars must be stopped."

"We shall give it our best efforts. For now, we have a long way to go, and we've lingered here long enough." He returned to the highway, and Laedron and Valyrie followed.

* * *

Upon entering the Shimmering Dawn's stronghold, Laedron wanted nothing more than to find a tub and soak in some cool water. He passed up the dining hall despite his hunger, entered the bathroom, and secured the door behind him. While cranking the handle on the water pump, he detected the faint odor of copper. *Old pipes. I'm likely the first one to use the bath in weeks.* An unused pot of soap confirmed his suspicion.

He cleaned his clothes with a simple spell, then plunged into the waiting water. Although he could clean himself with magic alone, he enjoyed relaxing in a bath. Not wanting to tarry in the tub the rest of the afternoon, Laedron bathed quickly, dressed, and joined Jurgen and Valyrie at the dining table.

Piers entered from the hallway coming from the private gardens, looked around the room, and sighed. "Looks like it's going to be soup today."

"Why do you say it like that?" Laedron asked.

Piers stirred the cauldron hanging in the fireplace. "Caleb and your friend still haven't returned."

"What were they doing?" The thought of having to save Brice and Caleb from some unnamed danger gave him an uneasy feeling. Such a rescue would be far more difficult in the heart of the Heraldan church.

"You know... the usual."

"No, I don't know. Perhaps you could explain."

"Since your arrival, we've made plans to step up our operations, so to speak. They have gone to gather information from any reliable sources."

"And who are these sources?" Laedron asked.

"One of the consuls this time."

Jurgen raised an eyebrow. "You have a consul working with us?"

Piers smiled. "No, but we can acquire secrets all the same."

☙ Chapter Three ❧

Seeking Out Secrets

B rice heard the door close down the hall. "They're headed to the coast."

"Good." Caleb produced a thin bit of metal from a pouch on his belt. "We can get started. Ever handled a pick before?"

"No, but I was pretty good with a needle and thread back home."

Caleb rolled his eyes. "Picking a lock's a bit different from sewing. Pay close attention." He took a lock in his hand, and Brice leaned over to see.

"Most Heraldan locks have keys that look like this." Caleb held up a key in his other hand. "You turn this end, the bow, and insert the shank into the lock. The other end is called the bit, and the bit is what unlocks the mechanism."

Brice noted the grooves of varying lengths cut into the bit. "Why is it shaped like that?"

"Inside the basic warded lock, you have blocks in place. If the key isn't cut properly, you can't turn it." Caleb ran his fingernail through one of the slots. "You see?"

"I think so." Brice stroked his chin. "How do you open the lock if you don't have the key?"

"We'll get to that." Caleb waved his hand. "Do you understand how the key works?"

"Yeah, if the key doesn't get blocked, the levers turn and the lock opens."

"Good. Now, I'll show you how to feel out a lock." Caleb held up the pick, then slipped it into the lock. He closed his eyes while he slowly manipulated the pick with his fingertips. "All right. You try."

"What am I trying to do?"

"Put that end in there and feel around." Caleb pointed at the curved end. "You're a blind man feeling your way around in the world. Tell me what you *see*."

Brice crouched next to the lock and slid the pick inside. "I don't see why we can't just break it off. I mean, most locks aren't strong enough to resist an axe."

"That's all well and good, my simple friend, but you might not want people knowing their locks have been bypassed." Caleb smiled. "After all, we're trying to be discreet. What do you see in the lock?"

Brice closed his eyes, trying to envision the blocks. "I feel a circle at the back. Next to that, there's a short block." He steadied his hand and moved the tip of the pick further along.

"Anything else?"

"Yes," he said, tilting his head. "Two more blocks. The middle one is the longest."

"Any levers in the back?"

"Is that what you call those things sliding back and forth?"

"Yes. Good. Withdraw the pick."

Brice leaned back and looked up at Caleb. "So, what do I do now?"

"That depends. How many blocks did you find?"

"Three."

Caleb handed Brice a few pieces of flat metal, each similar to the probe. "Take these and lift the levers, those 'sliding things' you found in the back."

"Can't I use this?" He held up the probe.

"No, you don't use a probe for this. Notice the grooves?" Caleb ran his finger along the end of the pick. "They're designed to help you keep hold of the levers once inside the lock."

Brice nodded, then took the picks and inserted one. After wiggling it in the lock for a while, he heard a faint click.

Caleb apparently heard it also because he said, "Good, now the next."

Though he became frustrated throughout the process, Brice eventually picked each lever until the lock sprang open. He smiled proudly after the last.

"Don't be too proud of yourself just yet." Caleb folded his

arms. "These are the simplest of locks. They're common, but you'll have a hard time getting into everything."

"Well, give me something harder to practice on," Brice said, wiping the sweat from his forehead.

Caleb went to a wooden crate on the far side of the room and returned with a padlock. Brice was amazed at the ornate carvings and gold and silver inlays across the exterior of the padlock. He had never seen another lock to match its quality or beauty.

"I met my match in this lock. It took weeks for me to pick this one." Caleb handed it to him. "Here's the key, too."

"Weeks?" Brice eyed the lock, then held the key to a nearby candle. Slots and grooves of varying lengths were cut into every side of the key except the end attached to the shank. A series of holes had been drilled through it, as well. "What're the holes for?"

"Curved spikes within the lock. They make it even harder to get around inside the lock and pick it." Caleb smiled. "A masterpiece, that lock."

"Where'd you get it?" Brice couldn't keep his eyes off it.

"Some merchants from Qal'Phamet were selling sandalwood strongboxes and other things a few years back. You can keep that one."

"Keep it? How much?" Brice asked as if he had any money to offer.

"No charge. The merchants sold it cheap."

"Thanks."

"Don't thank me so fast." Caleb waggled his finger. "I've picked it once, but I never want to try again. You'll be ready to toss it into the sea by the time you're done."

"Thanks anyway, then. It'll help me learn."

"Oh, yes. It'll learn you, that's for sure." Caleb grinned. "Ready to do something more fun?"

"What do you have in mind?"

"Like Piers said, our purpose here is to gather information about the church—information we can use against them. He didn't tell you how we do that, though."

"Well? How?"

"This time, it's a daytime burglary, and I'll need some help in case things get tight. You up for it?"

Brice stared at his shoes. *Burglary? I wonder how upset the others will be with me.* "We have to break into someone's house?"

"What, are you afraid?"

"No, not afraid. How can we justify that?"

"Asks the one who came from an assassination mission against a priest? A *successful* one, I might add."

It looks like Piers has been spreading our business around. "Good point, I suppose."

Caleb patted him on the shoulder. "It's simple. I've done it a hundred times before. You wanted to make yourself useful, didn't you?"

"All right, fine."

With a nod, Caleb led him out of the chapel and into the street. "It's this way. In the Ancient Quarter."

"Ancient Quarter?" Brice asked.

"That's the middle of town. The newer portions of the city grew up around the ancient city of Uxidia, so that's what we call it."

Brice swallowed hardy. "What's there now?"

Caleb whispered, "The Vicariate, for one. Don't worry, though; we're not breaking into the Grand Vicar's house."

They turned a corner onto a wide boulevard which wound its way toward a high spot surrounded by walls. Behind the wall stood a huge golden dome, and at the peak of the dome gleamed the silver symbol of Azura—five hollow, elongated diamonds joined at one end and pointing outward like the petals of a flower. *Azura's Star.* Brice vividly recalled the meaning of the empty petals from his early childhood in the Heraldan church—a reminder to the faithful that Azura would return someday. To the right of the gates, a building constructed of vibrant red bricks seemed newer than the wall beyond, but Brice didn't ask about it; more serious affairs clouded his otherwise curious heart.

Please forgive me, Brice prayed silently as they passed through the portcullis. *I try to do only what is right.* He followed Caleb to a luxurious three-story home, then through an alley to the rear of the residence. Even the back of the house was well-maintained, and he figured it must belong to some snobby aristocrat. *I hope this is worth the trouble.*

Caleb glanced around before pulling out his picks. "Cough if you hear or see someone coming."

Unaccustomed to lookout duties, Brice did the best he could to eye the people walking the streets. He had no way of knowing if they were watching him back or if any of them knew what Caleb and he were doing at the end of the street, but he nonetheless tried his best not to appear suspicious.

Turning the knob and opening the door, Caleb pulled him

inside the house. Upon seeing the beautiful tapestries and lavish furnishings, Brice felt his heart rate pick up, and his palms became sweaty. *We'll surely be killed if we're caught in here.*

Caleb wasted no time moving across the tiled floor until he turned, apparently noticing Brice frozen in his tracks. Hesitantly, Brice joined Caleb near the stairs.

"Common thieves might waste their time picking silver from the cabinets," Caleb whispered, "but we'll be heading up to the sleeping quarters, where they'd keep their intimate belongings."

Brice matched Caleb's slow pace on the ascent to the second floor, each step laboriously made on the creaking wooden frame. *What sort of 'intimate belongings' are we here to find?* Brice wondered. *To risk our necks in such a fashion over gems or coin would be foolhardy. Information, he said. But what?*

Caleb crested the landing and slid along the wall like an assassin happening upon a sleeping victim. Brice matched his movements, creeping beneath the windowsills and being cautious not to bump into anything hanging on the wall. Caleb peeked around the first door, then closed it and moved on without saying a word. Looking into the second, he paused before slipping inside, and Brice followed.

Closing the door once he had passed through, Brice surveyed the room. A huge wardrobe dominated one side, and an equally large desk with a matching chair occupied the other. Beyond two glass doors lay a balcony, and bookcases filled with tomes and expensive keepsakes lined the rest of the available wall space. Caleb rushed to the desk, snatched up a handful of scrolls, and glanced through each one.

"I thought we were supposed to—"

"Don't worry. I'll put them back the way I found them," Caleb said, never taking his eyes off the parchment.

Brice glanced over the books on the nearest shelf, whispering the titles under his breath. *"The Tenet of Faith, The Miracles of Our Lady, The Heraldan Church: Foundation to Dominance."* He paused. "This is a priest's house?"

"Not just any priest." Caleb glanced over at him, then returned to the scroll. "If you pull out any of those books, remember to replace them the way you found them."

He struggled to keep his voice from cracking. "Whose house is this, Caleb?"

"Forane's."

Brice hesitated. He had trouble placing the name, but before he could ask, he remembered the conversation between Jurgen and Velan, the innkeeper in Pilgrim's Rest. *The Vicar Forane. She had been at the cathedral in Pilgrim's Rest to see the Southern Lights.* "But—"

"This one, yes!"

"What is it?" Brice fought the trembling in his hands, but it was no use.

"Listen to this." Caleb held a parchment near the window and read aloud.

Yes, madam, I am aware of your situation, and I thank you for your services thus far. You have made contact with a weak one in their ranks, and now is the time to increase his pay. Instruct him to keep a lookout for the priest Jurgen and tell him you will pay tenfold if he would see fit to do away with that problem. —D

Brice gazed at Caleb. "They hired an assassin for Jurgen?"

"Not just any assassin. Don't you see?"

"See what?"

"The assassin was Lester."

Brice was filled with surprise. "They had a spy in the Dawn Knights?"

"We have to go. We have to warn—" Caleb pressed his ear against the door. "Hide."

"Hide?" Brice whispered. "Hide where?"

Licking his lips, Caleb pointed at the balcony door. "We'll jump."

Brice stopped him when he opened the door. "We can't jump out there. It's twenty feet or better to the ground. We'll be seen, too." He searched for another option. "There, the wardrobe. Get in."

Brice waited for Caleb to get all the way to the back. Feeling a draft, he glimpsed the still-open balcony door, but he jumped into the wardrobe upon hearing footsteps coming from the hall. He closed the armoire and sat next to Caleb only moments before he heard the study door burst open. Silently, they arranged the clothes hanging above to hide them in case anyone opened the wardrobe.

"Collette!" a voice shouted, muffled by the sturdy oaken construction of the bureau, but still discernible. "Left my balcony door open again, fool girl!"

"Sorry, madam," another voice replied. "I'll—"

"No, I'll do it." The angry woman had neared the wardrobe, and Brice tensed at her shouting. *She's going to find us; I just know she is. And when she does, poof—a pile of ash or worse.*

"Letters scattered. Do you not remember me telling you the wind blows in from this side and tosses around all of my correspondence?"

"Yes, madam. Sorry."

A silence followed the girl's apology, then Brice heard a few footsteps going away.

When the steps paused, the woman shouted, "Have you been reading these letters, girl?"

"No, madam, I swear—" Even through the dense wood Brice heard the slap and the crying that followed.

The front of the bureau flew open, and he caught sight of a woman's face. *We're done for.* Hanging her silver and gold robe on the rod, the woman huffed and puffed with anger, then turned back to her maid. "Don't lie to me. If it weren't so difficult to find help these days, I'd have done away with you long ago." She slammed the wardrobe door closed.

The girl spoke with a sick desperation. "No, please. I knocked them over, madam. I didn't read the letters, though. I was cleaning. I forgot to pick them up when you called for me."

Brice stared at his shoes with pity in his heart. *I can only imagine the life this girl has, knowing she did no wrong, but admitting it nonetheless—only to keep from getting walloped again.*

"So long as you didn't read them," the older woman said, her voice no longer as angry. "Very well, I forgive you... this time. Prepare us some supper, and I'll join you in a while."

"Yes, madam."

Brice heard the door close, then the sliding of wood against the stone floor. The sound of cloth rubbing against leather followed, and he assumed Vicar Forane was seated at her desk. The scratching of a quill against parchment confirmed his assumption.

* * *

With no way to measure time, Brice didn't know how long it had been since Vicar Forane started writing, but he was thankful when he heard the chair slide against the floor and the hallway door open. Caleb, who had been perfectly still the entire time, let out a quiet groan as he pulled a shoe from behind his back.

Brice rose to his feet, but remained crouched since the ceiling was low.

"What are you doing?" Caleb whispered, tugging at Brice's pant leg. "It isn't safe to leave yet."

Turning back, Brice said, "I want to see what she wrote."

"No, get back in."

Ignoring Caleb's plea, Brice emerged from the dresser. Only a few steps brought him to the desk, and he leaned over to read.

My Lord,

To answer your question, no. None of the priests in Balfan know Jurgen's whereabouts, but he was seen in Pilgrim's Rest briefly in the company of some monks. We can only assume that he fled when the cathedral was attacked, but he hasn't yet resurfaced. I cannot agree more that having sorcerers in our country is a problem, and I work daily to discover their whereabouts.

My contact is overdue in returning my latest reply, but I have faith that he will accomplish the task I've assigned by your request. As always, you are correct when you say we must keep Jurgen from the consulship. Nothing is of greater importance to our goal.

As we agreed, I plan to meet our friend tomorrow night by the bell tower, and I shall demand to know why he has not answered my correspondence. If he does not attend, we may have to seek other ways to find and eliminate the pretender.

Your Servant, F.

The words shocked and surprised Brice so that he didn't notice the door creak open until it was too late. He gasped and turned to run, then saw the face of a girl looking back at him, a fresh bruise marring one side of her otherwise pretty features. He wanted to run, to flee, to jump out the window, but he stood and stared, and the girl made not a sound. Brice couldn't tell if she was too frightened to scream, or if she held her tongue so as not to alert her mistress. With apparent reluctance, the girl finally stepped through the door and closed it behind her.

"I suppose you mean to do my mistress harm," she half-whispered. "I knew the day would come, but I never thought it would be so soon."

"No, miss."

"No?"

"We mean her no harm, not this day."

"Then you spy upon her. Will you undo her?"

If only it were that simple. Brice sighed. "Probably. Eventually, we hope. Why do you remain quiet with burglars in your house?"

"The house isn't mine. My only purpose here is to make sure it stays clean and its residents well-fed." The girl touched the bruise and winced. "Some days are better than others."

"If you won't turn us in, will you help us leave?"

She nodded. "This way."

Before following her into the hall, Brice fetched Caleb from the wardrobe. "I'm going now if you'd care to join me."

"Two of you?" the girl asked. "Follow me." They followed her to the stairs, where she whispered, "The dining room is below the stairs."

"Here." Caleb crouched beside her, keeping his voice low. "Climb onto my back."

"What?"

"A single set of footsteps. Once I'm down, you'll come back for Brice to do the same."

Brice grinned widely. "Brilliant."

"No time to waste." Caleb pointed over his shoulder, and the girl climbed onto his back. Once at the bottom, she slid to the floor, whispered to him, and pointed down the hall. Caleb disappeared around the corner, and the girl returned to the top of the stairs. Holding her on his back, Brice made the trek down the steps.

"What are you doing, girl?" Vicar Forane's voice echoed through the house, and Brice stopped dead in his tracks on the first floor. "Running up and down the stairs and disturbing my peace of mind?"

"The waste baskets, madam. I've finished the upstairs."

Hearing nothing more than silence in reply, the girl climbed off Brice's back and led him down the hall. She opened the door and pushed him inside. "I'll come back when the mistress sleeps."

Brice glanced around the paltry room. A small bed—probably too small even for the thin, short girl—lay against the far wall, and a nightstand with a lone candlestick sat beside it. Brice and Caleb occupied the remaining floor space, and even with so little furniture, the room was quite cramped. *The only thing left to do is wait.*

* * *

After what seemed like an eternity, the door opened and the girl entered. The only way she fit was because Caleb had taken the liberty of sitting on the bed.

"Vicar Forane is upstairs in her chambers. I'll show you out."

Brice stopped her before she opened the door. "You could come with us."

"No," she said, dipping her head. "I'm too close to the end of my servitude to leave now."

"Servitude?"

"My father disobeyed the church's doctrine, and I was forced to serve to pay penance for his wrongdoing."

"That makes no sense." Brice shook his head. "Why didn't he pay for it himself?"

"They can't force a nobleman who is also head of the household to pay penance in such a way. The burden falls upon his heirs; it fell to me."

"What, if I might ask, was his breach?" Caleb asked, rising from the bed.

"He'd been seen by his accuser philandering with other women. Though this is commonplace when done in secret, he became boastful to the wrong ears."

Brice raised an eyebrow. "So you would be punished for your father's indiscretions? It hardly seems reasonable."

"Then you're clearly not from this land. To the church, it's quite reasonable—so reasonable, in fact, that it's become an unwritten law. Now, I'll never see my father again."

"Wait... I thought you said you'd be released soon enough."

She sighed. "My father's dead. He passed away while I've been in this house."

"How?"

"His way with loose women brought disease to him. Now I serve in an attempt to save his soul, that he won't burn in the hells with Syril." She folded her arms. "Don't worry about me. I'm fortunate to be in this house; others have it far worse than I."

"Worse than being beaten?"

"*Much worse*," she replied, as if she'd witnessed the atrocity firsthand.

Brice averted his eyes. "Very well. Show us to the door, if you would."

She led them to the darkened hall and the door through which they had originally entered. "Be on your way and good luck."

"One last thing," Brice said, offering his hand. "What's your name?"

"Does it matter?"

Caleb opened the door and grabbed the tail of Brice's shirt. "Let's not waste the opportunity. Come on."

"Your name, miss?" His hand remained outstretched, and she finally took it.

"Collette. Now, *go*."

Once he had passed the portcullis, Caleb started to run, and Brice struggled to keep up. Brice grudgingly maintained the pace, staying within reach of Caleb's fluttering cloak the entire way back to the Shimmering Dawn headquarters. Out of breath and sweaty, they burst through the door to find the others gathered at the large dining table.

"Have you led anyone here?" Piers asked without any apparent concern for their haggard appearance. His concern obviously lay with the safety of the headquarters' secret location.

"N-no." Caleb bent over and rested his palms on his knees, sucking in air.

Marac closed the door they'd carelessly left open.

Piers said, "What's gotten into you? You both look like you've seen a ghost."

"We've come from… the Vicar Forane's house…" Caleb choked out.

Piers gestured at the chairs. "Have a seat, you two."

"Vicar Forane's house?" Jurgen leaned toward Brice and Caleb as they sat. "Genevieve Forane?"

"Yeah," Brice said before taking a swig from a nearby mug. "That's the one."

"What did you find, pray tell?" Jurgen asked.

"Correspondence. Letters between her and someone else, the Grand Vicar, I think."

"And what did they say?"

Brice glanced at Caleb before responding, "You're in danger."

"What, specifically, did they say?" Jurgen demanded.

Caleb answered, "Lester was a traitor. He was working for Forane, and his task was to have you killed. We were all nearly caught up in his plot."

"Bastard," Piers said. "That little, sniveling cretin. Had us all dancing to his tune, did he?"

Brice nodded. "Almost. She doesn't know what's happened to him, and she wrote that she wanted to meet him tomorrow night—by a bell tower."

"The city has many bells, but it is host to only one such tower," Caleb said. "That is where the meeting will take place."

"Were you able to procure one of these missives to use as proof?" Piers asked.

Brice shook his head. "We couldn't. She would've taken it out on the girl."

Piers narrowed his eyes. "What girl?"

"The servant girl Collette. She discovered we were in the house. She could've turned us in, but she didn't. We wouldn't have escaped without her help."

Piers put a hand on Caleb's shoulder. "Have our whereabouts been disclosed?"

"Not from what I saw. Either Vicar Forane doesn't know our location, or she hasn't written of it. Surely even Lester wouldn't have been that stupid."

"Shouldn't you relocate?" Laedron asked. "We can't accept the lack of evidence as an assurance of safety."

Piers rubbed his chin. "No. If she knows, we must keep up appearances. This could be a boon for us, though."

"How could this, in any way, shape, or form, be a *good* thing for us?" Laedron asked.

"We could send someone to meet her tomorrow. To keep up the ruse."

Laedron stared at Piers. "And how do you plan to accomplish that? Lester's dead, isn't he?"

"Yes, that he is, but perhaps someone else could win her confidence. Perhaps Lester had someone else helping him from our own ranks." His hand landed on Caleb's shoulder.

"As you wish, Master," Caleb said.

Brice studied Caleb's face—the downward turn of his eyes, the quiver of his upper lip, and the lack of regard for the locks of hair crowding his face. *I can't let him go alone. He's afraid—genuinely scared. He must not be accustomed to face-to-face confrontations.* "I'll go with him."

"You will not," Laedron said quickly. "You've already gotten yourself in enough trouble."

"Who will, then? You can't let him do this on his own."

"It already carries a narrow chance of success if he's goes by himself," Laedron said. "I doubt she would believe a total of *three* of the few Dawn Knights left in town would be willing to defect."

"Laedron's right, but I still don't want Caleb going alone." Piers returned to stand beside his chair. "Brice could go with him, but only to observe the happenings. I cannot do this myself, for she may be able to recognize me."

Laedron huffed, then threw up his hands. "All right. Just don't get yourself hurt out there. Should she attack, bring word of it here. *Do not* act alone."

"Agreed." Brice slapped Caleb on the back. "Ready for

another adventure?"

Caleb nodded, but he didn't seem excited.

"Then it's settled." Laedron turned to Jurgen. "What will you do?"

"I am still having trouble believing what I've heard. It's difficult for me to believe that Genevieve Forane would have ill intent toward me. That's not like her."

"Explain, please."

"When I was still a member of the consulship, she was kind to me, to everyone with whom she had dealings. She aided me in every way, in everything I ever asked of her. It simply does not make sense."

"Perhaps she found someone else in power. You did say you were supposed to be the Grand Vicar," Laedron said. "She may have been paying homage to the prince to get close to the king."

Jurgen gave him a long stare.

"Pardon the expression. I only meant to demonstrate the point."

"I don't believe it was that way. Believe me when I say that I think something has changed. That letter read nothing like the Genevieve Forane I knew before I left. Something's changed."

"Either way, she's placed herself on the other side of a fine line. We must consider her to be the enemy."

Jurgen threw up his hands. "Fine, then. I cannot argue based upon what we've been presented."

"So, what will you do?"

"Tomorrow, I'll go to the consulship to claim my seat." Jurgen took a deep breath. "I want something from you, though."

Laedron appeared to be confused. "What could you possibly need from me?"

"To go with me. To watch over us whilst we're inside the Ancient Quarter and the Vicariate."

"Impossible."

Hearing the word cross Laedron's lips gave Brice a strange feeling. *Lae's never said* impossible *before. What has gotten into him?*

Jurgen shook his head. "Not impossible."

"Then how?"

"The militia commander, Dalton Greathis. If I were to write a recommendation, you would be hired on without reservation."

"Hired on? You mean the guard, don't you? The militia?" Marac asked, displaying a dumbfounded expression.

"Yes, my young friend."

"Won't they figure us out, though? We're not from here—not by far. Why would they believe us?"

Jurgen grinned. "I've known Master Greathis for years—from my church duties and in personal life—and a recommendation from me would get you in the door. So long as you don't say anything foolish, few questions would be asked. Besides, Heraldans are descendants of the original Midlander settlers— Sorbians and Cael'Brillanders. You look like them for the most part. Anyone who might recognize you would likely dismiss any suspicions if you were wearing guard's clothing."

Marac gazed at Laedron, who was rubbing his chin as if deep in thought. "You can't be considering this."

"Why not?" Laedron asked. "What better things have we to do?"

48

"Eliminating Tristan, for one, and taking care of Vicar Forane might be a good start." Marac fixed his eyes on Jurgen. "Right?"

Laedron nodded. "Those are all our goals, Marac, but Jurgen has work to do before we can accomplish any of it. We can't just march into the Vicariate and slay them both."

"He's right," Jurgen said. "I have work to do, and I'm not convinced Vicar Forane is the enemy."

"Not convinced?" Brice got to his feet. "What, do you not believe me?" *It seems nobody believes me. Seems as though no one takes me seriously around here.*

"It's not that, not by far." Jurgen walked to his side and patted him on the shoulder. "She may be influenced or otherwise forced to act in this manner. I only mean for us to wait until we can verify where she stands."

Nodding, Brice lowered himself into the chair. "Very well." He turned to Laedron. "So, you and Marac will be parading as guards. Caleb and I will meet Vicar Forane, and Jurgen and Valyrie are going to the consulship."

"That's about the size of it," Jurgen said. "I think we should send someone to the Ancient Quarter wellspring each night to keep in contact and coordinate our efforts."

"Agreed." Laedron took a sip from the cup before him. "May the Creator aid us in our mission."

ᔆ Chapter Four ᔕ

Returning to the Consulship

Valyrie heard a knock on the door, and her eyes flicked open. Her dreams had kept her in twilight the entire night, somewhere between being asleep and a groggy consciousness. She could still hear her father's tortured screams, leaving her with a sick feeling. Since her father's death, she could barely recall or remember the finer details of what had passed. In that moment, her life had changed forever.

Even the low light of the lantern caused her to squint, and the haze of suddenly waking blurred her vision. "Just a moment." She covered her nightclothes with a long robe and opened the door.

Jurgen stood dressed in his priestly garb. "I thought we might get an early start. In truth, I'd much prefer to be there before Tristan arrives. It may make his dreadful gaze easier to bear."

Her eyesight finally returned to normal, and she could see the darkened halls past him. "What's the hour?"

"One, maybe two hours before dawn. I'll wait in the common room." He turned and walked away, and Valyrie closed the door.

Though she wanted to give parting words to the others, she decided simply to pack her things and leave. After dressing, she met Jurgen in the common room, and they departed the headquarters.

Upon passing a familiar street, she said, "We're not far from the inn."

Jurgen glanced at her, then returned his gaze to the road ahead. "Yes, no more than two or three blocks."

She wondered how long it would be before her uncle got word of her father's passing. *I hope he doesn't find me when he does. The man's never liked me. I'd surely find myself given up as a ward of the church.* Her thoughts drove her to miss her father even more. She knew he would have never allowed that to happen, but he was gone.

Jurgen led her along the familiar boulevard, which opened to the view of the Ancient Quarter. Before Jurgen had returned, she would often visit the ancient structures and dream up stories of people and places long ago, and when she told her father her tales, he took it harshly. *Quit fooling around, girl,* he would say. *You're wasting your time. Learn a trade, do it well, and get hired with a noble family with sizable wealth.*

As they passed the rich mansions, she smiled. *Like that one, Father?* she mused, observing a seneschal holding a cumbersome ledger while being chastised by his employer, a well-dressed noblewoman who had probably never lifted a finger to do her own work. *That would have been a better choice?*

Jurgen entered the portcullis of the Ancient Quarter first, and he quickened his pace. The familiar gray and tan stones seemed more vibrant inside the Ancient Quarter, as if washed and maintained on a regular basis.

"Slow down," Valyrie said, picking up speed. "Why are you so hasty?"

"These are the consuls' houses. I don't want to be seen."

Once beside him, she slowed to match his pace. "You'll have to be seen eventually. Isn't that why we're coming here?"

He raised the cowl over his head. "Yes, but not too soon. We must go to the steward's house."

"The Ancient Quarter has a steward?" She recalled the last time the local steward had visited the inn—to collect taxes and make sure everything was on the up and up. "What's the need?"

"He handles the housing assignments in the Ancient Quarter, amongst other things. Vicars aren't required to pay rent, but we must check in." Jurgen stopped at a door fronting a common house smaller than the others she'd seen, but by and large better than the domiciles of the lower quarters. He knocked and received a muffled, unintelligible reply from within.

"Yes?" a man asked, opening the door. "Oh, it's you. We weren't told of your visit, Vicar Jurgen."

"With war swirling on our very borders, I thought it best to make my way back. I'm in need of a place to stay, along with my charge."

The man stepped back inside, leaving the door ajar. Sorting through a cabinet of drawers, he produced a key, then returned. "Here you are, Your Grace. Anything else I might do for you?"

"No, and I prefer to announce myself at the consulship today. No need to spread the word prematurely." Jurgen exchanged a smile with the man and took the key. "I'll let you know."

"Very good. And good to see you back, Your Grace."

After giving the man a nod, Jurgen walked with more confident steps, seeming to know the way without instructions. Valyrie followed him to the end of the row, and they stopped in front of a smaller townhouse set off from the street. Though not as large as those close to the entrance of the Ancient Quarter, the house had been constructed with the same fine materials. The yellow bricks gleamed in the morning light, and the exposed wood of the supporting posts shined as if freshly lacquered.

Jurgen slid the key into the lock, then pushed open the door. Inside, a staircase led to the second floor, and the first floor seemed to be some kind of storage area—too small and uncomfortable for a living space. Upon reaching the upper level, Valyrie took note of the narrow build of the house, the open floor plan, and the stairwell along the western wall. Each section clearly had a specific purpose—a writing desk, a sofa, and a table with chairs in the back, and each area had been plotted with no more room than necessary to perform its function. *Tight, but comfortable. Like the inn in many ways, but much nicer.*

The memory of her former home fell upon her like a ton of heavy timbers, and she collapsed to her knees, tears streaming from her eyes. "He's gone, Jurgen! My father's dead and gone, and he'll never be back!" The surreal feeling suddenly transformed into a very real, very present ache in her heart. Each time she thought she caught her breath, the air escaped her body like water from a bucket riddled with holes. She wept for her dead father and felt a whirlwind of emotions—the anguish for his loss, the contempt for his plans for her, the mistakes for which she could never apologize.

Jurgen rushed to her side and took her by the hand. "Come, have a seat on the chair."

"They killed him! How can we help those men? How can we help men who would do such a thing?" She tried to restrain herself, but she couldn't contain her rage.

"We were betrayed, Valyrie," Jurgen said. "It's my fault. I see that now."

"Yours?" She wiped her eyes, shocked by his statement. "How could it be yours? You didn't kill my da."

"I may not have thrown the dagger, but his blood is on my hands. He was killed on my account. My return to this city triggered a chain of events that led us to our present circumstances."

"Don't blame yourself, Jurgen."

"Then you cannot blame those men, for their error was in trusting their friend. All we can do now is right the wrongs and stop this war. What's done is done, but we will always remember these sacrifices."

"I miss him. Creator! All of our future moments lost by the utterance of a lie. All of them, Jurgen, destroyed by a traitor."

Jurgen closed his eyes, a frown forming his wrinkled face. "I miss him, too. Arthur was a dear friend, but we have little time. We can either wallow in our pain or do what we must to end this fighting."

She wrapped her arms around her body. "I shall help you. I'm trying to be strong."

"Be strong, but not so much that you lose what makes you who you are." He brushed his finger against her chin. "Such is the path to callousness and a cold heart."

Who could want this man dead? She had known Jurgen since before she could remember, and he had shown her nothing but kindness and compassion. Remembering those years past, she recalled more recent events. "They beat you, didn't they?"

He seemed almost disheartened by the question. "Yes, but don't concern yourself with that now. Such thoughts will only make it harder to do what we must do."

"How can you move past them so easily? Even if done based on the word of a liar, the wounds aren't closed by simple apologies."

"I'm an old man, Valyrie. This isn't the first time I've had hardships." Jurgen sighed when she gave him a cross look. "No, the sting remains, but sometimes we must overlook smaller grievances to do our duty. Would I have liked to beat Piers as he did me? Perhaps. But we'd be no closer to our goals. We have no time for petty revenge, and like our sorcerer friend said, we need the help."

Sorcerer friend—Lae. He had tried his best to hide his attraction to her—an attraction she shared, in fact—when they had first met. Had circumstances been different, she might have pursued those feelings, but her father was dead and a war raged. "Have you known him long? Our sorcerer friend, as you put it?"

"Long enough to know he's grown wiser since our first meeting. Long enough to see he's good at heart. Perhaps mages aren't the demons the church proclaims them to be."

"I never agreed with that line of thinking." One of the many arguments she'd had with her father came to mind, about sorcery's place in the world.

"No?"

She shook her head. "Blanket statements have never sat well in my mind. The church would have us believe that the Al'Qarans are barbarians, but are they not known to sail the seas for trade? To build wondrous palaces and, somehow, keep cities in the farthest reaches which are not swallowed up by the desert? Surely not the behavior of the witless."

"I can see your father did not instill in you his dislike for foreigners."

"He tried, but his attempts were for naught." She smiled. "He always said I had the will and stubborn nature of my mother."

Jurgen paused, then grinned, seeming to drift through distant recollections. "Like the sky calling the ocean blue, is it not?"

"Yes, you knew him well."

"Come," he said, offering his hand. "Let us be off to the consulship. I hate the thought of being in that place, but I dread the thought of our doing nothing."

* * *

Nearing the structure, Jurgen slowed. Valyrie couldn't tell if his reduced pace was caused by the daunting size of the consul chamber or the number of people milling around in front of it. The building stood taller than most of the others in the city, the golden dome atop the perfect cylinder extending nearly ten stories into the air. Massive marble columns with gold and silver inlays ringed the chamber, the arches between them adorned with gold and silver banners. A huge censer hung by a thick chain from the ceiling, the incense burning within filling the room with a pleasant scent like roasted lemons mixed with fresh pine needles. Though Valyrie had seen the consul chamber many times before, she always stood in awe of it.

Seeming to recognize Jurgen, the commoners stopped and whispered to each other. They were apparently filled with warmth and excitement at his approach because the words spoken under their breaths changed to a dull chant, then mixed with applause until the entire square cheered his every step.

"It would seem the people are joyous at your return, Vicar," she whispered.

Jurgen gave her a smile, then turned and waved at the crowd. "Thank you. Azura bless you." Entering the arched hall to the central chamber, he whispered, "And may she watch over me here, too."

Valyrie felt small and miniscule, more so than usual, and not because she was thin; the size and grandeur of the assembly room filled her with angst. *So many eyes watching us enter already, and the place is but half full.* Long, sturdy desks made rings around the room, each set atop a terrace of steps extending high above in every direction. The rings terminated opposite the entrance at a wide platform with a throne glimmering with gold, silver, and jewels. *That must be where the Grand Vicar sits. Only the highest would be placed on such a chair.*

A man rushed over. "Vicar Jurgen? We didn't expect you. Can we help you?"

Jurgen removed his fine overcoat and draped it across the man's arm. "I've come to sit at the consulship, of course."

"Y-yes, as you wish," the man said.

"Can you point me to an empty seat, Chamberlain? Or have things changed since I've been gone?"

"No, of course. Please, this way." The chamberlain escorted Jurgen to a desk on the floor, and Valyrie followed, her footsteps echoing no matter how lightly she walked. "I hope this is fitting, Your Grace, on such short notice."

"Fine, worry not. When arriving without warning, a traveler must take whatever he can get."

"Your Grace is kind." The chamberlain bowed, then scurried away to attend the other vicars.

Sitting, Jurgen extended his hand to offer Valyrie a chair at his side. "The chamber is different since last I sat within these walls."

"How so?"

He studied the walls as if they had an answer scrolled across them. "The priests are anxious and uncertain. You can tell by the looks on their faces and the trembling of their hands."

Sudden drumming startled her. She scanned the circular balcony lining the wall high above. The drummers beat the solemn tune for the Grand Vicar's approach, a rendition she remembered well. Then she saw him on the raised platform, a platform which extended all the way to the Grand Vicar's palace to the east. His silken robes shined with dyes of silver, gold, and purple. Atop his head sat a thin golden circlet—a mark of his office and the least impressive of the jewelry he wore. The magnificent onyx ring on his hand caught her attention as it seemed to shimmer with an artificial vibrancy. Beneath the pomp and pageantry, his pale skin and blue eyes were a stark contrast to his jet-black hair.

Sitting on the ornate throne, Grand Vicar Tristan IV gazed over the crowd until the drums stopped. "Vicars," he said, then didn't speak again until the room grew quiet. "We are at the precipice. All that we have worked toward is under threat of being undone. The Albiadines will not join us, and the Lasoronian claim they are stretched too thin across the swamps."

The Almatheren Swamp? She recalled the tales told by her father and others of the dangers and undead within those wetlands. The Vicar's words were met with haughty sighs from the assembly.

"We must stand on our own against the Sorbian enemy, it would appear—well, with our only friends, the Falacorans." Tristan clasped his hands.

Valyrie had seen a Falacoran once, a gruff man dressed in darkened armor adorned with studs and spikes. The Falacorans were known to be deeply religious and strong supporters of the Heraldan church. The Falacorans, strong, resilient warriors and craftsmen, were the church's perfect ally—a military arm to protect it from those who would see it demolished. She briefly imagined the sketches of massive cathedrals and castles she had seen books, the structures rife with arches and steep roofs. Falacorans had both a preference and a need for high, angular architecture. It reflected strength and power and had the added benefit of keeping snow from gathering too thick in the colder months.

"Our blessed church cannot stand on its own. Even with the help of the Falacorans, we will see great difficulty in the coming days without tightening the reins. Sorbia is a strong, proud nation, and it is a safe haven for the heretical sorcerers. To once and for all rid ourselves of this dark menace, I propose to this consulship a measure to fight this war. I ask you all to confirm and anoint me Protector of the Faith."

"No!" one of the other Vicars shouted amidst the gasps and whispers of the assembly. "We've governed ourselves for hundreds of years without one."

"And during that time, we've seen no threats as serious," Tristan said. "Is now not the time for strong, confident leadership?"

"Yes, but—"

"Then, we must do this, lest our holy land be ravaged by the heathens!"

Jurgen stood. "Vicar Aberlin is correct, Your Grace."

Valyrie clenched her fists under the desk when the Grand Vicar turned their way. A look of surprise dominated his features at first, then he gave a stern glare. "Vicar Jurgen, we weren't aware you would be joining us."

"I've come with worry, Your Holiness, for I have heard rumors recently of trouble abroad."

"You have heard correctly, Vicar. The witches of Sorbia threaten our very existence with their unjust war."

Jurgen stood and walked onto the floor the way a performer would enter a stage, then turned to face the congregation. "Yes, an unjust war indeed. Of course, war is rarely justified."

"Then join with me in doing what is right," Tristan said.

"We must do what is right, yes. I cannot agree with you more, but declaring Your Holiness as Protector of the Faith seems a bit hasty. After all, we must remember our history. The last time this body did such a thing, the power wasn't returned to its proper place once the threat was resolved."

Tristan stood and cast off his cloak. "You dare question my loyalty to the church? To this assembly?"

Jurgen respectfully bowed toward the platform. "Your Holiness, I only mean to say that such steps are not necessary at this juncture."

"Not necessary?" a woman shouted from the gallery. "The enemy is loose in our own country. Perhaps you didn't know since you've been cloistered in Balfan this entire time, or have you been?"

Fishing, Valyrie mused. *Be careful here, Jurgen.*

"I've heard the rumors, yes," Jurgen said, apparently unwilling to divulge anything more. "And I give my condolences to His Holiness for the loss of his brother. May he rest with Azura."

Tristan relaxed on the throne. "I thank you for your kind words, Vicar, but we are still no closer to a resolution on this matter. I call for a vote."

"A vote, yes. What a magnificent idea, Your Holiness," the woman said. Valyrie craned her neck, but she couldn't see the woman.

"Agreed," Jurgen said. "Whatever suits His Holiness and

Vicar Forane shall suit me."

Forane. The hairs on the back of her neck stood on end.

When Tristan clapped his hands, chamberlains approached, placing a sliver of parchment before each clerk.

What in the hells do I do with this?

Jurgen took a seat next to her and whispered, "Tristan will pose the question to the assembly, and we record our answer. The chief amongst the chamberlains will record the result and report his findings. The Grand Vicar is not allowed to vote unless it is tied."

"What if they vote for it? What will we do?"

"Fret not. I take the worried looks from the majority of the consuls as a sign it shall fail. Regardless of the outcome, we will find a way."

Tristan stood and leaned against the rail. "Here me now! Those in favor of my anointing to the status of Protector of the Faith, record 'yes.' Those who would oppose should record 'no.'"

"We, of course, will say 'no.'" Jurgen pointed at the scrap and the quill. "Write the response."

After the chamberlains collected the votes, the chief went through each one. He then stood and walked to a podium near his seat. "By the grace of Azura, we congregate to do her will in all things. It is the will of the consuls that Grand Vicar Tristan IV not be anointed—"

The chamberlain's voice was drowned with both the cheers and boos erupting throughout the gallery. Tristan stood and exited the chamber the way he had entered, apparently unwilling to face the crowd or speak another word that day. Jurgen chuckled under his breath, then dipped his head to Vicar Forane when she raced past them, heading for the main entrance.

"That went well," Valyrie said, shaking her head.

Jurgen grinned. "We are fortunate it went that way, for I fear what might have come to pass if he'd succeeded."

"Is it not dangerous, though? To anger him in such a way?"

"That's the point, isn't it? The last thing our faith should do is have us living in fear. If I put myself in danger, it is so others can be free of an iron grip."

"Though you don't think so, I still think you're brave for doing this."

"Brave?" Jurgen lowered his voice. "No, our Sorbian friends are brave. I am only doing what I should have done a long time ago."

"Very well. You would know better than me," Valyrie said. *I just hope all of this is worth it in the end.*

"Of course. Come. When the Grand Vicar departs, we are released for the day."

ᖚ Chapter Five ᖚ

Militia Matters

nother day in the enemy's homeland. Laedron rose from the bed and donned his clothes. *Better get to it. One step, then the other.* He concealed his scepter and wand as best he could and went in search of his friends.

In the common room, he found Marac sharpening his sword at the dining table.

Laedron closed the door after entering. "I think it's sharp enough, my friend."

"Never sharp enough. The blade must be ready." Marac slid the whetstone along the length of the edge. "I won't be caught helpless again."

"Being captured worked in our favor this time. No worries."

"It could've turned out much differently."

"But it didn't."

"But it could have," Marac said sharply.

"Are you well?"

Marac let out a chuckle. "As well as can be expected. I'm deep in the enemy's territory, but we play games of politics and intrigue."

"Things must be handled with delicacy, Marac. I'd like nothing more than to rid this world of Andolis Drakar, but we must do so carefully if we're to survive."

"And how long must we wait? Weeks? Months? Or years, perhaps? How long will it take?"

Laedron put his hand on Marac's shoulder. "No matter how long it takes, we must stay the course. This plan is the best chance for success."

Marac lowered his head. "Very well."

"Don't worry." Laedron patted him on the back. "We'll see some action today, but first, I must make sure Jurgen and Valyrie are preparing themselves to leave."

"They've left already."

"They have?"

"You seem disappointed. I would've thought you'd be pleased they got to it."

"Yes, but—"

Marac smiled. "You wanted to see the girl off, did you?"

"No. Well… yes. To wish them a safe journey."

"It's more than that. I can see it."

Laedron took a seat next to him. "I... um..."

"Say no more. I already know how you feel."

"How did you know?"

Marac leaned back in his chair, having finally laid the sword on the table. "I've known you for as long as I can remember. I've never seen you behave that way around other girls."

"Is it that obvious?"

"To me, sure. I doubt she realizes it, though."

Laedron folded his arms across his chest. "I feel horrible for her. She's just lost her father, and now she's wrapped up in our schemes."

"By her own will."

"What?"

"She's old enough to know what she's doing, Lae."

"Is she? Perhaps, but I can't help but thinking she helps us because she has no other choice."

"She mentioned her uncle, didn't she?" Marac asked. "She could've gone to live with him."

"From what I understand, he's unbearable to be around."

"It's still a choice. She chooses to be here with us—with you."

"Maybe you're right."

Marac smiled. "Of course I'm right. I'm always right."

"Unless I am," Laedron said, letting out a laugh.

"Oh, you got me there. I'm right until the ol' archmage starts arguing me up and down the Midlands. Can't be denied."

Laedron poured a bowl of stew from the fireplace pot and returned to the table. "Once I get a bit of this in my belly, I'll be ready if you are."

"Go ahead, I've already had some. One thing I won't miss is the food in this place."

"Won't argue with you there." Laedron poked a chunk of overcooked meat with his spoon. "This stuff's fit for a dog."

"Not even a dog, but you'd better eat up anyway. You need your strength."

Maybe this will help it go down, he thought, snatching a piece of bread from the plate.

After eating, Laedron brushed his shirt free of crumbs, then took the scroll sitting on the end of the table. "Jurgen's note to get us in the militia."

"Good." Marac sheathed his sword and wrapped his cloak about his back. "At least we'll get to walk around a bit. Where is this place, anyway?"

"Near what they call the Ancient Quarter. We passed it on the way to the sea."

"Then, lead the way."

Laedron followed the same path Jurgen had taken him on earlier. On the trip to the seaside, he had kept his head down most of the way, but he decided to take in the sights and sounds of the city. The buildings were closer together in that end of the city than anywhere he'd seen in Morcaine, but many rose as high as three stories. In his homeland, the houses and businesses were made of carved stone and wood, but the Heraldan homes and shops were built of timbers, brick, and plaster. *Maybe they lack quarries. Or perhaps the expense would be too great.*

Every window and doorway had some religious decoration of some kind, and the symbols made Laedron feel even more foreign. He wondered if the people glancing at him as he passed could see that he wasn't Heraldan. *Don't give yourself away. They can't know. There's no way for them to know.*

The houses and shops had well-trimmed grass occupying the open space of each lot, a feature he found strange, yet somewhat pleasant. People in Sorbia, from his recollection, cared little about how their lawns and shrubs appeared. The grass had been allowed to grow long around the passage, and the people apparently cut back bushes only when they threatened to block a door or a window. The only flowers to be found on a Sorbian's tract were wild and grew at random. The Heraldan houses sometimes had a number of planters or even beds of fertile earth set aside for flowers. *That's likely the reason the air has a certain perfume at all times. These flowers are everywhere.*

Turning the corner, Laedron spotted the golden dome of the consul chamber in the distance and thought of Valyrie. *I hope Jurgen keeps her safe.*

A cart caught his attention, and he approached the vendor.

"Might I help you, young man?" the seller asked.

Laedron's stomach churned with delight at the smell of the hot rolls, and he reached in his pocket. "How much?"

"A pence apiece. How many?"

"Four should do." He offered the copper coins to the merchant and received a thin cloth full of buns in exchange.

As they took to the road once more, Marac said, "You won't be eating them all on your own, will you?"

"Of course not." Laedron gave him two.

Honey bread? How fine. Laedron savored the roll after he

popped it into his mouth. Then, he ate the second, trying not to look like a hungry beast. Marac didn't fare well in hiding his pleasure, either.

They arrived at the militia headquarters, and Laedron found the building peculiar. It was the only structure in that end of town built entirely from red bricks—a rich, bright red, as if the color itself had a significance.

Upon entering the main hall, Laedron stopped one of the guards. "Might you tell me where I can find Master Greathis?"

"Master Greathis? What business have you with him?" the guard asked, impatience in his tone. He wore a gold and silver tunic with the coat of arms of the theocracy on his chest—a gold and silver shield beset by Azura's Star.

I'm beginning to get sick of that symbol, Laedron thought, studying the man's tunic. *It's displayed on everything here—shops and houses, the flags, the coins, and even the people themselves.*

Marac stepped forward. "We mean to join up, of course."

"You can do that without seeing Greathis." The soldier pointed down the hall. "Go to—"

"We must see Greathis himself. We were sent here by Vicar Jurgen," Laedron said, producing the scroll.

The man glanced at the scroll. "Very well. Third floor, all the way back."

"The stairs?"

The guard sighed and gestured toward the nearby door.

"Thank you."

On the third floor, they walked toward the rear of the structure, stopping when Laedron spotted a sign reading, "Master and Commander of the Militia Dalton Greathis." Laedron hoped the long, stuffy title didn't accurately reflect the man to whom it referred. He took a deep breath before knocking on the heavy door.

Receiving a muffled response from inside, Laedron opened the door. "Master Greathis, I presume?"

"Yes, yes, come in."

The office was resplendent, but the décor was markedly different from any other place Laedron had seen in the city. The room contained an Azuran banner at the center of the rear wall, but he couldn't place the furniture or any of the other decorations. Looking past the desk, he also noticed the man wore dark armor with studs and spikes all over it.

"And who, pray tell, are you?" The man's words were sharp and crisp, and his voice carried a throaty accent.

"Um... Laedron, and this is Marac. We've come to join the militia at Vicar Jurgen's request."

Greathis's eyes widened. "Vicar Jurgen? Has our friend returned from the city of Balfan?"

Laedron handed him the scroll. "Yes, Master Greathis. I—"

"Dalton." He read over the parchment, then stamped a small piece of paper with his signet ring and handed it to Laedron.

"Sire?"

"Any friend of Vicar Jurgen may call me Dalton, for we are friends by association. Just Dalton."

"Very well." Laedron glanced around the room again, taking in the strangeness of the place. "You're not from the theocracy, are you? I feel as if I've journeyed to a new land just by passing through your door."

Greathis laughed. "Not the first time I've heard that. I hail from Falacore, and these are my possessions."

Falacore. The icy north, the land of the fabled warriors. "What is a Falacoran doing so far from home?"

"His duty, of course," Greathis said. "We have a close relationship with the church, and it is not as uncommon as you might think. Many of my predecessors have also been Falacoran. Our skill in battle makes us apt at training men for patrolling streets or for service on the battlefield."

"We won't need any training," Marac said.

"Won't you? A wise man once told me that he who knows everything knows nothing. I've found it to be true."

"He means no disrespect." Laedron glanced at Marac before returning his eyes to Greathis. "To say it better, we are prepared for duty now and require no further instruction."

Greathis dipped his head. "Very well. Jurgen wouldn't have sent you unless he had faith in your abilities. What are your specialties?"

Laedron's gaze fell to the floor. "My friend here is skilled with a sword."

"And you?"

An array of weapons flooded his mind. *Which one? What's easiest to use? I carry none of them!*

"No need to be bashful, friend," Marac said, stepping past Laedron. "He fights with a dagger."

"A dagger? Interesting…"

Though Laedron had only handled a knife for carving fish, he figured he could use it better than anything else. "Yes, daggers. I'm sorry. I know it's an unusual weapon to master."

"No, it's quite all right." Greathis clasped his hands. "I've seen wonders performed with the shorter blades."

Laedron exhaled lightly so as not to appear nervous, then grinned at Marac.

"The armory is on the first floor," Greathis said. "There you may acquire your tunics and arms from the quartermaster. Give that order to him once you find him."

"Thank you… Dalton." Laedron bowed, and Marac followed him to the first floor. Hearing shouting from down the hall, Laedron rushed forward and located the source of the racket, a man with a longsword at his hip and sergeant's chevrons on his sleeve.

"On the left! Damned fools! No, the other left!" the sergeant yelled. "All the way against the wall and two high."

Not wanting to draw the man's ire, Laedron waited for the sergeant to finish his diatribe. "Are you the quartermaster?"

"Aye, Sergeant Wilkans. And who are you, boy?"

"New recruits, come for our tunics and weapons." Laedron showed Wilkans the missive that Master Greathis had given him.

Wilkans put his hands on his hips. "Well, you'll have to wait. We're reorganizing the stockroom right now."

"Perhaps we can help," Laedron suggested.

"Maybe. Do you know left from right?"

"Sire?"

"It's a simple question, boy," Wilkans said with a sigh. "Do you know your left hand from your right?"

73

Laedron nodded.

"Good." He turned to yell at the men inside the stockroom, "Maybe somebody with some sense about them can get this done!"

Laedron gestured for Marac to come with him, and they both grunted at feeling the weight when they lifted the crates. Per Wilkans's detailed instructions, Laedron and Marac moved the heavy boxes across the storeroom and stacked them. Finishing, both of them heaved sighs and did their best to wipe the sweat from their brows.

Entering the room and inspecting the work, Wilkans said, "Good, many thanks. Let's see about getting you some supplies."

I can't believe I'm doing this. Laedron eyed the symbol on his new tunic. *Everything I've come to despise is embodied in this emblem, a symbol I will have emblazoned across my chest.* He shook his head, then donned the garment over his shirt and pants.

"Need any arms?" Wilkans asked.

Laedron pointed at the daggers across the top of the weapons rack. "I could use one of those and a sheath."

Wilkans obliged, then turned to Marac. "I see you already have a sword. You can use your own or one of mine. I care not."

"I'll keep my own, thank you."

"All right. Have you a route yet?" Wilkans asked.

"A route? No," Laedron replied.

Wilkans led them down the hall to a room with a large table holding a map of the city. He rubbed his chin and studied the map. "This here would be a good one." With his finger, he traced a series of narrow streets near the Ancient Quarter.

"Anything we should know about it?" Laedron asked.

Wilkans cleared his throat. "Some have gone missing along this route before."

"Gone missing?" Laedron raised an eyebrow. "How many?"

"Three, and the answer to your next question is two months."

"Without a trace?"

"Nothing that we could find. No bodies, no blood, no witnesses." Wilkans handed Laedron a pair of whistles, each attached to its own chain. "If you get in trouble, signal for help. We run patrols tighter since those disappearances."

Laedron gave a whistle to Marac, then put the other around his neck. "Very well, Sergeant."

"Get to it. Report anything unseemly to me or Master Greathis. Get a bit of sleep before you go out; you're on the night patrols, and you start at sunset and keep on 'til sunrise. The militia quarters are on the second floor."

* * *

"I'm bored already," Marac said, kicking a stone down the avenue.

The sun had just dipped below the horizon, and the lantern lighters were busy on their appointed rounds. They had done little more than eat a heavy meal at a nearby tavern and ensure that old women had no harassment or trouble when trying to cross the roads.

"You're always bored." Laedron swatted Marac on the arm.

Marac scoffed. "What are we doing? Walking along while waiting to be killed under mysterious circumstances?"

"Giving Jurgen peace of mind."

"I've never seen a city so tight. What more could he need?"

Laedron grinned. "We got in, didn't we?"

"Good point."

"Loosen up, Marac," Laedron said. "Creator! I never thought those words would cross my lips."

"You're telling me!" Marac rolled his shoulders. "Nothing a good night at a tavern wouldn't cure."

"Don't even think about it. When we're done with this, you can have as much ale as you can stand, but not before."

"Yes, Da."

"Oh, stop it. You know how important our task is. We have no time for loafing."

"Yeah, yeah. I know."

The night marched forward, and even Laedron felt ungratified and listless as the evening progressed. *I pray we don't have weeks of this ahead of us.* They returned to the militia headquarters once Laedron caught sight of the first rays of the morning sun. Collapsing on his bed, he heard something crinkle against his hair. Reaching behind his head, he found a scroll held furled by a red ribbon and a bit of wax.

❧ Chapter Six ❧

Dealing with the Enemy

Brice sat quietly in his room, the lock Caleb had given him in hand. The decorations, the inlays, and the mechanism all captivated Brice unlike anything—or anyone, for that matter—he had ever encountered. Each time he slipped the probe into the keyhole, he closed his eyes and envisioned the little world within, the blocks, levers, and shafts. Opening the lock and claiming victory over its intricacies would be proof that he could open any door or chest which barred their progress.

He was beyond frustration, but he remembered the feeling well. In Reven's Landing, Brice had had run-ins with many looms that had given him fits, and he had been tempered like steel to be patient and resolved when machinery malfunctioned. The lock he held, though, was not in need of repair. In fact, his goal was to make the lock work against its purpose and give up that which it protected.

"Still playing with that?" Caleb asked.

Brice blinked. With his attention fixed on the lock, he hadn't noticed Caleb enter the room. "Trying to figure it out."

"It'll have to wait. It's time for the meeting."

"Already?" Brice turned to see only darkness through the window. "Sorry, I hadn't noticed the time passing."

"Quite all right. Made any progress?" Caleb opened the door and led the way into the street.

"A little. Halfway to getting it open, I should think."

Caleb smiled. "Then you're close to the surprise."

"Surprise? What surprise?"

"It wouldn't be a surprise if I told you, now would it?" Caleb chuckled. "You'll get there. For now, keep your mind on the task at hand."

Brice nodded. "Where do you want me once we get there?"

"There's a well in the courtyard. You shouldn't have a problem hearing us from there." He passed Brice a mug. "Lie behind it with this in hand and hide yourself from view of either of the walkways leading to the tower. If anyone happens upon you, act like a drunkard and make your escape."

"What about you?"

"Don't worry about me. I can take care of myself." Caleb displayed a dagger at his hip.

"I hope you're good with it."

"I am."

Brice likened the sight of the bell tower to the lighthouses of Sorbia and Cael'Bril. The stone structure seemed old compared to the rest of the city, but the well-kept lawn indicated that the building had not lost its utility over the years.

Caleb stopped at the intersection of two roads opposite the courtyard. "You go. We can't be seen together."

Brice nodded, then hoisted the mug in the air. Once he reached the iron gate of the courtyard, he swaggered across the lawn and belted out a tavern tune with a drunken slant. Having taken a winding, indirect path to the well, he collapsed next to it and closed his eyes. After what seemed like an eternity, he heard footsteps on the cobbled path. Not long after that, he heard another set of steps.

"Who are you?"

Brice recognized Forane's voice.

"Caleb. I'm all that's left of us. Lester's dead."

"And who is that?" Forane asked. "Why do you speak in such a familiar way, young man? As if I should know this Lester of whom you speak?"

"Don't toy with me, madam. You think Lester could've accomplished the task on his own?"

"Maybe, and maybe not." She held a long pause. "If you were involved with Lester, how much did I pay him?"

"Pay him?" Caleb asked sharply. "You mean to tell me that

bastard was paid? He told us it was for the good of the order!"

If I didn't know any better, I would've believed that one, Brice mused, trying to keep his mouth from bending into a smile.

"Keep your voice down, fool," Forane whispered. "You would see us discovered?"

"I apologize, madam, but I hate being used. Good thing he's dead, or I would've killed him myself."

"How did he die, exactly?"

"He went alone—against my advice, I might add—to take care of… our friend. He crawled back to our spot with a slash in his belly. It would seem the vicar has better protection than we thought."

Forane, seemingly without any regard for Lester's death, continued, "Matters are further complicated. The man has returned to the consulship, and we are in peril of losing control."

"Surely not, madam, for you are—"

"Don't. I have no time for flattery or games, young man."

"What would you have me do?"

"Nothing as of yet. I have something else in mind to take care of him. If we are unsuccessful, I will contact you again—here, two nights hence."

"Might I ask what you intend to do?"

"It's none of your concern. Worry only for yourself. Should we succeed tomorrow night, I shall pay you the other half of the money owed to Lester. If not, it will be up to you to earn it."

Brice heard the flap of a cloak, then footsteps growing distant. He peeked over the stone wall of the well to see Caleb exiting the courtyard. He waited until he thought it was safe to leave, then walked back to the Shimmering Dawn.

Forane's plotting deep and wide. We must warn them somehow. Reaching the last street before the headquarters, Brice took one last look around to see if he'd been followed, then he entered the building and heard Caleb relaying the essential details of his conversation with Forane to Piers.

"She didn't say where or how?" Piers asked.

Caleb shrugged. "No, she wouldn't reveal it. I can only assume it will be wherever Vicar Jurgen is tomorrow night."

"We should expect any possibility." Piers ran his fingers through his hair. "With Lester's failure, they could have anything in mind and may have little regard for subtlety or stealth."

Caleb folded his arms. "How do you think they will come for him?"

"When dealing with the theocracy, there are a number of possibilities. Anything, Caleb. Anything at all."

"Should we shadow Jurgen?" Brice asked. "You know, to keep an eye on him?"

"No, impossible," Piers said. "Forane has seen Caleb's face, and she would likely see you two in the district. If they were to attack, you two couldn't be seen helping Jurgen. No, we must contact Laedron and Marac; his safety will be theirs to handle."

Brice took a seat across from Piers. "And I thought breaking into houses was dangerous."

"We're not out of the fire yet, not by any means." Piers took a quill and scrawled a message on a piece of parchment. "I shall prepare a missive for our friends. Brice, you will take it to them."

"Where?"

Piers rolled the scroll, wrapped it with a red ribbon, and dripped some wax for a seal. "To the militia headquarters. The red brick building near the Ancient Quarter."

"That's what that was?" Brice took the missive. "Right. I'll be back."

"Good. Hurry back, but you must make sure you aren't followed. The stakes are high in this game. The same goes for you, Caleb. I shall devise how we will handle the vicar."

❧ Chapter Seven ❧

An Army in the Holy Land

After waking and dressing, Valyrie found Jurgen seated at the dining table.

"Good morning," Jurgen said, turning to her when she came into the kitchen. "I thought you'd never wake."

She rubbed her eyes. "You jest, Vicar. I've risen well before the rest of Azura."

"Come, have some of this. I fetched it from the mid-market just before dawn."

She thought fondly of the mid-market, a series of stands just outside the gate of the Ancient Quarter where one could acquire the freshest produce and dairy if the buyer came early enough. "Smells wonderful."

"One of my favorite recipes," Jurgen said, then put the plate before an empty seat and offered her the chair. "Apple bellies."

"What's an apple belly?"

"A dash of cinnamon and sugar, a spoonful of butter, all wrapped up in sweet dough and twisted at the end. Oh, and the slices of peeled apple at the center, I can't forget to mention those."

"But why the name?"

Jurgen smiled, lifting his pastry by the twists at either end. "See how it dips low, like the belly of a pig?"

Nodding, she took a bite and savored the rich flavors. The taste reminded her of the apple cobblers she'd enjoyed on numerous occasions at the inn, but more buttery.

Having already finished most of his by the time she had started, Jurgen waited until the last bite passed her lips. "You seem troubled."

"My dreams trouble me. I can think of nothing but the dagger which pierced my father's heart."

"The nightmares will fade in time. I have them myself, but I keep faith."

She dipped her head, swallowing the last bit of her breakfast. "Do you think we'll make any headway today?"

Jurgen frowned. "You say that as if we've done nothing. Blocking Andolis from becoming Protector was an important step."

Andolis. Tristan IV. "He still rules. Though he does not possess the title, he remains in power, right?"

"Indeed, but the powers of a Protector are sweeping and total. As Grand Vicar, he suffers some restrictions. Only through small steps can we hope to make a change, and the first was yesterday. Today, we continue along the path. We can do nothing more."

She leaned back to take the pressure off her full stomach. "I fear for the future, near and far away. If we don't do something soon, the war will claim more and more."

"I know, and I share your concern. Come now to the consulship; we'll make no progress sitting here." He slipped on his ceremonial garb and led the way out the door.

* * *

She sat at Jurgen's side, and again the drums roared throughout the chamber as the Grand Vicar made his entrance. Valyrie glanced at him, and then she stared at the onyx ring on his finger. The pulsing, shimmering glow didn't come from the sun or the candles and torches ringing the auditorium. The stone itself glowed with an unnatural light. *How can that be?*

"Brothers and sisters," Tristan said, then waited until the assembly grew silent. "I must apologize for my hasty exit yesterday. The stress of how best to serve our most holy church has weighed heavily on my mind of late, and the path is unclear at times. I spent the night in my private chapel praying that Azura would guide my hand, and I believe I have come to a solution.

"Vicar Jurgen is correct. Anointing a Protector will do us little good in these times, and we have yet to exhaust all of our options."

Valyrie did her best to keep her face from telling her feelings of confusion and doubt at his words.

Tristan opened his hand to Jurgen. "You were right, my brother. Rise and be recognized."

Jurgen stood, then bowed to the other vicars. A light applause echoed throughout the room. Valyrie could tell by the looks on the vicars' faces that they were just as bewildered as she.

Tristan turned to the assembly. "Azura has shown us through her actions that even in the most dire of times, we must demonstrate our restraint and faith. Consuls, I yield to Vicar Forane, who has news for us from Balfan."

"Thank you, Grand Vicar." Forane emerged from the sea of consuls, and Valyrie was able to match a face to the voice she had heard the previous day. "It has come to my attention by way of a messenger that we are now under siege. The Arcanist ships we refitted for battle were unable to break the blockade, and Sorbian troops..." She lowered her head for a moment. "Forgive me, for this news may be difficult to bear. Soldiers from Sorbia have landed and surrounded Balfan in the night."

Valyrie felt fear tainting the once-serene halls of the Vicariate. The vicars gasped and muttered profanities. Even Jurgen, who she had thought unshakable, seemed to be uneasy.

"Those are the facts," Forane continued. "The city isn't expected to resist for long since they haven't any walls or a force capable of repelling the enemy."

"Master Greathis," Tristan said, sitting on the throne. "Pray tell, how long we can expect to hold out?"

When she heard heavy footsteps, Valyrie turned to view Master Greathis. He was adorned in Falacoran armor and spoke with the throaty, dense accent of that country. "A few months, I should say." Greathis walked to the center of the chamber just below the Grand Vicar's perch. "The militia can keep them out for some time, but we won't last forever, and we won't force out or dislodge a professional army."

Tristan quickly rose to his feet. "Then, we must raise an army of our own."

"We cannot," Jurgen said, standing. "The procurement of soldiers is not the church's business."

"You would see us destroyed, our hallowed ground trampled underfoot of the invaders, our great cities lying wasted?" Tristan asked. "The enemy has now come to our gates, Jurgen, and we must do something about it!"

Jurgen cleared his throat. "Can we not negotiate? Make a compromise with the Sorbians?"

"Negotiate with the aggressor?" Tristan asked. "Why would they speak with us? The way I see it, their plan goes quite well for them. They have declared war and invaded us, and they are making progress."

Valyrie recalled Laedron's story of the attack at the Sorbian mage academy. *The Grand Vicar lies, or he does not know the truth. Gustav... Andolis must know the actions of his own brother.*

"And who would we recruit for our fledgling army, Your Holiness?"

"Well, people from the city. *They* would have no problem

coming to the defense of their homes."

Jurgen walked from behind his desk. "Yes, the young ones of our own capital. The untrained children, strangers to battle and war. They would be slaughtered outright, and that would be an atrocity, one committed by us, not our enemies."

"Then what else is there, Vicar Jurgen? I'm all ears for a solution."

Jurgen rubbed his chin, standing in the center of the hundred or more people in the consulship, all of them silent and still. Valyrie likened him to a defenseless animal in a cage surrounded by hungry hunters preparing to make a kill.

"Tell them, Your Grace," Valyrie said, standing. "Tell them of what we discussed earlier of your service as an emissary." She tried her best to conceal the lie with a concerned tone.

Jurgen eyed her for a moment. "Yes. I had discussed the option with my clerk earlier."

"Well, tell us more of this great plan," Tristan said.

"Your Holiness, if it pleases the consulship, I could go to Balfan and negotiate with the Sorbian commander to get them to leave our lands peacefully."

Tristan stood and shook his head. "The only thing they would accept is surrender. We both know that."

"Perhaps, but perhaps not. A nation such as Sorbia does not rise to its status by being barbaric and unreasonable to compromise." Jurgen clasped his hands. "I feel such a course would be better than sacrificing our inexperienced young men to the jaws of war."

"It can't be permitted," Forane said, walking onto the main

floor across from Jurgen. "Azura stood on the battlefield against insurmountable odds once, and now we must follow her example. Send the defilers to the hells where they belong!"

"Forane and I are in agreement." Tristan returned to the throne. "I request a vote on the question, Chamberlain. All those who would be in favor of raising an army to defend our most holy church, respond 'yes.' Those who would oppose, and see us destroyed outright, respond 'no.'"

Jurgen sighed, then returned to his desk. "We, of course, will respond with 'no,'" he whispered to Valyrie.

The chamberlains collected the votes with the same efficiency as the previous day. The room became silent while the chief chamberlain counted and tallied the votes.

Eventually, the chamberlain stood. "By the grace of Azura, we congregate to do her will in all things. It is the will of the consuls that an army *not* be raised."

Unlike with the last vote, the chamber remained silent with the announcement.

Tristan stood with disappointment riddling his face. "Thus is the will of the consuls. Tell me, Chamberlain, the count in favor and of those against."

"Half of the assembly plus one dissent the question, Your Holiness," the man said, then took his seat.

"It would seem half of you—plus one—would see our church destroyed. To see it annihilated by the invaders, to see our precious cities in upheaval and our people enslaved. Very well." Tristan put his hands on the iron rail and leaned toward the consuls. "If this body is unable to do what is needed, I shall act on my own. I shall raise the army we so desperately need."

Jurgen shot out of his chair. "It cannot be! You have no authority to override this body's will, Andolis." His words were received with shouts from the gallery expressing disdain for Tristan.

"Enough!" the Grand Vicar shouted. "If none of you have the strength to see this done, I must preserve us."

"You have no power to act on our behalf, especially not when we've said no." Jurgen pointed at Tristan. "You have no right."

"I am Tristan IV, Grand Vicar of the Heraldan church. Sworn to uphold and defend the church in all matters, chosen to lead us in accordance with Azura's teachings and to protect that legacy. Do not presume to tell me what is and what is not in my power, Vicar Jurgen. I shall see us through the night and into the morning, with or without your help." Tristan turned and walked toward the exit.

Jurgen called out, "Wait, Your Holiness."

Tristan paused, then turned to look at Jurgen. "What need have you for me?"

"A compromise."

"I'm listening."

"Instead of an army, we could increase the size of the militia. That would serve our goals, would it not? Provide better protection for the city when the siege comes?"

"That won't remove the Sorbians from our shores," Tristan said. "You and I both know that."

"Perhaps not, but it would help keep them at bay. If we begin training new men now, we would stand a better chance to resist the invasion when it reaches our gates."

"Fine, then." Tristan returned to the throne. "Chamberlain, the question shall be to the raising of more militia for our defense. An answer of 'yes' will... let's say, double the current number of guardians."

Jurgen returned to his desk. "Our answer will be 'yes.'" Valyrie scribbled the vote on a scrap of parchment and handed it to a passing chamberlain.

Once the votes had been collected and tallied, the chamberlain announced, "By the grace of Azura, we congregate to do her will in all things. It is the will of the consuls that the militia *shall* be doubled."

Valyrie stood, joining Jurgen and the other vicars in applause. For the first time, Tristan cracked a slight smile and almost gleamed with kindness. *I wonder if that goodly smile is truly benevolent.*

"We've done good works here today, Vicars," Tristan said. "We shall now adjourn for the remainder of today. Master Greathis, execute the will of your consuls and find men willing and able to defend our holy church."

"Your Holiness!" Greathis snapped to attention, then left the chamber.

"It will only be a matter of time before he has his army," Jurgen whispered. "The church is endangered, but the vicars aren't quite ready to commit to the idea of a standing army."

Valyrie leaned close to him. "Surely you can stop that."

"Who is to say that I would want to stop it? If things were to worsen, even I could change my mind. Though the Drakars have perpetrated wrongs, I would still not see Sorbian troops looting and burning our sacred places."

"Maybe you should meet with the Sorbian general without Tristan's knowledge." She stopped abruptly and lowered her head when a group of vicars passed. "They might listen to you."

"And if they don't? I would be labeled a traitor publicly, and if I were captured, Tristan would never ransom me back after the trouble I've given him."

Valyrie shook her head. "I wish we could go to the guard with this. It seems Master Greathis could easily solve the problem."

"Though I've known Greathis to be neutral, I cannot maintain an expectation of anyone based upon my experience. After all, Forane is much different since the last time I saw her. No, we must act with the utmost caution. We must assume all are potential enemies unless otherwise proven."

Valyrie looked up saw a group of vicars standing before them.

"Vicar Griffinwold," Jurgen said, dipping his head to the eldest amongst them. The man, judging by his robes and jewelry, seemed equal in both age and status to Jurgen.

"Winfred," Griffinwold responded, and Valyrie likened his accent to that of a Falacoran, but sharper and with an aristocratic bent. *Lasoronian, perhaps?* "We've known one another too long for that, Aldric."

Aldric? Valyrie had never heard Vicar Jurgen's first name. Not even her father had referred to him so informally.

"How might I help you gentlemen?" Jurgen asked, eying the two standing with Griffinwold.

"Causing quite the disturbance, are we?" Griffinwold asked. "It would seem you are drawing battle lines with His Holiness."

"I only do what I feel is right and proper, what I feel Azura would will."

Griffinwold smiled. "Indeed. I was just remarking to Vicars Tumolt and Carrenhold about the spectacles demonstrated before us, and we began thinking that perhaps Vicar Jurgen might care to join us for our midday meal?"

"I would be delighted to join you. Could my clerk come along?" Jurgen asked.

Griffinwold displayed a broad grin. "So long as she shares our disdain for the current situation."

"It is safe to say that she does."

"Good." Griffinwold gestured toward the grand entryway. "Let us go. I know a quiet place where we can speak."

* * *

The sign outside the establishment stated, "The Refined Palate," and from the moment Valyrie entered, her eyes and nose were assaulted with all manner of delectable sights and smells. Having not eaten much since her father's passing, her body responded strongly to the offerings of the tiny restaurant.

"A shame this place doesn't see the kind of business befitting of its quality," Griffinwold said, taking a seat at one of the large, empty tables.

"I've always understood the food comes at a price here." Jurgen sat next to him and offered Valyrie a chair at his side. "A price not all are willing to bear."

Griffinwold waved at the serving maiden. "Bring us a feast to rival that of the palace, and as quick as you can. I starve!"

"So, you dislike the current circumstances?" Jurgen asked once the maiden left to fetch the order. "I've been discontent since I heard rumors of priests training in miracles of an offensive nature —battle spells, as mages would call them."

"What sane man could like them? If we train as mages, are we not mages ourselves, the very thing we hope to avoid? Though I am Lasoronian, I do not follow blindly, a behavior many of my Falacoran allies failed to unlearn after the War of the Eagles."

"The War of the Eagles, yes, and the Zyvdredi influences. I've never truly understood the relationship between Falacore and Zyvdred, Winfred. It seems... complex." Jurgen grinned at the serving maiden when she brought a round of drinks.

"Zyvdred, yes. It has long been a protectorate of Falacore, a place whose mystery is surpassed only by the strangeness of its inhabitants. In the black mountains, they practice old rituals and even older magic, and they rarely pass their borders for anything other than trade. Little is known about what goes on deep within that country, but the Falacoran monarchy maintains close ties. The only certainty is that strange beasts and men live in those isolated reaches, and few dare to venture there."

Valyrie toyed with her salad, removing unwanted bits from the pile. *I've never understood why rich people like onions on everything.*

"Perhaps I shall never understand it. I would think a nation as strong in the faith as Falacore would impress Azura's teachings upon the Zyvdredi," Jurgen said.

Griffinwold gave a dismissive nod. "It seems strange, does it not? I've been told that the Zyvdredi maintain their old ways, and the Falacorans can do little to change that, no matter how much they try. Besides, sometimes I think their King Elson keeps up the relationship only to have his hand in everything within his reach."

"One day, perhaps." Jurgen sipped from his cup. "But, as you were saying…"

"Yes, the matter at hand," Griffinwold said, snatching a fresh roll from the basket as soon as it landed on the table. "It would seem you mean to stand between the Grand Vicar and his army. You make dangerous enemies, Aldric."

"The church was never meant to fight wars of conquest. I feel this entire situation has gone too far."

"Wars of conquest? You mean of defense, don't you?" Griffinwold eyed Jurgen for a moment. "Or has Aldric Jurgen come across some new information?"

Valyrie stared at her lap, refusing to look any of the men in the eye. The full reality of the situation gripped her mind; she was seated across from the Lasoronian *vicar primus* and his associates, and Jurgen had let down his guard at a dangerous time. *Please, think of something*, she thought, as if to will the notion into Jurgen's head.

Jurgen sat for a long while, seeming to ponder his answer at length. "Yes."

Griffinwold's eyes brightened. "Yes? That's it?"

"If I tell you these things that I know, you and your friends shall join me in danger." Jurgen paused, studying each man's features. "Your expressions tell me that you are prepared to hear the truth."

"Tell it, Jurgen," Griffinwold whispered, evidently aware he was missing a piece of the puzzle. "What have we been denied?"

Here it comes. Valyrie closed her eyes. She only hoped that the words crossing Jurgen's lips would be well received, or Jurgen and she would be making a trip to the nearby prison for a prolonged stay.

"I have been in contact with a sorcerer, and he has advised me of some rather grim news—the truth of what happened, how this war started. The Morcaine mage academy was attacked preemptively... by Gustav Drakar."

"You, Jurgen? Approached by this sorcerer?"

"Yes. I know it may be difficult to believe, but I assure you that this is the truth."

"I knew it," the man across from Valyrie said, his accent crisp and posh. "Why would Sorbia declare war upon us out of nowhere? I never bought it for a second."

"You'll have to excuse Vicar Carrenhold," Griffinwold said. "His disdain for Tristan comes from a constant disrespect—"

"Disrespect?" Carrenhold asked. "That's putting it lightly."

Griffinwold bowed slightly. "Yes, the Grand Vicar gives him fits about his being from Albiad and their inability to help us in this war. He's shown disdain for me, being that I am Lasoronian, but he gives Carrenhold hell. Go on, Jurgen."

"Gustav and his men massacred the Sorbian mages, then fled. His death is the result of his own misdeeds, and I feel that His Holiness knows the truth, but keeps it from us."

"Then we must do something," Griffinwold said. "This war is

a farce."

"That is what I've been working toward these many days. I want to see this war ended and its true reason known—and those who are responsible punished." Jurgen took a piece of meat from a serving tray. "We must find a way to remove Tristan from the Vicariate."

"And who did you have in mind to replace him, Vicar Jurgen?" Vicar Tumolt asked.

"This isn't about me, if that's what you are implying." Jurgen sighed. "I have no great aspirations. I only want what is best for the church, and I can assure you that Andolis Drakar no longer works toward that end."

"Spoken like a *true* Grand Vicar." Griffinwold swatted Jurgen on the shoulder. "Said by the kind of man we need leading the church in these harsh and uncertain times."

"Do what you will once Tristan is gone, but until that day comes, our work lies unfinished. Good day to you, gentlemen. We shall speak more of these things when there is need." Jurgen stood and exchanged embraces and goodbyes with each of them, then led Valyrie out of the restaurant.

"Will you take the throne if offered?" Valyrie asked once they were on the street.

"Perhaps. If Azura wills it through her consuls, I would serve, but we needn't concern ourselves with such things at this juncture."

"Yes, Your Grace."

"For now, we continue going to the consulship to make sure Andolis doesn't do any more damage. We must also send word to the others."

"How?"

"I shall prepare missives, and you'll take them around. If I were to go, it would put our friends in even more danger."

Jurgen opened the door of their assigned house, closing it behind Valyrie. "You shall deliver these letters." He sat at the writing desk and scribbled notations, then handed them to her. "I wrote them in the form of a journal in case they are read by our enemies. Go quickly. First to the militia for Laedron and Marac, then to the headquarters."

She turned toward the door.

"Oh, and take this," Jurgen said, removing his Azura's Star brooch from his robe. "No one will trouble you while you wear it."

"What will you do?"

"I'll remain here until you return. Be swift."

"Alone?" she asked.

Jurgen patted her on the arm. "If they were to come for me, little would stand in their way. Go."

* * *

She arrived at the militia headquarters and found a guardian standing post outside the front door. "I have correspondences."

"For Greathis? Third floor—"

"No, these are for two others. They joined recently. One with black hair and dark blue eyes, thin, and the other had brown hair and eyes to match. Bigger fellow."

"They'd be on the second floor with the other new ones. On

the right, miss."

"You haven't seen these two before?"

The guard chuckled. "Based upon the details provided, you've described half of the regiment. Good evening."

"Sorry," she said, her cheeks warming from the embarrassment. "I'll find them."

Once on the second floor, she found Laedron and Marac in their sleeping quarters. They were dressed in uniforms of the militia, a stark contrast to the plain clothes they normally wore.

"Jurgen sends news." She handed Laedron the missive.

"Not as grave as the other news we've received, I pray." Laedron passed her a rolled parchment. "This was left in our room while we were out. Found it this morning."

She unfurled the parchment.

The meeting with our lady has gone well. Make yourself available around the Ancient Quarter and our holy friend's new home, and keep a good eye out. The time nears. —Your Confessor.

"Your Confessor?" she asked.

"Piers." Laedron sighed. "When I thought I was going to die by his hand, I begged that he take my life and spare you and the others. I said... too much, but in hindsight, it's better that I did."

"Will you two be close to us?" She tried her best not to plead for their protection. "We're near the west end of the Ancient Quarter."

"Of course," Marac said, sheathing his sword at his hip. "We're assigned a route that takes us near where you're staying. Don't worry."

If only it were that easy. "Thank you. I have more to deliver, so I will be off before it gets late. All the best."

"Are you well?" Laedron asked.

"As well as can be expected in these times."

"I can't disagree. I hope we'll see you again soon, and under different circumstances."

৩৯ Chapter Eight ঙ৶

The Lost Militia

Laedron watched her walk down the hall until she was gone from sight. "It's good to see her in higher spirits."

"You call that 'higher spirits'?" Marac scoffed.

"If you'd seen her mourning in the chapel, you'd agree with me."

"If you say so." Marac placed a shield on his arm and buckled it.

"Never thought I'd see you using one of those again."

"I'd rather take a blow to this hunk of wood and iron than my fleshy bits, if I can help it."

"You stand a good chance, I'd say. The thing's more than half your height."

"Let's get on with it. My feet are begging to roam the cobbles for hours on end."

"No need to be dry about it, Marac. At least now we have a useful purpose in the scheme of things." Laedron gave him a good-natured poke. "Brice has seen more action than you in this city thus far."

"Oh, so we're competing now? Little thimble's got a long way to catch up to Marac Reven."

Laedron laughed, leading the way through the hall and into the street. He soon found the beginning of their appointed route, the mouth of a narrow back street near the western wall of the Ancient Quarter. *It couldn't have been a well-lit street, now could it?* Laedron sighed.

Marac's face radiated his concern. "Everything all right?"

"Yes, yes. I only wonder what we'll find along this road."

"This one's as good as any other. We've been in tighter spots."

"Let's get to it, then. It's not going to patrol itself."

With the sun setting on the horizon, Laedron watched the lantern lighters scurry through the streets. The light posts gave off a dim ambient glow, just enough for him to make out important features, but not enough to clear the shadows that gave him anxiety. *How entertaining it will be for our assailants when I draw this dagger. I know more about fishing than wielding this thing, and that's pathetic indeed.* He was glad to have Marac at his side; he knew the miller's son had paid close attention to sword training.

Marac walked over to the first business they encountered, turned the knob, and jiggled the door in its frame.

"What are you doing?" Laedron asked.

"Making sure it's secure. If we're to be militia, we might as well do it right."

Laedron checked the next door. "What do we do if they're unlocked?"

"Reach in and lock it, I suppose. You'll have to forgive me. I'm a bit new to this whole patrolling thing."

"We just have to stay close to Jurgen's apartment. I'd die if anything happened to him."

"Don't you mean *to her*?" Marac asked.

"What? No, of course not. Don't be silly."

"What's silly about it? Has your training made you cold to any possibilities other than the mission?"

"Now's not the time. We have a war to stop."

Marac gave him a cross glare. "All duty, eh? What will become of you when duty ends and all that remains is a tired old man?"

"I have some time before that, I should think. Plenty of time by my calculations."

"Wait too long, and you'll find things passing you by, my friend. Wait, yes, but no longer than you must."

"We're too different, and her father just passed. I don't want to simply be a replacement for someone she's lost."

"No, she doesn't strike me as that type. She's willful, and she might even be as stubborn as you. From my limited experience, I could say that you two have several things in common—a love of books and knowledge, a quiet demeanor, all wrapped around a fiery, passionate center."

"All of that aside, I doubt she's interested in me. I've been in her embrace, but it was only to comfort her in her grief. Nothing more."

"Then bring her back from the darkness, Lae. Give her hope. Won't you at least try?"

Laedron stopped.

"Well, won't you?" Marac took him by the shoulder. "What's gotten into you? I'm sorry if I offended, but it's—"

"Look. Just there," Laedron said, pointing down an alley. In a wider part of the alleyway, a pair of shoes—clearly still worn by a body—lay exposed, and the person to whom they were attached wasn't moving. Laedron could gather little detail since the body was mostly concealed behind a few barrels.

"Oh, probably a vagabond. We're militia, right? Let's check him out." Marac approached, looked over the tops of the barrels, then turned back to Laedron. "It's a militia guard, Lae. He's not moving."

Laedron walked around the barrels and crouched beside the man. Searching for wounds, he said, "There's no blood. Nothing. He isn't breathing."

"Roll him over." Marac walked to the other side of the man and hunched over him. "Check his back."

"Nothing there, either. No blood, nothing." Laedron scanned the distance when something made a noise in the next alley, a sound much like a pan hitting the ground. "What was that?"

Across from them, a man cowled in black robes took off down the opposite street. Laedron caught a glimpse of red symbols on the back of the man's cloak, small, indistinguishable characters written in two vertical rows from his shoulders to the hem.

"A killer? Marac!" Laedron sprang to his feet. With Marac's heavy footsteps on his heels, Laedron pursued the shadowy figure through the alley. Laedron turned the next corner and heard the sound of a sword being drawn behind him—Marac readying himself for a fight. He drew his dagger. *Better this than nothing, I guess.*

Rounding the next corner, Laedron felt a sting on his throat and recoiled out of reflex. He remembered that same feeling when Heidrik, Gustav's minion who had tortured Marac and Mikal, had lashed him in the face. The feeling was unmistakable and familiar, the warmth of blood flowing across his skin. He turned and plunged the dagger into the cloaked man as hard as he could. Laedron's breathing hastened while his target's slowed and became shallow. From the amount of blood on his hands, Laedron knew that he had hit his mark and hit it well.

The man's dagger dropped from his left hand, and a bit of wood from his right, as he collapsed. A pool of blood spread slowly and soaked his garments.

Laedron took a step back to keep his boots from getting drenched. Laedron's eyes widened when he realized that the length of wood was, in fact, a wand. "It's a mage, Marac! Have I killed one of our countrymen?"

"Keep your voice down, Lae." Marac leaned down and removed the cloth covering the man's face. "Doesn't look like any Sorbian I've ever seen."

"We haven't seen them all. What if he's like us? What if he was on a mission, too?"

"If he was on a mission, I doubt it came from the same people we serve. Look, a tattoo on his neck. Unlike anything I've seen before."

Laedron turned the man's head to the side, and the tattoo on his neck was illuminated by the lantern light. "It's a word."

"A word? What does it say?"

"*Kivesh*."

"Kivesh?" Marac asked. "Well, what does that mean?"

"Nothing. It's a name."

"How can you read it?"

"It's written in an old language. Zyvdredi."

Marac's face twisted with apparent shock and fear. "Zyvdredi? Here?"

"It would seem so." Laedron rummaged through the man's pockets. In the belt, he found a black cloth pouch.

"What's that?" Marac asked.

Without responding, Laedron opened the purse and pulled out a handful of black stones, each etched with a runic symbol that he couldn't place, symbols similar to the ones along the back of the man's cloak. A few of the stones sparkled with an artificial glow as if reverberating with energy. The others only reflected the light of the lantern posts.

"What are those, Lae? What does all this mean?"

"I don't know." Laedron returned the stones to the bag and put it in his pocket. "I'm going to hold on to them until we know for sure."

"What do we do now?"

Laedron retrieved the man's wand and tucked it into his other boot. "Back to the dead guard. I need to see what I can discover about the body. It may lend a clue."

Marac led the way back to the militiaman's body, and Laedron searched the area for any sign of onyx stones.

"Nothing here. Nothing more than we already know, which isn't much."

Laedron reached for his wand, but Marac grabbed his hand before he could draw it.

"If we're to do this, we'd better try the old-fashioned way — find witnesses and look around. If you're discovered, we'd be in deep water."

Laedron stood with a sigh, then turned when he heard a door close behind him. "Where was that?"

"Couldn't tell," Marac said.

Believing the source of the sound to be close, Laedron knocked on the door opposite the dead guard, then listened intently. He heard the shuffling of feet against a wooden floor on the other side, but no one answered. He knocked again.

A muffled, "Go away!" came from beyond the door.

"I won't go away. Open, in the name of the militia," Laedron said, trying to sound serious and authoritative.

The door creaked open only an inch or two. "What ye want?" The voice was that of an elderly male, probably crotchety and set in his ways, but little else.

"Did you see what passed here not long ago?" Laedron asked, pointing over his shoulder.

"No, and we don't want any trouble. Go away."

Before the man could slam the door, Laedron forced it open just enough to lodge his boot in the crack. "We're not done here. If you've seen anything, you need to tell us."

"What are you doing there?" a voice shouted from up the alley. The jingle of metal armor matched pace with footsteps, and Laedron recognized the newcomer as one of the younger militia guards.

"Investigating a crime," Laedron replied. "Go get more guards. The killer is up this street. Take the next right, then turn right again. There you shall find him in a puddle of his own blood. Go!"

"You caught the one who did this?" the elderly man behind the door whispered, opening the door. "Is it true?"

The man wore a long, white beard identical to his hair, both unkempt and dirty. He gave off a horrible odor reminiscent of sweat and spoiled milk, and his clothes were those of a beggar.

"Yes," Laedron said, trying to hide a grimace. "Now, will you tell me what you saw? Or do you insist on playing this game even still?"

"Lower your voice, young man. There are ears that might overhear us. Come in, and I shall tell you what I saw."

Entering the cramped domicile, Laedron was thankful he hadn't eaten anything recently because the smell and conditions within the pitiful house would have surely made him lose his stomach on the floor.

"What in the hells is that smell?" Laedron asked, unable to contain his disgust. "Are you harboring the dead beneath your floors?"

"My soup, young man. Sounds like you wouldn't care for any."

"If it's putting off a scent like that, I think I'll pass," Laedron said, and Marac waved his hand in agreement.

"Well, have a seat, then." The man gestured at a pair of rickety wooden chairs set around a matching table, then took a seat across from them. "Name's Clarence."

Laedron sat and folded his arms. "Laedron, and this is Marac. What did you see?"

"That young fellow there, the dead one, he was walking along and tapped another fellow on the back when he reached the barrels. They exchanged words too quiet for me to hear, then I saw a glimmer of light."

"A glimmer of light?" Laedron asked, his interest piqued. "What did it look like?"

"Swirling, vibrant, and red. It wrapped around the guard, and only a few moments later, the militia man collapsed."

"The man who did this, he had symbols along the back of his garb? Red embroideries?"

"Yes, and a scarf across his face." Clarence paused. "Am I safe here?"

"Worry not. That one will trouble you no more." Laedron stood. "Anything else?"

"That's the best I can remember. What do you think this means, if you don't mind me poking my nose around in it?"

"We know not," Marac said, "but we shall find out. Keep your doors secure and report anything else you remember to Master Greathis."

With a nod, the old man stood and let Laedron and Marac out. Laedron heard the slide of metal locking the door behind them once they reached the alley.

Seeing more militia approaching, Laedron pointed at the dead guard. "Take this one back to the headquarters, and you'll find his murderer on the next street. Bring that one's body to Greathis, too. We'll keep up the patrol in case there are more."

Once they had gotten farther up the alley and clear of the militia, Marac asked, "Do you mean to tell them about the stones?"

"No, not yet." Laedron patted the pocket containing the black pouch. "I mean to do a little investigating before I reveal that piece of information."

"What if Greathis could tell us more?"

"At worst, he might know exactly what they mean and not tell us anything because he works for the same people. He is Falacoran, after all. At best, he would know and tell us, but the risk far outweighs the good that might come of it."

"You're right. So, you think it's not an isolated incident? A lone murderer on the prowl?"

"No, not from what we saw. A name tattooed on his neck written in Zyvdredi, these stones, and magic—no, he's working for someone else, but I don't know the purpose. We've come upon the identity of the killer and the reason guards have come up missing, but it creates even more questions."

"Let's keep searching. Perhaps there are more clues around here that we're not seeing."

Laedron shrugged. "Maybe. It's worth a shot. If we don't find anything, we should go see Greathis to feel him out and see what he can tell us."

They continued patrolling for over an hour. Nothing seemed

unusual or out of the ordinary, as best he could tell. He decided they should go visit Master Greathis, and Marac agreed.

* * *

When they arrived at the militia headquarters, Laedron took in the spectacle in front of the building. A squad of guards, with Greathis among them, were gathered around the dead body Laedron had found and the one he had caused. Several dozen regular citizens crowded the streets, craning their necks to see.

"Shouldn't we take this inside?" Laedron asked. "It would appear a crowd is gathering."

"Sergeant Wilkans just informed me of what happened, as I only just arrived myself," Greathis replied. "Yes, bring the bodies inside and bar the doors. The rest of you, get on with your duties. Half of the city remains unwatched with you all here."

Once inside, Laedron recounted everything that had happened, being careful to leave out the parts about the stones and the magical occurrences.

"No wounds. Not even bruising from strangulation," Greathis said, searching the dead guard's body. "He was too young to die of anything natural. How did he die?"

"I wish I knew." Laedron shrugged. "We found him like this in the alley, and we searched for weapons or a cause of death. None could be found."

Greathis turned to the other body. "Looks as if you are skilled with a dagger after all, young man. These symbols on his cloak, do they mean anything to you?"

Laedron swallowed deeply. "No, Master Greathis. I've never seen anything like them before."

"I fear we may have mages afoot," Greathis said, tracing the embroidery with a fingertip. "I haven't seen runes like these in a long time."

"You've seen them before?"

"Not exactly like these, no, but the style reminds me of mage writing." Greathis rubbed his scruffy chin. "The Sorbian army is in Balfan, and we now have what seems to be a dead mage before us. Infiltration?"

Laedron had some difficulty keeping the details sorted in his mind. The war, in the minds of the Heraldans, had been started by Sorbia, but he knew Gustav and his hired hands had made a sneak attack to cause it—the academy burned and toppled by their torches and incantations. If nothing else, Greathis seemed either not to know what had actually passed or refused to reveal his knowledge of those events. The former would be good news for Laedron, proof that Greathis was not part of the scheme, but the possibility of the latter gave him pause and reason not to trust the militia commander. *For now, I'll need to keep some things secret.*

"How long since the first militia guard went missing?" Marac asked. "Didn't Sergeant Wilkans say two months or so?"

Greathis sighed. "Yes. It began just prior to the opening of the war, and that is why I feel the Sorbian mages had something to do with this."

If only he knew he was speaking in the presence of a Sorbian mage. He's ready to lay the blame on us, though, regardless of the fact that he's probably never met or even seen a Sorbian sorcerer. Well, knowingly seen one.

"Sorbian or not, we should be on the lookout for others such as this," Greathis said. "I thank you for bringing this to my attention. Should you find anything else, let me know. Of course, I can only hope that it was an isolated incident and that we'll see no more murders of my men."

"Yes, Master Greathis. We'll return to our patrol." Laedron gave Marac a nudge, then walked out the door and down the street.

Marac glanced around when they were by themselves. "Quick to blame the Sorbians, isn't he?"

"He has nothing else to go on," Laedron said. "It looks awfully suspicious, and for a Heraldan, it's not a far stretch to believe the Circle could have done this."

"Do you believe it, Lae?"

"Of course not, don't be silly. I can't even tell you if anyone from the Circle is still alive, aside from those taken into the Shimmering Dawn."

"What if it *is* Circle mages, though? Ones that you don't know? Maybe they've come here for revenge."

Laedron stopped and gave Marac a long stare. "I can't discount the possibility. It's out of character for a Circle mage, though; we don't go around killing random people."

"He wasn't a random person, though," Marac said, turning a corner into an alley. "He was a militia guard, a symbol of Heraldan authority, and the closest thing they have to a military."

"Yes, but why? Why kill militia guards just before a major attack on your own academy?"

"I don't know. What are you getting at?"

"I mean to say that we're clearly not privy to every piece of the puzzle. What if some act by the Circle mages did cause the war? What if it wasn't a preemptive sneak attack? Instead, what if the attack was merely a response to some other grievance?"

"We can speculate about the reasons, but it will do us no good. For now, we're walking a thin line between reality and what we can prove, and falling on either side puts us in grave danger."

Marac turned. "Do you hear that?"

Stopping, Laedron closed his eyes. "A whistle. From the Ancient Quarter… Jurgen!"

৩৯ Chapter Nine ৫৬

Trouble in the Ancient Quarter

Valyrie brushed a concoction of butter and seasonings onto the goose, turning it on the spit to ensure each side had a liberal application. Night had fallen over the city, and with Jurgen's missives delivered to each recipient, she had been given the task of making a meal for them. Her first night in the house had left her with an unsettled feeling, much like the one she'd had the night her father died, a feeling of homesickness and a longing to return to something familiar.

"Smells delightful," Jurgen said, looking up from his papers at the writing desk. "I wasn't aware the house came stocked with all manner of spices."

"It didn't." Valyrie wiped her hands on a scrap of cloth. "To cover my steps, I visited the market and purchased some spices before going to the headquarters. If anyone had been following me, I don't see how they could have kept up after that."

"A wise move."

"A few more minutes on the goose, and we'll be ready to dine." She sliced a carrot and dropped it into the bowl with the rest of the greens. "I've made a salad, too. I saw how eagerly you ate the one at that restaurant."

"The Refined Palate?" Jurgen stood and joined her at the counter. "Since Griffenwold paid, I thought it would be disrespectful not to indulge."

"Then, I made it for nothing?"

"No, no. I only mean to say that I didn't favor the one from earlier. Yours, however, looks splendid. Yes, I think I shall enjoy every bit of what you've made. Thank you, Valyrie."

She couldn't tell if he was lying to make her feel better. "I hope so." She sighed, leaning against the counter.

"Is everything all right?" Jurgen asked.

She nodded. "Just tired. I haven't had much sleep lately—the moving around from place to place, the nightmares, the fear."

"Nightmares? Your father?"

"Sometimes, sometimes not. In one of them, I find myself locked in my cell in the basement of the Shimmering Dawn. That's the one I have the most." She paused. "I hear your anguish as they beat you, and I'm waiting for my turn, for whatever they have in store for me. Every time I see Piers's face, it reminds me of the terror I felt."

"Our dreams have a strange way of reminding us of our deepest fears." Jurgen took the salad bowl and sat at the small dining table. "They also have a way of showing us our greatest hopes, despite the darkness."

"It's silly to indulge in dreams," she said, sitting next to him. "The bright or the dark, they're all the same—not real and fleeting."

"The same way it's nonsensical to deal in fables and tales untrue?" Jurgen gave her a grin. "I know someone who fancies doing just that. Don't allow yourself to grow bitter from this."

"Perhaps Da was right about the whole thing. Had I become a seneschal, I'd be far removed from any of this plight."

"Yes, perhaps," Jurgen said. "But what sort of life would you have as a bookkeeper for some noble? Living is something not done from writing desks and with your nose deep in ledgers. Not at all."

"What do you suppose, then? After all of this is said and done, what is to become of me? I have no trade and no money, and I won't go to my uncle. I can't."

"I know not, but if I survive this, I wouldn't see you cast out in the streets. Your choice will become clear to you in time."

"Thank you." She went over to the goose, carved a few pieces, and gathered them on a dish. "Just right. The outside is crispy while the inside is tender and juicy."

"Wonderful, thank you," Jurgen said when she returned to

the table. "Shall we pray?"

Pray? She remembered the practice, but prayers had rarely been said in her home. "Yes, that would be fine." She bowed her head and closed her eyes.

"Azura, protect us in this dire time and show us the way. Give peace to Valyrie, for she suffers greatly outside of your grace. Pass your blessings unto her that she might have satisfaction in your name. Bless our meal that it might provide sustenance and resolve against those who would not do your will in all things. Be it so."

Valyrie repeated, "Be it so," and opened her eyes. She took a portion of meat and a bit of salad.

After a while, Jurgen broke the silence. "You were right."

"About what?"

"The goose. Perfectly cooked. I applaud your efforts."

She smiled. "It was rare that we'd have a goose, but I managed. Cooked it about the same as I used to prepare roast duck."

"Quite fine." Jurgen turned his head. "Did you hear that?"

"Hear what?"

"Yelling, perhaps?" He stood and approached the window. Valyrie got up to stand at his side.

On the street below stood four men, three militiamen and a fourth man opposite them, some twenty paces away. The guard in the front was pointing at the fourth, a man clad in black from head to foot. Valyrie spied red markings along the back of the man's cloak, but she couldn't derive their meaning or purpose. All she knew for certain was that she had never seen such markings.

The guard leader stepped closer to the man, and the

unknown man held up his hand. Valyrie was left breathless when she recognized what he held in that hand—a wand. "Mages? Here?"

Jurgen took a deep breath, his eyes widening. "They've come for us, Valyrie."

"Who? Who are they?"

"I do not know. Go to my room and retrieve the weapons."

"Weapons? What weapons?" she asked, trying to control her panicked breathing.

"I procured two swords." Jurgen pointed. "Get them. It seems we shall need them in due course."

Bursting through the door, she searched the room and found the swords leaning against the bed. *I wonder if Jurgen's ever used these. No matter. Fighting gives us a better chance than doing nothing.*

She crept to the window when she heard a loud noise outside, and she caught a glimpse of a bolt of lightning before it fizzled out of existence. One of the militiamen lay dead, smoke rising from his chest. Trembling, she watched the two remaining guards rush the man in black. One of the militiamen blew hard on his whistle. The chirp echoed off the buildings and into the night air.

Please, take him down. She eyed the swords in her arms. *If left to us, we'll fare no better than the dead man.* A blast of swirling flames took one of the militiamen to the ground. The other grappled with the man in black, trying to wrest control of the wand. In the chaos of the struggle, a stream of fire shot from the wand, igniting the roof of a house across the street. The flames quickly swept across the roof, and people ran out screaming.

With apparently all of the strength he could muster, the militia man pulled the mage's hand to his right. Valyrie saw the tip of the wand pointing her way, and she took a few steps backward. An explosion deafened her and incinerated half of the room in a flash of light. She felt the floor give way, and she reached out through the smoke and debris flying through the air, catching a plank before she fell through to the first floor.

A haze came over her, and she felt the prickles of wood splinters lodged in her skin. *If you can feel that, you're still alive. Pull yourself up before the next spell!* With all her might, she tried to lift her body onto the landing, but it was no use. She looked below, and though she thought she would survive the fall, landing in a pile of broken wood, nails, and bricks made her think twice about letting go. Glancing up, she saw a hand close to her face, and she grabbed it.

Jurgen pulled her up, then brought her into the common room. "The swords, where are they?"

"I don't know," she said, shaking with fear and pain. "They might've fallen."

"No matter. We have to get out of here." Jurgen helped her to the stairs. When they had made it halfway down, the top of the house exploded in a firestorm. He ran, almost lifting her off the ground as he pulled her behind him, and burst through the door into the street.

She stared at the man in black, his eyes seemingly full of rage upon seeing them emerge from the burning structure. Losing no time, Valyrie grabbed Jurgen's hand and ran toward the closest portcullis leading out of the Ancient Quarter.

She spotted two militia guards running up a narrow lane, and she didn't stop running until she reached them. "Mage…" Leaning over, she rested her hands on her knees and tried to catch her breath. "A man in black attacking—"

"Val," one of the guards said.

She squinted. "Lae?"

Laedron took her hand. "Attacked you? Creator! You look like you've been through the hells."

"I'll be fine, but one of the militia fights with him still. You've got to stop him."

Laedron turned to Jurgen. "Return to headquarters with Valyrie. We'll take care of this one. Tell Piers what has passed here and have him send help."

She took Laedron in an embrace. "Be careful. We'll see you back at the chapel."

The hug seemed to last an eternity, the safety of Laedron's arms filling her with a warmth she hadn't felt for a long time. Clearing his throat, Laedron returned her to Jurgen's side, then took off with Marac toward the west gate.

❧ Chapter Ten ❧

Crossing Wands

L aedron peered through the entry into the Ancient Quarter with a heavy heart. He recalled how powerful Gustav had been, and he only hoped that he had a chance at fighting the mage who was somewhere beyond. Then, he caught sight of a man in black rushing toward them, probably in pursuit of Jurgen and Valyrie.

The man stopped a hundred paces away and stared at Laedron and Marac, seeming to study them as they approached. Laedron paused after passing the portcullis and reached into his boot.

"No," Marac said, readying his shield. "You can't."

"We stand no chance otherwise." Laedron drew Ismerelda's scepter.

"Houses ablaze ahead," the man yelled, starting toward them again. "Several men dead, and a madman slashing about. I must leave this crazed place."

"Not so fast." Laedron held up his rod. "The houses may be on fire, but we'll handle that in due time. The madman of whom you speak is you, Sorcerer, and we shall deal with you now!"

"Deal with me?" The man chuckled, then raised his wand. "Since you've made it clear that you know what I am, why don't you simply let me pass? We'll forget the matter, and you'll live."

The man must not have noticed what Laedron held, and Laedron decided to use that to his advantage. *If he doesn't know I'm a mage, he might not notice a ward spell on Marac's shield.* Laedron whispered an incantation under his breath, concentrating on the ruby set in the scepter. Marac's shield glowed dimly with a silver vibrancy not unlike the color of its paint, and Laedron moved to stand behind him. Pushing Marac forward, he maintained the spell, and Marac continued at a steady pace and drew his sword.

The man in black sighed. "Another group of militia who don't know a good deal when they hear one, it would seem. Very well. Only a bit of time wasted."

The sorcerer flicked his wand while speaking a spell, and a lightning bolt flashed across the open ground, squarely striking Marac's shield. Marac faltered for a moment, but pushed forward again once he had recovered.

"Wooden shield? That's fine. How about a little fire?" the man shouted, raising his wand once more. With the utterance of some words, a ray of flames shot from the end of the man's wand and crashed into Marac's shield. Though Laedron could feel the heat warming his flesh, he kept his concentration strong. *A loss of focus will mean my death and Marac's. I won't let my friends down again!*

"What's this?" The man sounded nervous. "Unaffected? Impossible!"

His head aching, Laedron released the spell and stepped out from behind Marac. "No, not impossible, not when magic is involved."

"You... what do you know of magic?"

"Enough." Laedron flicked his wrist and shouted an incantation before the man in black could react. A swirling black and red stream of energy struck the man's hand, causing him to drop his wand.

"Another sorcerer? How can this be?" The man grasped his wand hand and winced. "How can this be?"

"You shall have plenty of time to think about the answer to that question in jail."

The man laughed and reached for his fallen wand, but Laedron quickly cast again, shattering it.

"No, no more spells," Laedron said. "You're coming with us."

"What is the meaning of this?" a voice shouted from Laedron's right. "What are you doing?"

Laedron glanced in the direction of the voice, then closed his eyes, regretting that he had displayed the rod in public. He had become the focus of a squad of militia who had happened upon his flank. He was unable to keep the cold chills from racing up and down his spine, the fear of being half a world away from his home and fully exposed before those who would see his kind dead.

On his knees, the man in black raised his face to the sky and cackled. Even though the man surely knew he was condemned to death, he seemed to take pleasure in the fact that he wouldn't be alone on the gallows. Hatred and anger welled up inside Laedron, and he counted the guards, considering for a moment if he could defeat them all.

"Drop it," Marac said, tapping Laedron on the hand with the flat of his blade. "Put the thing down and come peacefully with us."

Good, Marac. At least one of us stands a chance of getting out of here alive. Laedron put his scepter on the ground and held his hands outstretched at his sides.

"They're in it together," the other sorcerer started before taking Marac's boot to the face.

"Enough out of you, fiend." Marac picked up the rod, and the guards approached. "We'll take them to the headquarters. Master Greathis will surely want to question them."

An older militia man, a sergeant, if Laedron remembered the insignia correctly, stepped out in front of the others. "What has happened here?"

"I came upon these two quibbling in the street, then this one…" Marac pointed at Laedron. "… shot a spell at that one. I'm glad you showed up when you did, for I might have been killed."

"What's this business about you two being 'in it together?'" the sergeant asked.

Marac shook his head. "I knew this one when I joined, but I didn't know he meddled in the dark arts. Had I known that, I would've gone to Greathis much sooner."

The sergeant narrowed his eyes. "I see. We'll let Master Greathis sort this out." He turned to the squad and pointed at the other sorcerer. "Pick *that* up and bring it along."

* * *

His hands bound in chains, Laedron fell to his knees in Greathis's office. The guards threw the man in black down beside him, and Marac stood to Laedron's left. *I might as well get used to living in chains if I survive this. It would seem the only thing I can do well is get captured.* Greathis sat quietly behind his desk.

"We caught these two sorcerers in the Ancient Quarter," the sergeant said.

"Leave us," Greathis replied with a harsh tone. Laedron figured the tone was directed more at him because Master Greathis hadn't looked at anyone else.

The sergeant left and closed the heavy oak door behind him. The room remained silent for what seemed an eternity.

Greathis studied the man in black. "What's your name?"

The man laughed.

"Tell me your name."

"Why should I?"

"Because," Greathis said, standing and walking around the desk, "if you do not, you'll rot in prison until you do."

"If you even knew the people I work for, you'd know how

empty your words are. Put me in your prison, but I'll be out before dawn."

Greathis turned to the door. "Wilkans!"

Sergeant Wilkans opened the door. "Commander?"

"Lock him up, and go under heavy guard. Search him well before leaving him alone, then bring all of his possessions—clothes, wands, everything—to me."

"Yes, Master." Wilkans dragged the man from the room.

"Perhaps some time in the stockade will loosen his tongue." Greathis sat on the edge of his desk. "I already know your name, so we can skip the introductions and move straight into the matter at hand."

Laedron nodded.

"What in the hells is going on?" Greathis asked. His tone was kinder than the one he'd used with the man in black.

"We heard the whistle coming from the Ancient Quarter, and we made haste. Jurgen is a friend of ours, and we wanted to make sure no harm had come to him."

Greathis's right eye twitched. "Go on."

"Just before the west gate, we ran into Jurgen and his clerk, and they told us of the chaos. We went forward and met that man —the sorcerer—inside the Ancient Quarter. He tried to lie, but we saw through it. We engaged him and stopped him then and there."

"Engaged him. You mean with magic, right?"

Laedron closed his eyes and slowly bobbed his head. "We had no other choice but to—"

"No other choice?" Greathis slammed his fist on the desk. "As if everyone goes around playing with wands and magic? As if it's something innate and natural to do? Do you realize where you are, boy?"

"I know how it must look, Master, but—"

"How it must look? A recruit wearing my colors and throwing spells into the night? 'Ole Greathis has lost it,' they'll say. 'He let a mage into his little regiment. Jeopardized the whole of the theocracy, he has.' You've made me into a laughing stock!"

Marac stepped forward. "Few saw us, Master Greathis, and those who did were mostly running away and screaming."

"And you! Don't think you're out of trouble in the least. As far as I'm concerned, you're just as guilty as this one." Greathis took a deep breath. "To think, my militia has been infiltrated by a mage. Azura! You're not Sorbian. Tell me you're not."

Laedron dipped his head.

Greathis let out an angry growl. "I can't believe it." Greathis gave Laedron a puzzled look. "Why would Jurgen send you to me or even help you? You're blackmailing him, aren't you? Turned our dear priest into a spy for your dastardly cause? No, no... a forgery. You forged the letter to gain my trust, didn't you?"

"He came willingly," Laedron said, frustrated at the accusations. "And he aided us without threats or bribery."

"Why, Sorcerer? If I may call you that, or would you prefer *Sorbian dog*? Why would Jurgen assist you against us?"

"We share the same goal."

"And that is?"

"To end the war."

"Why would a Sorbian be interested in ending a war that the Sorbians started in the first place?"

Laedron stared into Greathis's eyes. The man exhibited disbelief and wonder, not what Laedron would expect to see from someone helping the Drakars. "We didn't start the war. This war began with an attack on the Morcaine Mage Academy, a sneak attack perpetrated by Gustav Drakar and a band of your militia."

"You lie," Greathis said in a dismissing manner. "All of my men have been here with me this entire time. They couldn't be in two places at once."

Laedron shrugged. "Perhaps they only wore the uniforms of your men, then. Either way, the war was started by the Drakars, not by the Sorbians."

"This makes no sense to me. What you claim cannot be true."

"Can it not? Since we've joined your ranks, have we done anything other than help you? We found one of your men slain, caught his killer, and reported the incident to you. We stopped the one in the Ancient Quarter, too. Why would we do those things if we meant you harm?"

"To get on my good side?"

"Is that what you would expect of a sorcerer sent to infiltrate you? You can't believe that."

"I don't know what to believe," Greathis said, folding his arms. "Where is Jurgen? I would hear this from his lips before drawing any conclusions."

"I can take you to him, but only you. No one else."

"Ah, yes, so you can lead me into a trap?"

"If I wanted to kill you, I could have done that already," Laedron said. "You won't be harmed. I swear it."

"Well, if Jurgen trusts you, perhaps I can. You haven't killed him yet, at any rate." Greathis took a cloak from his chair and affixed it about his neck. "Lead on, Sorcerer, but no tricks. And the shackles stay on."

* * *

Laedron led Greathis to the abandoned chapel. He took a deep breath, then opened the door and entered with Greathis following close behind. Once inside the common room, Laedron saw Jurgen and Valyrie seated at the large table, and Piers was treating Valyrie's numerous cuts and scrapes.

Piers glanced at Laedron, then did a double take and drew his sword. "You've brought *him* here?"

"Shimmering Dawn!" Greathis shouted, reaching for his blade.

"Wait, calm down." Laedron waved his hands, the chains of his shackles jingling. "Just calm down. We're here to talk things out, not to make trouble, right?"

"You should have told me we were coming to the Shimmering Dawn—traitors, brigands, and thieves." Greathis spit on the floor, then extended his hand to the priest. "Come, Jurgen. They shall hold you prisoner no longer."

"They do not hold me hostage, Dalton," Jurgen said. "I am a guest of these traitors, brigands, and thieves, as you put it."

"A guest?"

"Yes, of course." Jurgen wiped his hands on a rag and approached Greathis. "By your presence here, I can only assume you've been told the truth. Ah, but I can tell by the look in your eye that you don't believe it."

"What this sorcerer has said is impossible. It cannot be," Greathis replied. "How can you be so quick to believe his lies?"

"You never knew it, but I've maintained correspondence with the Shimmering Dawn of Sorbia for quite a long time. Don't you see, Greathis? Training priests with miracles of war, outfitting vessels with weapons, hoarding supplies, and restricting our borders? The Drakars knew war was imminent, but they claimed the Sorbians were responsible. Meklan Draive sent this sorcerer and his knights to me for help, to aid them in ridding the world of one Gustav Drakar."

Greathis's eyes widened. "You, Jurgen? You helped them kill the Grand Vicar's brother?"

"Draive wouldn't have set his people on such a task without cause." Jurgen sighed. "I helped them for my own purposes. I wanted to leave this land. I just wanted to get away after what the Drakars had done to me and to our people."

"And you thought it best to aid these assassins with their task? There's no honor in that."

Brice and Caleb entered from one of the side rooms. Upon seeing Greathis, Caleb drew his sword, but Jurgen held up his hand and said, "No need for that. We're only talking."

Caleb replaced his sword, but continued to eye Greathis warily.

Jurgen continued, "You speak of honor? It was honorable to attack and kill innocent people in Morcaine? To start a war and keep an entire nation—our nation, Dalton—blinded by lies? No one wanted to believe me, but the Drakars are the poison in our cups. Now you see what they have done, but you do not believe it because you have been conditioned by their treachery for so long."

"What has gotten into you, Vicar? I've never heard you speak so forcefully," Greathis said.

Jurgen took a deep breath. "I apologize if my tone was harsh. Nearly being assassinated must have put me in a volatile state. Tristan shall have to try harder next time."

"That's a serious charge, Jurgen. Have you any evidence of that fact?"

"We found letters." Brice walked over and stood next to Jurgen. "In Vicar Forane's house. They've been trying to kill him for quite some time."

Greathis extended his hand. "The letters, you have them?"

"Sadly, no," Brice replied. "So as not to draw suspicion, we left them there."

"Then my men shall readily find them upon a search of her residence, yes?"

Brice nodded. "Of course. In her private office on the second floor."

"Why didn't you come to me, Jurgen? Why the secrecy, the plotting?"

"We didn't know on which side of the fence you stood," Jurgen said. "We had to be sure, and I'm glad that you're willing to do what is right."

"This will have to be handled delicately." Greathis closed his eyes and massaged his eyelids with his fingertips. "We will go to Forane, search her residence, and arrest her. You'd better hope the evidence is there."

"And Tristan?" Jurgen asked.

"That will be up to you, Vicar. My men will escort you to the Vicariate on the morrow, and you will be allowed to present your charges to the consulship. Only by the will of the assembly can we detain a Grand Vicar, and I shall not impede upon the law. Without the law, we have nothing."

Jurgen took Greathis's hand in a firm embrace. "Thank you, Dalton. You'll be remembered as the man who saved the church from utter destruction."

"No, that honor belongs to you, sordid as the path may have been to get to this point. Remain here, and I shall send a detachment of guards for you."

Laedron held up his manacled hands. "Care to take these off?"

Greathis produced a key. "Come to the headquarters within the hour and retrieve your things."

"I'd like to come with you to arrest Forane," Laedron said.

Greathis raised an eyebrow. "After all that has passed?"

"Yes, if it's the same to you. If she and her friends have been studying offensive spells, it'd be best if I came along."

"You're probably right."

Marac joined them outside. "You're not going anywhere without me."

"Me, too," Brice said, closing the door behind them.

Laedron gave them a broad smile, then followed Greathis to the headquarters.

* * *

Within the hour, Laedron, Marac, and Brice stood in a hall with Master Greathis and a handful of militia. The hour was late, and Laedron could feel the tension like a thick cloud of anxiety hanging over their heads.

"Men," Greathis said. "Tonight, we are going to search Vicar Genevieve Forane's residence for seditious documents. An anonymous witness has told me letters detailing an assassination attempt are inside her house, and we mean to locate them. If we should find anything indicating wrongdoing, she shall be arrested."

Greathis's words must have struck a nerve in the guards because they gave one another disconcerted looks.

"Steel yourselves, men. We have a secret weapon with us, one who has joined the militia only recently. More recent still, he told me of his abilities, his prowess with magic."

"Magic's condemned by the church," one of the guards said. "If a mage be among us, Azura won't."

"Silence!" Greathis glared at the men until their whispers ceased. "If what I am told is true, we will need his help. Azura will be with those who serve justice, so we have no worries."

"I won't let you down," Laedron said, stepping forward. "I will show all of you that not all mages are to be feared. Some can be useful and even helpful, regardless of how you may feel about us."

"He brought me back to life once," Brice said. Laedron surmised that Brice's support hadn't benefited them because the guards' faces were riddled with bewilderment.

Laedron glared at Brice. "Why do you keep bringing that up?"

Brice grimaced. "But... it was important to me."

"Fine, yes. I'm glad that you're with us, and we'll leave it at that," Laedron said, turning to the door.

"Is that true?" Greathis asked.

Laedron replied with only a nod, then left. The others joined him in the street, and they traveled to Forane's residence in the Ancient Quarter.

๑ Chapter Eleven ๑

Serving Justice

Outside Vicar Forane's house, Greathis ordered, "Cover all the exits, men. Take her alive, but defend yourselves if she attacks."

Laedron watched the guards surround the residence, then turned to study the building. Fresh yellow paint had been carefully applied to every brick, and the lacquer on the exposed wooden frame still sparkled in the torchlight. On either side of the heavy wooden door stood well-trimmed bushes covered with white flowers. Not a single crack could be found in the steps leading to the front door.

Greathis walked toward the door, seeming either unafraid or careless of the possibilities of what might happen. He knocked three times, each rap of his iron gauntlet against the wood producing an echo.

After just enough time to make Laedron apprehensive, the door creaked open, and a young girl stepped out. "How might I help you gentlemen?"

"We've come to see your mistress," Greathis replied. "Could you tell her to come speak with me?"

With a deep bow, the girl disappeared inside, and not long after, Laedron heard a woman ask, "What did they say they wanted?" from somewhere inside.

"They didn't say. Only said they wanted to see the mistress of the house, m'lady," the girl replied.

A woman stepped outside, pulling a robe tight around her body as if trying to hide her night clothes. "Ah, Master Greathis. I didn't expect you this evening."

Laedron observed Brice holding the hilt of his sword tightly, and he followed suit by reaching within his garments to find his scepter. Glancing at Marac, Laedron noticed his hand shaking, but he had a tight grip on his blade. *He's afraid. If she doesn't come peacefully, I shall have to act quickly.*

Greathis bent at the knees, seeming to gain better footing in anticipation for a fight. "I'm sorry to come here with the hour so late, but I've heard disturbing news, rumors that only you could lay to rest."

"Rumors, Commander? What sort of rumors?"

"I shall have to take a look around inside. Do you mind?"

"Mind? Look, Greathis, there's nothing wrong here. Perhaps you might find some true criminals in the low quarter, someone deserving of this harassment."

"I'm sorry, madam, but there most certainly *is* something

wrong here. Stand aside."

Forane squared her shoulders, putting her hands on her hips. "And if I don't?"

"Then, I shall have to detain you."

Laedron drew his wand, concealing the subtle movement from Forane, then whispered an incantation.

Forane's tone turned from obstinate to hostile. "Detain *me*? Do not forget your place, guard."

She flung open her robe and withdrew a black metal rod. Marac and Greathis drew their swords in unison, but before she could utter a word, Laedron nudged Greathis aside and flicked his wrist. A blue blast of energy shot from the ruby scepter, ensnaring Forane in a web of energy. The guards must have heard the spell because they clamored to the front of the house.

Laedron concentrated on his spell, tightening the fibrous twine until Forane's arms were forced down to her sides. The young girl emerged from the doorway, snatched the rod from the vicar's hand, and tossed it over to Brice. She then gave Forane a shove, sending the woman to the ground.

"Thank you, Collette," Brice said, placing the rod into a pouch at his side.

"Bind her hands." Greathis handed a set of manacles to one of his men. "And put a gag in her mouth."

Brice led the way into the house and upstairs to Forane's study. Pushing open the door, Laedron spied innumerable scrolls lying strewn about the desktop. He walked to the writing table, and Greathis joined him.

Greathis read each of the letters, his expression hardly

changing the entire time. Finally, he said, "Madness. All of this."

Brice approached. "Mad it may be, but it is still the truth."

"Take all of these letters and deliver them to my office," Greathis said to one of the guards, then he turned to another militia man. "Once we're done here, seal the house. No one in, no one out."

They both replied, "Yes, Master."

"Genevieve Forane… I can't believe it."

Laedron folded his arms. "Vicar Jurgen couldn't believe it, either. Why does no one think this woman is capable of what she's done?"

"Before this war business, she was kind, kinder than any woman I've ever met. Sincere, friendly, and abiding to all who approached her. She's changed dramatically in a short period of time."

"Perhaps she might be able to tell us why," Marac said. "Now might be a good time to ask."

"Yes, yes. Let us return her to the headquarters."

* * *

Marac stopped Laedron just before the entrance to the militia building. "Lae, mind if I have a word?"

Laedron nodded.

"I-I'm having a little trouble." Marac flexed his hand. "Ever since I was captured, I've had this tremble. It started off innocent enough, but it's grown worse since we arrived in this city."

"What do you think it is? A sickness?"

"No, not a sickness... not unless you consider cowardice to be an ailment."

"Cowardice?" Laedron asked. "You've stood at my side in the face of danger. I wouldn't consider that cowardly, not in the least."

"Yes, I've stood by you, my friend. I've yet to swing my sword in anger against a foe, however, and I fear what may happen if it is required of me. Every time we face off against one of these mages, I can't keep myself from shaking."

"It's natural, Marac. The fear reminds you that you're still alive."

Marac closed his eyes and sighed. "I wish I could be as brave as you."

Laedron was speechless. Marac never seemed to be afraid, no matter what they had faced. Laedron had often wished that he was as fearless and brash as his friend.

"In time," Laedron said, "these feelings will go away. What happened to Mikal was horrible, and we should always remember it, but we can't go through life dwelling on it. We have to forge ahead and get through it together, brother."

"You've never faltered, Lae. You've led us through thick and thin—"

"And I was just afraid as everybody else, maybe more. When we were young, do you remember Calvert telling us stories about the great warriors and adventurers?"

With a tear welling in his eye, Marac bobbed his head.

"How they were always brave and never backed down? How they fought with their dying breaths if needed? When they were hurt, they laughed at death and mocked the enemy?"

Marac bobbed his head again.

"That's us, Marac. A few hundred years from now, they'll tell stories of Marac Reven, of Laedron Telpist, and of Brice Warren—how they fought bravely and never backed down, how they laughed at pain and spat upon the enemy, no matter how daunting. For now, we have to live it, and the living part isn't so easy. The tales tell us what we should aspire to be, not what we must be when we begin the journey."

Marac wiped his face. "All right. Let's see what Forane has to say about all of this. I'm tired of feeling around in the dark."

They met Greathis in his office, where Forane lay on the floor, gagged and bound in chains. She seemed more like prey caught in a trap than the horrible monster her letters portrayed. *Surely she must be putting up an act.*

Greathis pawed through the confiscated items spread across his desk. "A black rod, letters to someone named 'D' about assassinating Vicar Jurgen, and other suspect materials. We have been busy, haven't we?"

He received a grumble in reply.

"Remove her muzzle so we might hear what she has to say for herself," Greathis said, gesturing at the woman on the floor. Marac obliged.

"You'll never get away with this, Greathis," Forane snarled. "Employing a mage in your militia? You'll join me at the gallows."

"We'll deal with that issue when it comes up. *If* it comes up, I should say. For now, I have some questions for you."

She smiled. "Ask, but don't expect me to answer."

"Why would you conspire to kill Vicar Jurgen?"

"Me? I would never do such a thing."

"Come now. No need to waste our time with these games."

"Who's playing games? I know nothing."

"Shall I read an excerpt of your correspondence, woman? 'Instruct him to keep a lookout for the priest Jurgen and tell him you will pay tenfold if he would see fit to do away with that problem for us.' Who was this mercenary?"

"We already know that," Laedron said. "His name was Lester, and he was a member of the Shimmering Dawn."

Forane turned her head. "And how do you know that?"

"You met with one of our informants near the bell tower the other night. You offered him payment if he would do away with Jurgen."

"You seem to have all the answers already," Forane said. "What do you need from me?"

Laedron produced the black sack and emptied the onyx stones into his hand. "For starters, you could tell me what these are for."

She laughed and turned her head. "I'll never tell you."

Greathis peered at the stones. "She doesn't have to tell. I know what they are."

Forane gazed at Greathis with apparent surprise.

Laedron said, "We found them on one of the mages in black. What can you tell us about them?"

"A tool of Necromancers, I'm afraid. Have you ever heard the story of Vrolosh?"

Laedron exhaled heavily. "Several times."

"Then you should know what they are."

"They were never mentioned."

"It would seem the Falacorans kept the story intact while some of the details fell through the cracks in more distant reaches," Greathis said. "Long ago, Azura stood against Vrolosh, Master Necromancer and servant of Syril. Vrolosh and Syril agreed that Vrolosh would be given even greater power in exchange for new souls. A deal with a demon.

Syril imparted the knowledge of creating these stones, known as soulstones, in order to ease Vrolosh's task. The souls would be captured in these and given to his master in darkness, presumably for eternal torment."

Greathis paused. "The passage of the original story goes like this:

And into the stones Vrolosh cast their souls,

To trap and bind them in shards of darkest night.

For the master, always the master—Syril, the prince of hate."

Laedron felt a little sick, realizing that the stones giving off a faint light contained the essences of dead men. "Those mages were collecting souls for Syril?"

Greathis shrugged. "Perhaps, but likely not. A lesser known part of the tale tells of how Vrolosh disobeyed Syril, instead choosing to use the power of the stones for his own ends. That, as some would believe, is what made it possible for Azura to defeat Vrolosh at the end of the Great War. Vrolosh's arrogance and thirst for new heights of power made Syril turn his back on the Necromancer."

"What are they used for now?" Laedron brought his hand close to Forane's face. "Some kind of dark ritual?"

Forane licked her lips and eyed the soulstones as if the mere sight of them instilled a feeling of want. "They're meaningless to you. You could give them to me…"

Greathis crouched beside her and shouted, "What are they for?"

"Many things," Forane said, lowering her eyes. "If I tell you, will you give them to me?"

"I might consider it. Go on." Greathis stood and leaned on the front of his desk, folding his arms.

"Augmentation."

Laedron considered her simple response. He thought the effects he had suffered when he had returned Brice to life—his hair graying, the sudden appearance of wrinkles on his face. The purpose of the stones became clear to him.

"And what is that supposed to mean?" Greathis asked.

"I think I know," Laedron said. "The harvested souls can be used for powerful spells that would normally be fueled by the essence of the conjurer."

"Yes, young sorcerer," Forane said, smiling as if filled with accomplishment and satisfaction. "Now, give them to me."

"What would you use them for, Vicar?" Laedron asked.

"They have promised me immortality, and by these stones do I acquire it."

"Witch!" Greathis slapped her across the face. "You would sate your appetite upon the souls of men—my men and any others that you can find? Why would you do such a thing?"

She spat a bit of blood onto the floor. "Andolis and Gustav told me that the teachings were a lie. They showed me the truth, and they promised that I could live forever, as they do."

Greathis raised an eyebrow. "Live forever?"

"They're Zyvdredi, you fool. The immortal enemies of the Uxidi, the truth seekers... the great ones."

"I had my suspicions, and this confirms them," Laedron said. "When I fought Gustav in Pilgrim's Rest, he spoke the ancient language of Zyvdred."

Marac gave Laedron a look of astonishment. "You knew, but you told no one?"

"I didn't know at the time. I knew he was a mage by his use of the old spells, but I had no idea that he was actually Zyvdredi."

"Do many people go around reciting ancient tongues in your presence?" Greathis asked.

"No, but it's common amongst elder mages, and I'll leave it at that."

Greathis turned to Forane. "Why did the Drakars need your help?"

"They needed someone familiar with the consulship and the Grand Vicar, someone with influence. Someone who could get them close to His Holiness."

"You mean to tell me that they killed Daris the Second?" Greathis asked. "They murdered the former Grand Vicar?"

"Of course they did. How else could they take power?"

"And Andolis and Gustav being from Darkwatch? All a farce?"

"A cover story to validate their claims. We knew no one from Darkwatch would come this far to prove otherwise. They can't keep the undead off them long enough to do anything else but fight."

Greathis rubbed his forehead. "How did they kill Daris?"

Forane didn't speak, but glanced at the stones.

"They took his soul, didn't they?" Greathis asked.

She stared at the floor.

"Why do you look away as if you're ashamed to reveal it? You took stones like these in trade for your loyalty with full knowledge, did you not?"

"The process isn't pleasant," she said. "I've seen it performed before. Andolis has a staff, and it has soulstones throughout."

Greathis shook his head. "Have you any idea the amount of people you've killed or put in harm for your avarice? No, don't answer that. I can't hear any more from you, traitor."

Forane slinked across the floor toward Laedron, her chains rattling. "Can I have them now?"

"You'll be fortunate if you live another night," Greathis said, taking her by the throat. "Wilkans!"

The sergeant came through the door so quickly that Laedron suspected he had been eavesdropping. "Yes, Master Greathis?"

"Take this witch to the dungeon, to the depths where sunlight will never shine upon her." Greathis looked her in the eyes, anger and hate twisting his features. "However many years you've gained from stealing souls will only keep you in that hole longer."

"You promised to give them to me," Forane pleaded as she was dragged from the room. "Give them to me!"

Greathis closed the door. "Things are much worse than I thought."

"What can be done? Have Jurgen go to the consulship in the

morning?" Laedron asked.

"No," Greathis said, rubbing his chin. "It cannot wait that long. Every minute a Zyvdredi sits upon the throne of Azura, our people are in grave danger."

Brice said, "But I thought you couldn't arrest a Grand Vicar."

"That is true, but the circumstances have changed. No, Andolis Drakar has seen his last sunrise as Tristan the Fourth. I will assemble my men, and we will go to the palace and capture him." Greathis gave Laedron a grin. "I would appreciate your help if you would give it."

"You have it," Laedron said, and Marac and Brice nodded in affirmation.

"And you have my sincerest apologies."

"What for, Master Greathis?"

"For the fact that you've come here despite all odds and in the face of great danger, that you've been falsely condemned by the church, and that you've proven to be my best ally even though you have every reason to be my worst enemy."

"We only mean to end this war and return things to the way they were. Nothing more."

"Nothing will be the same after this. It cannot be."

❧ Chapter Twelve ☙

Storming the Palace

Greathis, at the front of fifty militiamen, led the way toward the Vicariate Palace at the heart of the Ancient Quarter. The column passed the consulship building first, then marched parallel to the platform connecting the palace to the consul chamber.

"That walkway was designed to give the Grand Vicar greater security when going between the palace and the consulship," Greathis said, seeming to notice Laedron's awe of the massive structure. "Early in the morning, you could catch a glimpse of His

Holiness on his way to the assembly."

At the end of the platform stood a tower, which Laedron estimated to be ten stories or more above the walkway. *Probably another five stories below that. Andolis could be anywhere in there or the palace beyond, and he may have any number of mages guarding him.*

Close to the steps fronting the complex, Greathis increased his pace, and the militia matched him. They stopped halfway up when the huge double doors at the top opened and Andolis emerged.

"What draws you to my door at this late hour, Dalton Greathis?" Andolis asked. Laedron thought it was strange for him to still be wearing ceremonial robes around the palace that late at night. "To what do I owe the pleasure of your company?"

"Genevieve Forane, and you shall meet her soon enough. You are under arrest for conspiring against the peace." Greathis unsheathed his weapon, and the militiamen readied theirs.

"Do you forget the law, Guardsman? A reigning Grand Vicar cannot be removed by the likes of you, regardless of your charges. I can only be dethroned by the will of the consuls."

"I shall not suffer you to remain in that office, Charlatan. Your lies and plots have brought nothing but misery and sorrow, and we shall abide you no longer." Greathis inched up the stone steps, his men following.

"Then, you leave me no choice," Andolis said as black-cloaked men joined him on either side. Even from a distance, Laedron recognized the garments and the runic symbols embroidered on the men's garments.

Andolis retreated into the palace, and Greathis raised his

sword. "For Azura!"

The militia guards rushed up the stairs amidst a storm of spells from the black mages. The night sky was illuminated by a deluge of colorful light, with the red of flame and the white of frost joining the light blue sparkles of electricity. Laedron focused on the nearest mage, trying to keep his mind and eyes off the guards falling at either side.

Almost there, Laedron thought, then a blast of energy sent him to the ground, dust and fragments of stone flying through the air. His ears rang and his vision blurred from the sudden explosion at his feet, and his legs burned like hellfire. *It can't end this way.* He ran his fingers past his knees to see if the rest of his legs were still attached to his body.

He felt holes in his pants and the wetness of blood, but surmised his body was still intact. Then he saw Master Greathis lying beside him. The mangled guard captain was gasping his last breaths. A hand came through the haze to wave in front of his face, and Laedron grabbed it.

"Are you all right?" Marac shouted over the roar of the battle.

"I'll make it," Laedron said with a grunt, struggling to stand. "We must get to Andolis."

"Brice!" Marac shouted. "You help Lae up the steps, and I'll lead. Stay behind me."

With his arm wrapped around Brice's shoulders, Laedron limped up the stairs. Marac held his shield at the ready. Fragments of wood and iron splintered off the hauberk as they went, and Marac dropped the bent, broken remains of the shield on the ground once they had reached the top.

A mage turned toward them, his wand outstretched, and Marac rushed him before a spell could be cast. Marac plunged his sword into the belly of the man, the dark crimson of the blood indicating a deep, vital strike. Withdrawing the blade, Marac spun around with a slash, severing the mage's head. He moved on to cleave another sorcerer in the chest and kicked the dying man down the steps.

"Inside," Marac said, pointing at the door. "They can handle the rest. Andolis is ours."

Brice helped Laedron through the door and pointed to the left. "There he is!"

Marac turned and ran down the corridor, but Andolis escaped into a passage behind a thick oaken door. Twisting the knob, Marac said, "Hells, it's locked!"

Laedron staggered down the hall, then produced his scepter. "Stand back. I'll burn it down."

Brice shook his head. "No, we have no idea what may be behind the door. Something flammable? Andolis waiting for us? Let me. I'll do it nice and quiet."

Nodding, Laedron leaned against a table, while Brice knelt at the keyhole. The circular room had three exits—the one Laedron had entered through, the locked door, and an open arch leading to a raised walkway, presumably the one normally traversed by the Grand Vicar on his way to the consulship. *We must be at the base of the tower*, Laedron mused.

Brice inspected the lock for a few seconds, then reached into his belt to retrieve a thin bit of metal. Laedron took the opportunity to mend his wounds with a healing spell, and though he couldn't close them completely, he was able to stop the bleeding and ease the pain into a dull ache.

Laedron heard a click, and Brice turned around with a proud smile.

"Let's get him," Laedron said.

"Wait." Marac approached the open archway.

Laedron moved to Marac's side, and before he could ask, he saw what had captivated Marac. The night sky had a sheen of yellow which brightened to an orange glow, and the clouds were moving. Observing the heavens, Laedron noticed that the clouds were swirling around a focal point—the tower itself. He took a step backward when a stream of red lightning struck the platform beyond the arch, cracking the stone and sending bricks flying through the air.

"We must hurry." Laedron pulled Marac back inside and opened the door.

Immediately inside the door, a stone staircase spiraled upward, and Laedron began a hasty ascent. He became winded the farther they climbed and was out of breath by the time they reached a ladder leading up to a wooden trap door. "Only a bit more now."

Marac climbed the rungs of the shoddy ladder, then pushed open the trap door. Past him, Laedron could see that the sky seemed to be burning. Flames swirled about the heavens, and thicker bands of searing red lightning mixed with them. He could hear faint chanting beneath the thunderous roar of magic, and he rushed up the ladder behind Marac.

Once on the roof, Laedron took in his surroundings. The city of Azura was aglow from the blinding light of Andolis's spell. *What in the hells is he doing? Trying to burn the entire city?* Like the finger of Syril, red flashes of lightning indiscriminately struck straw roofs, setting them aflame. At that height and with all the commotion, Laedron couldn't tell for certain if people were escaping the burning buildings.

Andolis stood on the opposite end of the tower's roof, his left hand raised to the sky and his right holding a long staff. The wooden staff was carved into a wicked shape with thorns and spines fashioned into the shaft. The pole had a bend throughout its length, suggesting a subtle crescent or the look of a longbow. Along its exterior, soulstones were set into the wood, and each of them glowed and sparkled with red light. Laedron likened their appearance to a flame burning behind glass, but rays of energy seemed to be emitted from the sigils carved in the onyx.

"Andolis Drakar, we come for you," Marac said, his sword high as he neared the mage. "Put down the staff and end this madness."

"End this madness? What a wonderful thought." Andolis lowered the staff, his eyes meeting Marac's. "Perhaps I shall end the three of you. Yes, I think that would be more fitting."

Marac lunged at Andolis. The mage knocked Marac's sword away with the end of the staff, then smacked Marac across the face with it. Brice let out a growl, rolled beneath the staff as it swung overhead, and slashed at the mage's arm.

Andolis hissed, a cut beneath his elbow dripping blood. Brice's proud smile transformed to a look of fear when the mage flicked his staff and shouted a phrase. The spell sent Brice flying across the roof with a blast of white energy. Laedron glanced over at his friend's body, then yelled his spell and aimed his rod at Andolis.

A shockwave pulsed from the tip of Laedron's scepter, and Andolis was thrown toward the edge of the roof, his momentum only stopped by one of the merlons at the edge of the battlement. Marac raised his sword high and ran toward the sorcerer. Andolis twirled his staff, blocking Marac's attacks. The clang of steel against the hardened wood of the staff echoed louder than the storm of flames churning above their heads.

Unable to get a clear aim for a spell, Laedron watched in horror as Marac slashed at Andolis, his sword deflected after each swing. Andolis struck hard enough to spin Marac around, creating time to cast a spell, an incantation which sent Marac flying backward and over the side of the tower.

"No!" Laedron shouted. "You've killed countless innocents, and you've killed my friends." Laedron raised his scepter and leveled it at Andolis. "Now, you die."

"I think not," Andolis said. "I shall be the only one leaving this place alive." Andolis waved his staff and uttered an incantation.

Laedron was quick to cast a spell to counter the lightning bolt flying at him. Striking Laedron's magic shield, the lightning splintered, arcing like the bolts he'd seen shooting across the sky. Once it dissipated, Laedron flicked his rod and shouted the words, sending a stream of flames at Andolis.

Countering, Andolis cast a spell, and the air swirled violently around him, the flames joining the air like a tornado. Then,

155

Andolis shifted and hurled the column of air and fire back toward Laedron.

After a tumble across the roof, Laedron stood several feet away, his clothes steaming from the superheated perspiration all over his body. Andolis had missed, but just barely. Through the whirlwind of spells which followed, Laedron and Andolis shouted phrases and waved their weapons, while bobbing and weaving to dodge the other's attacks. Laedron felt as locked in an improvised dance, and the final measure of the music would draw silent with one of their deaths. The fear he felt in his heart weighed greater than any he had come to know prior to that day, and he knew that one misstep, one false move, would finish him.

He felt the sting of Andolis's icebolt from the center of his body to the tips of his extremities, and the feelings of anguish and defeat that followed were no easier to accept. Glancing down, Laedron saw that a solid shard of ice had pierced him just above his sternum, and judging by the fact that he was still alive, he figured the spell had missed anything vital. He could still feel his heart beating in his chest, but with every pulse of blood, a chill surged through his body. Laedron saw doubled, blurry outlines of Andolis, then his face hit the ground as hard as Andolis's spell had struck him in the chest.

He had been bested by the enemy, and the world as he knew it would cease to be, instead becoming a place shrouded in darkness, pain, and torment for all who inhabited it. Lying on the ground, Laedron let his thoughts drift, flashes of visions of his life and the lives of his friends. Then, he saw people huddled in misery in distant, foreign places, people he had never met, but who shared in his defeat.

Tears welled in his eyes for Ismerelda, who had died by the hands of another Drakar, for Master Greathis, who had been killed on the steps of the palace, and for Marac and Brice, who had followed him only to lose their lives so close to victory. Laedron cried for Valyrie, who would never see her father again, and for her father, whose death would go unavenged. Then, his emotions changed into anger, an insurmountable, insatiable hate for the man who approached to gloat over him while he lay dying.

The pain lessened as the ice bolt faded from existence, Andolis having obviously released the spell. A perfect hole—an inch or two in width—remained in his chest, but it didn't hurt; the freezing cold had numbed the area, though it wouldn't be long until the effect wore off.

"Are you crying? For what do you shed tears? For my men whom you killed? No. For your own shortcomings and lack of training? For the defeat itself? Why do you weep?" Andolis asked, inching closer with each word.

Laedron's entire body trembled, a cocktail of fear, anger, and adrenaline coursing through his veins. "You... mustn't..."

"Mustn't I? What? I mustn't finish you off? After all the trouble you've caused?" Andolis glanced at the scepter sitting a few feet from Laedron's hand, then he smiled. "No, I think I shall be done with you, boy. Then I shall continue my plan to rid the world of your kind, your impure and reckless brethren who should never have been taught the secrets of magic in the first place."

Laedron considered Andolis's words, feeling as though he

was only a pawn in a much greater, far older game about which he knew nothing. *A war between the Zyvdredi and Uxidi over control of magic? They used the church to hasten the demise of all mages except those born in Zyvdred?* Laedron had only a passing thought of the possibility. Given that he had seen neither the Creator, nor Syril as of yet, he considered his options.

Laedron lifted himself an inch or two off the ground. "You've done well—"

"Where do you think you're going?" Andolis asked, kicking Laedron in the face.

The popping noise and the flow of blood from his nostrils let him know his nose had been broken. Doing his best to set his nose straight despite the insufferable pain, Laedron said, "You've done well thus far, Andolis. Turned the church on its head, even using it as a tool to rid the world of us. You've made one mistake, though, don't you see?"

Andolis put his left hand on his hip, the other tightly grasping the staff. "What mistake is that, whelp?"

"You've taught others, priests, the secrets of magic. You have yourself done that which you hate."

"You think I don't have a plan for that? With the rest of you gone, it would be easy to do away with the priests I've taught. A necessary evil, my little friend, much like the one I shall serve you with now. Once I'm done with you, I'll finish my spell and be away from this place. Imagine it, boy, a firestorm, a torrent of fire to last at least the next hundred years."

Laedron was confused for a moment, then he realized how Andolis planned to accomplish the feat—the soulstones. Laedron saw the full use—the terrible use—of the soulstones to their maximal effect: making magic permanent by the use of a proxy, a fresh soul depleted in the casting of a spell.

Andolis raised his staff high.

Laedron braced himself for the finality of his death. The time had come for the Zyvdredi to claim his prize. Andolis spoke his chant slowly, as if savoring each dark word as it crossed his lips. In his other hand, Andolis presented a black stone, and his plan quickly became apparent.

Laedron writhed in agony at the thought of being trapped forever inside an onyx gem, his soul used to power the spells that would lay waste to men and nations. Laedron reached for the dagger at his belt, but then remembered that Brice had taken it. *Not even a chance to end my own life before he can draw out my soul.*

Laedron closed his eyes, unwilling to look at the dark violet light swirling around his body. Much to his surprise, the chanting stopped with a grunt from Andolis. Opening his eyes, Laedron saw a sword protruding through the mage's chest with blood squirting around the edges of the blade. Andolis's face told of his shock and dismay, apparently aware of his impending death, reminding Laedron of the time he had practiced captivation magic with Ismerelda. Laedron almost pitied Andolis and would have given in to the emotion had he not known Andolis's true personality.

He should have felt relief at watching Andolis's limp body fall and Marac standing—alive—a few feet away, blood-drenched and wearing a look of deep satisfaction, but he didn't. The mage's words riddled his mind, and all the miles traveled thus far notwithstanding, Laedron felt as if they had only begun the journey.

Laedron's arms and legs grew numb, and his breathing became shallow. His vision cloudy, he lay still on the ground until he could see only darkness. The last thing he heard was Marac's voice shouting his name, and then he heard nothing.

❧ Chapter Thirteen ❧

Toying with the Fates

Marac reached down, grabbing Laedron's hand tight in his own. "Stay with me, Lae! Can you hear me?"

Laedron didn't respond, but Marac noticed movement across the roof. *Won't you stay dead, bastard?* He took a firm grip on his sword and rose to his feet. Then, he realized Andolis lay dead and still where he had fallen. The movement came from further away.

"Oh, my head," Brice said, sitting up.

Crouching at Laedron's side again, Marac shouted to Brice,

"Laedron's hurt badly. We have to get him out of here."

Brice took the staff from Andolis's dead hands and the ring from the corpse's finger, then returned to Laedron's side. "You get that arm, and I'll take this one." He pulled Laedron's limp body forward.

Marac eyed the staff and the ring. "What, we're looters now, Brice?"

"No, no. The ring glimmers like the stones in the staff. It could be important."

Please, don't die. Azura... Creator... whoever is listening, please, save my friend, Marac prayed, lifting Laedron by his other arm. "Be careful with him, but we must hurry. To the headquarters. Jurgen will know what to do."

They lugged Laedron's seemingly lifeless body through the streets with little more than surprised looks from passersby. Buildings burned, illuminating the night sky, and the total chaos gave no one time to ask questions or share concerns. Marac and Brice ended the race across town at the door of the Shimmering Dawn headquarters.

Marac burst through the door and yelled, "Jurgen! Help!"

Without delay, Jurgen and Valyrie joined them at the door and helped carry Laedron the rest of the way into the room.

"What happened?" Valyrie asked.

"Greathis decided we would take Andolis and the palace tonight," Marac said.

Jurgen's face twisted with confusion. "What? He told us—"

"I know what he said. After Forane's confession, he decided we had to act quickly. He's dead, Jurgen, Greathis and many of his men, and Laedron's not far behind. Help him!"

Jurgen led them to Laedron's room, and they laid him on the bed. The priest examined his body. "A great deal of damage has been done. If you value your friend's life, you'll leave me to my work."

"I can't leave him," Marac said. "Not in a time such as this."

Jurgen pressed his hand firmly against Marac's chest. "You must give me time and space to work. Now go!"

He breathes still. Marac glanced at Laedron one last time, then begrudgingly walked out, and Brice and Valyrie joined him at the long dining table.

"After all we've done for him, Jurgen had better fix this."

"What if he can't?" Brice asked.

"He better find a way. I'm not losing Laedron now. No, not now. We finally accomplish what we've come here to do, and he dies? No, I won't have it."

"He's hurt pretty—"

"Not another word," Marac snarled. "That is a possibility I will not accept. Do you not understand? He *will* survive."

Every crackle of the fire grated on Marac's nerves, his temper rising with each second that passed without news. Staring at the closed door to Laedron's room, he pondered what might be happening on the other side. *Does a longer wait mean they're getting good results? Or does the delay mean my friend has taken a turn for the worst?* The uncertainty had a dual effect on his mind. Until someone came out and told him, he didn't know whether Laedron was alive or dead, and although he preferred the former, the passage of time kept him from finding out the latter, leaving him with hope.

Few more precious, abrasive moments went by before the door slowly creaked open. Standing, Marac studied Jurgen's worried face.

Jurgen continued to wipe his hands on a scrap of cloth, and his head turned downward when he seemed to notice Marac watching him.

"I—" Jurgen began, then paused. "I'm sorry."

"Sorry?" Marac asked, wanting a better explanation. "What do you mean, 'sorry?'"

"I've done what I can. I don't see him lasting the night." Jurgen reached out to take Marac in an embrace, but Marac pushed away his hands.

"Sorry?" Marac shot past Jurgen and into the room, then looked at his friend lying on the mattress, his life draining away with every tick of the clock. *Lae. It cannot be. It can't end this way. No!* He fell to his knees next to the bed, gripping Laedron's cool hand. He could tell little life remained in the body. Tears rained from his eyes like a torrent of floodwater, and he wailed with desperation. Brice turned away, and Valyrie gasped.

He wondered how he could continue forward without his friend at his side. They had come so far together, yet Laedron lay dying. He fell further into the depths of despair when he tried to imagine telling Laedron's mother what had passed, that her only son had died trying to save a people who hated his kind. *Laren. Creator! How can I explain to his sister, my love, what has happened? How can I tell her that her brother will never come back?*

Putting his head on Laedron's belly, Marac felt the brush of a velvet cloth on his forehead. He sat up and noticed the black cloth bag still tied to Laedron's belt. Marac remembered what had happened in Pilgrim's Rest—Brice's resurrection. *If Laedron could bring Brice back, Jurgen can stop Laedron's death, for priests are gifted with healing magic. The stones. Augmentation, as Forane put it. There is a way!*

He snatched the sack, stepped out of the room, and forcefully took hold of Jurgen's arm.

Jurgen's eyes were full of heartache and regret. "I'm sorry, Mar—"

"No, it cannot end this way." Marac emptied the pouch into Jurgen's hand, then held up a stone with an unnatural glimmer. "Take this. You shall undo this, Priest."

"What?" Jurgen stared at the stone. "What do you mean? What is this?"

Marac tried to decide if he would lie or tell the truth. *I can't ask him to do this unless he knows full well what is involved. He must know the truth, but he will do what I ask just the same.* "A soulstone, Jurgen. To instill full healing and restoration in his body, to bring him back from death's door."

"No. No, you cannot ask this of me." Jurgen pushed Marac's hand away. "Not even Azura would do as you ask. What you speak of is Necromancy, preventing a death that cannot be stopped."

"I shall miss him as much as any of you," Valyrie said. "But this isn't right. No matter how much I want him to stay with us, what you ask is against everything Jurgen believes—what we all believe."

165

"What I speak of is fairness!" Marac punched the nearby wall. "We've come hundreds—no, thousands—of miles because of a war your people started, and we stopped the murders of your militia, took care of the Drakars, and soon, we'll end the war. Now, Vicar, it is time to repay your debt."

"He was wrong to resurrect Brice," Jurgen said, backing away. "Do you know what you ask? Meddling in the affairs of the Fates? Performing acts reserved for gods? He's too far gone for me to prevent his passing, Marac Reven."

"I care not. You owe everything to him, Jurgen. Take this stone." Marac raised the onyx gem close to Jurgen's face. "Keep him alive. Cast the spell, perform the miracle, whatever in the hells you want to call it, and repay him for everything he's done for you."

"And what soul might be contained within this gem?" Jurgen stared into it. "If there is a way to return that person to life, you would sacrifice this man or woman's soul?"

"Do you suggest we find some empty vessels to house these souls? I know no other way to house a soul other than to find a body in which to place it."

"Of course not."

"Then, use this essence and return our friend. He doesn't deserve to die here."

"No, it cannot be—"

"Then, you shall receive no more help from us, Priest." The sadness, the anger at Laedron's impending death, and his newly formed contempt for Jurgen clouded his thoughts and heightened his anxiety. "You'll be left to deal with the rest of this on your own."

"We won't help him?" Brice asked. "You can't leave him to finish this on his own. None of this is his fault; he's done nothing."

"That's precisely the point, Thimble," Marac said. "His idleness is the problem. He can save Laedron here and now, but he refuses."

"We still need your help," Jurgen said. "We require the knowledge of your countrymen to secure a lasting peace."

"Then, do what's right. Make him better or see your country laid to waste. Those are your only choices."

I can't believe I'm threatening a priest. Marac kept his expression harsh, and in the condition and circumstance he was, he didn't find it difficult to maintain his demeanor.

Valyrie ran to Jurgen's side. "You can't abandon Jurgen, not now. Laedron wouldn't have wanted you to give up and leave. Please, stop this."

Marac shook his head. "If he dies, Lae shall no longer be bothered with affairs such as these." He looked at Jurgen. "Will you do as I ask?"

"I can't do it," Jurgen replied. "It could condemn my spirit for eternity."

"Then let the act be of my will. I am the one who demands it be done, so the responsibility—for better or worse—is mine to bear. Do it, Jurgen."

Jurgen seemed to contemplate the proposition for quite a while, then he said, "Very well. Give me the stone, but know this: I do this on your behalf, and when I have finished, never ask this of me again. None of you may speak of this to anyone else, not ever."

Marac handed the soulstone to the priest, and Jurgen gave Marac a gaze that he would never forget, the priest's eyes piercing and penetrating him to his very core.

Once inside the room, Jurgen examined Laedron, then he peered at the window. "We need to take him somewhere secluded."

"The chapel downstairs should suffice," Valyrie said.

Without another word, Brice and Marac took Laedron's body down the stairwell at the end of the hall. They lay him on the shoddy stone altar, then backed away.

"Leave us," Jurgen said solemnly, clasping his hands together. "I need privacy for this."

Marac followed Valyrie to the door, then he nudged Brice because he seemed enraptured by the sight of Laedron upon the altar. "Come along. We've done all we can."

On the stairs, Brice said, "I just never could have imagined Laedron like that. He's not much older than we are, Marac."

"I know. Worry not, though." Marac took a seat at the long table once again, and he could only guess how long it might take. *Minutes? Hours? Until morning? Whatever it may be, it shall be worth the price to see my friend once more. To hear his voice, his encouragements. I'd settle for a tongue-lashing if only it meant he were here with me.*

After an hour had passed, he heard the sound of footsteps against stone, then Jurgen entered from the hall. After a long pause, Marac said, "Well?"

"It is done." Jurgen folded his arms. "Your friend will live, but he has not awakened."

Marac stood. "What can we expect?"

"I cannot say how long Laedron will be asleep, but we mustn't wait for him. We must find and speak to the Sorbian commander posthaste, as early as we can go in the morning."

"I understand," Marac said, nodding. "We shall aid you in that task."

"So long as you don't threaten me again."

Marac gazed at the floor, unwilling to look Jurgen in the eyes. "I can only offer my deepest apologies for my... outburst. Please, forgive me, Vicar. I only—"

"You don't have to offer up excuses. I've become tired of seeing so much death of late. I must remind you, however, that I will not perform a miracle with a soulstone again. To do so would be against what little of my principles I have left. I shall go to the consuls tomorrow and raise the question of negotiating, and hopefully, we will be able to leave the city by noon."

"I won't ask it of you again." Marac paused. "Thank you for what you've done, and I will go with you to meet my countrymen and negotiate for peace."

Jurgen went into his quarters and closed the door.

"Will this insanity ever cease?" Valyrie asked.

Marac bobbed his head. "For a time, it shall, but not forever."

"Goodnight." Valyrie glanced at him. "I suppose we will go and meet the Sorbians tomorrow."

"No," Marac said, stopping her. "You must stay here."

"For what? To protect me from the ravages of war?"

"To watch over my friend while I'm away. To care for Laedron. I don't trust his welfare to just anyone."

"You're probably right."

"Thank you."

"Goodnight." She disappeared into her room and closed the door.

"What would you have me do, Marac?" Brice asked.

Marac smiled and wrapped his arm around Brice's shoulders. "You'll be at my side for this. We'll need our best people for the time ahead."

Brice grinned. "I'd better get some sleep, then. Morning'll come faster than we know it."

"Yes, get some rest. We'll talk over breakfast."

✤ Chapter Fourteen ✤

An Exchange of Blood

E arly the next morning, Marac met Brice and Jurgen in the common room. Caleb and Piers had prepared a great feast—sausages, eggs, flat cakes, and fresh juice. While they ate, Marac eyed Jurgen, receiving only a dead stare in response.

"We'll be going into the city today, Caleb and me," Piers said, taking his cloak. "To check a few things out and make sure no more of those mages show up unexpectedly."

"Good, yes," Jurgen said, watching them leave.

"You think they'll agree to peace?" Brice asked, eagerly helping himself to heaping portions of food.

Jurgen had barely touched his meal, but he drank plenty of the juice. "Who can say? The only thing we can do is ask."

"I doubt they have much of a choice in the matter," Marac said. "We have quite a story to tell, and the Drakars—the whole reason for the fighting—have been done away with."

"No guarantee they'll agree to our terms, though." Jurgen leaned forward. "After their successes at Balfan, they may yet yearn to devour the entire country."

Jurgen stood and walked toward the door. "Coming?"

Marac joined him, and Brice was still shoveling handfuls of meat and eggs into his mouth even after they had passed the golden chalice in the square. Jurgen confidently led the way to the consulship chamber, and they were among the first to appear— behind only the chamberlains and the militia. Garnering a few odd glances from the arriving consuls, Marac took a seat at Jurgen's side and tried to keep a low profile.

Jurgen stood once the chamber had filled. "Vicars, we have been victimized. We have been tricked, and we have been defrauded. We were led to believe that a Lasoronian had ascended to our highest office, but in fact, a Zyvdredi plotted his way to the Vicariate Palace, assuming the title and rank of Grand Vicar."

Amidst the roars from the gallery, Jurgen continued, "We must undo what the Zyvdredi have done. We must go to the Sorbians and make peace."

"What proof have you, Jurgen? Where is Tristan?" one of the vicars asked.

"Tristan is dead, along with Dalton Greathis and a number of our militia."

Sergeant Wilkans stood. "It's true, all of it. I was there, and I didn't want to believe it myself. When men in black emerged from the palace and flung spells at us, I saw nothing other than the truth of it."

"Vicars, we must send an emissary to sue for peace, and I shall volunteer to go."

Vicar Griffinwold stood and joined Jurgen. "Surely, Vicar Jurgen, we can select someone other than you to send forth. Such a task is very dangerous, and I couldn't bear anything unfortunate befalling you."

"You are kind, but the responsibility sits upon my shoulders. I should have been stronger. I failed to serve this body once by indifference and lack of action, but I won't fail again. Begging the vicar's pardon, I remain a choice for this mission."

"As you see fit." Griffinwold bowed and withdrew to the gallery.

"Then, the question shall be, shall we send Vicar Jurgen to meet with the Sorbians to negotiate peace? If it pleases the chamberlain, I would ask for a vote by live voice." Receiving a nod from the chamberlain, Jurgen asked, "All in favor?"

In unison, seemingly everyone said, 'Yes.'

"And in opposition?"

His question met with silence. "Good. We will take some horses from the Vicariate Palace stables."

"*We*, Jurgen?" Carrenhold asked.

"Yes, my friends here. I will not be taking a complement of

173

militia on this journey. Should we fail, every man will be needed to guard the capital. I suggest, in my absence, that you continue the initiatives we have put forth. I would also advise we appoint a new militia commander."

"I offer up Sergeant Wilkans for the position," Griffinwold said, standing. "He has always been at Greathis's right hand, and he knows the responsibilities well."

Jurgen nodded. "All in favor?"

A resounding echo of 'yes' confirmed Wilkans as the new commander of the guard.

"I only promise that I'll do my best. Many thanks." Wilkans bowed before the consuls, then exited the room.

Jurgen turned to Marac and Brice. "Are you prepared to leave now?"

Although Marac was concerned for Laedron and wanted to stay, he knew his friend was in good hands. "We are."

Jurgen led them out the smaller rear exit, then to the side of the Vicariate Palace. Marac considered the stables to be like most others he'd seen until Jurgen called for the horses. Catching a glimpse of the snow-white geldings, Marac remained still until the horses were in full view. The horses, probably bred carefully for the solitary purpose of conveying a Grand Vicar, were groomed with an exquisite attention to detail. Beads of gold and silver were braided through their manes, their tails had likely been brushed every day, and the hooves seemed perfect—no chips, cracks, or marks of wear. He then beheld a coach near the stable's entrance, a white carriage adorned with gold filigrees and engravings.

Taking a quick peek through the window, Marac saw that the

sitting benches were upholstered with velvet and dyed a shiny gold, and he imagined that any who rode within would take great comfort from the seats.

Jurgen tapped him on the shoulder. "You can see the sights later. For now, we must endeavor to locate the Sorbian army."

* * *

As they rode, Marac recounted what had happened during the fight with Andolis Drakar. They kept a moderate gait so they could talk over the beating of hooves. The day waned into afternoon, the heat from the sun reaching its apex.

Brice slowed to a halt when he crested a hill, and Jurgen asked, "Why are we stopping?"

Hearing no reply, Marac came alongside his friend to see what was going on ahead. Brice's face appeared to be stuck in an expression of awe or fear. Marac couldn't quite tell which, but Brice's eyes were fixed on a single point in the distance. Marac turned and squinted, then he simply stared.

Soldiers stood on the side of the highway. Adorned in vibrant orange and subdued black, they carried all manner of weaponry. Marac immediately recognized the men as Sorbian troops, but his concern heightened when he peered to the east. Along another ridge of hilltops, men in darkened armor bearing the banners of Falacore were gathered, their spears and blades at the ready.

Battle lines. The Falacorans finally made it to the war. And numbered in the thousands.

"What is it? What do you see?" Jurgen asked.

Marac pointed. "Two armies. The Sorbians and the Falacorans, I think."

Jurgen joined Marac and Brice at the ridge. "They are just staring at each other?"

Brice nodded. "The calm before the battle. Sizing up their enemies, preparing the last bit of strategy before they loose the men upon each other."

A thunderous roar echoed through the air, the sound of thousands of men yelling to steel their resolve. Pouring like water down both sides of the hill, the footmen smashed into one other, and the indistinguishable voices mixed with the clanging of blades and armor. With the first clash of arms, men fell by the wayside, trampled underfoot by the advancing waves or slain outright.

"Azura! We're too late," Jurgen said, his eyes wide with shock.

Marac glanced at the nearby hilltops where the generals on horseback were separated by a sea of men. "No priests, no sorcerers—a battle of steel and mettle."

Countless men along the front line fell quickly after the opening moments of the battle, but the lines thinned after a few minutes. *That could have been us. Brice, Mikal, and me—even Laedron, had they taken him into the ranks—could have simply died here on this field, forgotten by history and remembered only by the weeping hearts of family and close friends.*

The troops paired off—Sorbian soldiers against their Falacoran counterparts—and fought with impressive skill. Both sides had clearly sacrificed their weakest troops first, treating them as fodder to the mouth of war, the armies going forward from that point only with those strong enough to survive.

A cloud of arrows from the Falacoran archers who had topped the eastern hills darkened the sky. Marac could tell the missiles found their targets because he heard screams erupt above the dull rumble of the thousands of men in the throes of battle.

The Sorbian cavalry quickly flooded into flanking positions. When they neared the archers, the cavaliers lowered their spears, then crashed into the line. In response to that move, the Falacoran horsemen rushed the exposed flank of the Sorbian mounted knights.

Chaos ensued, and Jurgen said, "Remain here."

Before Jurgen could take off down the road, Marac stopped him. "Where are you going?"

"To get help. This battle is the church's doing, and we have a role to play yet!"

* * *

Jurgen had been gone for a few hours when the fighting slowed. The loud roar of vigorous men engaged in martial warfare dulled and slowly became replaced with the moans of the wounded and dying.

"Where is he?" Marac asked Brice.

Brice shrugged. "Maybe he had trouble getting back."

Marac scoffed. "Only two roads lead out from Azura—the one we're on and the one that goes south. He couldn't have gotten lost."

"What do you think he has in mind?"

"No way of telling. I just hope he reveals it soon."

The battle had nearly drawn to a close, and it became clear that there were no winners on that field. Both armies had apparently been of equal skill since hardly any of the troops on either side remained without injury of some kind. He couldn't even see an unscathed horse in the mix, and men and beasts both lay strewn across the field like discarded grain on a mill floor.

Marac glanced over his shoulder when he heard the sound of horses galloping toward them from the south, and saw Jurgen leading the entire assembly of the consulship, minor priests, and a veritable army of carts and wagons.

"Have you brought them to see the disaster caused by their blind following?" Marac asked when Jurgen came close.

"That, and to do what we can for those who have survived."

"What will you do?"

"A miracle, I hope." Jurgen gestured to the priests, and they all took off down the hill toward the injured soldiers. "Save as many as you can, and load anyone who cannot walk into the wagons."

Marac turned to Brice. "We'd better help however we can."

With a nod, Brice rode down behind the priests, and Marac followed him. Nearing the battlefield, Marac could clearly see blood flying up with the clumps of dirt and grass as the horses ran. *Saturated. Soaked in blood.*

He reached the closest of the battle's victims and climbed off his horse. The boy's panicked breathing sent chills up Marac's spine. Blood was smeared across the young man's face, and his belly had been slashed open, probably by the sword in the hand of the dead Sorbian lying next to him. Marac felt pity for the Falacoran soldier, that he might die so far away from his home, friends, and family.

Then, Marac's heart filled with sadness when he saw nothing but peace in the boy's eyes. Where Marac had seen hope in his eyes, the boy's features relaxed, the look in his eyes replaced with an emptiness, a void. Marac turned his gaze upward slowly, looking at each of the men who lay dead before him. From that distance, he couldn't discern the number of soldiers by the groaning, but he could tell there were many.

The wailing was soon drowned out by chanting from hundreds of priests doling out healing miracles. *Miracles. Spells. What's the difference?* Marac mused, watching the priests. Their postures and gestures differed little from what he'd seen of Laedron. *Instead of wands, they have rings. Their words are spoken in Heraldict, and Laedron says his spells in Zyvdredi. Both concentrate in the same fashion.*

Marac heard the shrieking of a man nearby and saw the body of a horse rising with each howl. He ran to see who was trapped beneath the warhorse.

Marac couldn't believe his eyes. "Fenric?" He recognized the man as the king's brother, Duke Hadrian Fenric of Westmarch.

Fenric drew a dagger. "You've come to finish me? It shan't be that easy."

"No, my lord." Marac crouched and put his shoulder under the horn of the saddle. "We'll push together. On three."

Marac gave the count, then heaved upward, feeling the strain from the top of his head to the tips of his toes. Seeing Fenric pull his leg free, Marac lowered the horse's body to the ground.

Fenric gritted his teeth and grabbed his leg. From the unnatural twist, Marac surmised that the man's ankle was broken.

"Here!" Marac shouted at a nearby priest.

The priest joined them and inspected the injury. "You'll have to hold him down."

"Keep your hands off me, devil!"

Marac pressed against Fenric's shoulders, fighting the man while the priest inspected and healed the ankle. Fenric's body went limp for a moment, then the duke let out a scream to rival any Marac had heard on the field that day. By the time the young priest finished, Fenric had lost consciousness, probably from the excruciating pain.

"Get him on a wagon. He *must* survive this day," Marac said.

* * *

His hands and arms covered with the blood of other men, Marac returned to Jurgen when it seemed like all of the survivors had been located and loaded into the wagons. "What will you do now, Jurgen?" Marac asked.

Jurgen climbed atop his horse with a heavy sigh. "We take them all back, the Falacorans and Sorbians alike. Our task is to save as many as we can."

"You may consider speaking with Duke Fenric. He's the Sorbian general."

"Ah, I see. They've sent their best against us," Jurgen said, nodding and wiping blood from his hands with a handkerchief.

Marac glanced across the field of fallen soldiers. "It would seem the Falacorans sent their elites, as well."

"Indeed. The Falacorans have won the day, but only by a margin. They had but a handful more than the Sorbians still standing after the battle."

"Have you located their general?"

"Yes," Jurgen said. "He was killed in the fray."

"Then the Falacorans will likely want to pursue the war, right? Generals are most often high-born."

"No, they will do as we say. My plan still calls for ending the war."

"Will they?"

"Yes. Falacore is the one nation left that obeys the church. Years ago, all nations bowed to the Heraldan church, but not anymore."

Marac raised an eyebrow. "Just like that? No questions asked?"

"I think you'll find the Sorbians harder to deal with, my young friend. They will prove the most difficult to convince, even with this most recent devastation."

"I leave it to you. Far be it from me to question you on matters of politics."

"Good. We should return to the city with these men. I'll arrange for more to come for the bodies and bury them in a fitting manner or prepare them for the trip home if that is Fenric's will."

❧ Chapter Fifteen ❧

Keeping Watch

V alyrie heard Jurgen, Marac, and Brice leave, and snatched her Farrah Harridan book from the shelf before entering the hall. *Maybe I can finish reading this while I wait.* She eyed Laedron's door with apprehension, then sighed. Her thoughts ran rampant with all that had passed—the end of the Drakars, Laedron nearly dying, and her father's demise.

She was glad her father's body had been transformed to ash and spread along the coast. Though she missed him, she took some measure of joy from the fact that she couldn't ask Jurgen to return him to life. The knowledge of the possibility combined with the lack of the option gave her a kind of relief, an acceptance of her situation. Hearing Jurgen's argument and seeing Marac's rage, she could only imagine how strange and unnatural they both must have felt when Laedron was saved from death—a feeling she was glad not to have experienced.

She shook off her thoughts, then perused the larder. *A tomato... some parsley... ah, rabbit meat? These'll make quite a nice stew. Maybe, if we have time, I might teach these men how to cook something other than gruel.* She hastily assembled the ingredients into a clean pot—which wasn't easy to find—and hung the pan above the fire. Then, she went to Laedron's bedroom door. *No more putting it off.*

Laedron lay on the bed, his breathing slow and rhythmic and his eyes still closed. Confusion set in her mind as she neared, and she was unable to take her eyes off him. His hair showed no signs of gray at the ends, and his face and hands were smooth, showing none of the calluses from when she had first met him.

He still seemed to be in his late teens, yet all signs of aging had disappeared. *Jurgen's spell. It did more than simply return keep him from death. In fact, it's made him pristine in every way.*

Seeing him in such a way sent chills up Valyrie's spine. He was beautiful, truly handsome and perfect in complexion, and the awkward feelings she had felt when she first met him returned. Her father's death had done much to mask her attraction for him, but his being near death and being brought back from the brink drove her emotions to the forefront. She was glad Laedron lived, happy that he would wake.

She opened her book, an untitled, nearly forgotten work written by Farrah Harridan, and read the story, an alternate tale contrary to the church's doctrine. The tale depicted strange lands with mystical forests, and told of the wizard Azura, her staff held

184

high and magic spewing from her fingertips.

* * *

Nearing the end of the book, Valyrie looked up when she heard rustling. Laedron's face was wrought with pain, then he seemed to relax. Moments later, his eyes opened, narrowly at first, then wide. Valyrie was filled with astonishment. His irises were almost gray, instead of their former deep blue shade.

"How do you feel?" she asked.

He grunted, cleared his throat, and swallowed before replying. "My body aches. What happened?"

She looked everywhere but at Laedron's eyes. "Your friend Marac returned you here. Andolis is dead."

"That's not all, is it?" Laedron asked. He rubbed his chest. "No marks. Not even bruising. What happened, Val?"

Her name on his lips sounded sweeter than it ever had, and she was unable to keep the truth from him. "You nearly died, Lae. Last night, your life almost came to an end, yet you were saved."

"Saved? By who?" Laedron asked, his tone tainted with confusion and even some irritation.

"Jurgen," she said simply.

His eyes widened. "It cannot be. Did he survive the spell? A fool! He should never have attempted it at his age. Where are they, anyway?"

"They've gone to make peace with the Sorbians at Balfan."

He scoffed. "Then he lives. Probably haggard with more wrinkles than he had before, yes?"

"No."

His brow crinkled in confusion. "How is that possible?"

She swallowed deeply. "He used one of the stones—"

"The stones? Expended someone's essence?"

She nodded.

"No... he couldn't. How could he do that?"

"Marac was very persuasive," she said, averting her eyes.

"Marac!" He slammed his head backward into the pillow. "I can't believe he would want such a thing."

"Can't you? He's very close to you, Lae. He wouldn't let go."

"He should have. Do they have any idea whose soul they used to augment the spell?"

"No."

"Some militiaman, no doubt. The stones from the black pouch?" Laedron searched his belt for something, but he apparently didn't find it.

"Yes, that is where he found them."

"I'll have to have a talk with him. He shouldn't have done that. We don't know what happens to souls used in such a way. We're talking about eternity here."

She took his hand. "Please, don't be angry with him."

"How can I be anything else? He's done something unspeakable. He forced Jurgen's hand to augment a spell, expending an innocent soul in the process."

"He only wanted you back, Lae." She wrapped her other hand around his and squeezed. "I can't say that I didn't want it, too, and I suspect Jurgen didn't have a problem going through with it. He protested, yes, but he performed the spell."

"Do you know what you're saying?"

"Yes, Lae." She drew close. "Your death would have driven a dagger through our hearts."

His expression softened, then he sighed. "No matter what I may think, it cannot be undone now. If it can, I don't know the way."

"Accept this as a second chance. A second chance at life." She smiled. "Can you honestly say that you would rather be dead?"

"No, it's not that. It's a difficult position. I can't disapprove of being alive, but I dislike the method. That's all."

"The method aside, I'm glad you're back with us." She averted her eyes when she felt her heart longing to be closer to him.

"You, Val?"

She leaned backward and spoke with a casual tone. "Yes, why wouldn't I be?"

He grinned. "Yes, of course. We're friends, right? Friends appreciate one another's company."

Do I want to leave this as a friendship? She knew that she would have to be the one to make the first move because it seemed that Laedron didn't know a way to approach her since her father's death. Though she knew by his stilted behavior in her presence that he had a strong attraction, she wanted to be sure. *With tact, then. I have to find out if he truly feels the way I think he does.*

She felt a change of subject might be best to get him to loosen up. "You've come a long way, haven't you, Sorcerer?"

"Yes. It feels further than it probably was."

She nodded. "I feel the same somehow. Even though I've

lived here my entire life, I feel like a stranger to this city now that my father is gone."

"Have you considered what you will do?" Laedron asked. "You know, when we've finished with all of this."

"I…" She paused.

"You don't have any idea, do you?"

"I do, but I am afraid to say." She turned her eyes downward.

"Why would you be afraid?"

"Embarrassment."

Laedron sat up and adjusted his pillows. "You don't have to feel ashamed. I'll be quiet about it if that's what you want."

"Well, Jurgen said that I will always have a place to stay—he'll make sure of that—but I don't want to live a cloistered life. I want to go out into the world and explore, see adventure, and learn of new lands and new people. I yearn to hear tales of great heroes in lands I've never seen, to taste the food I have only read about in books."

"Why is that something to hide? I don't find it unreasonable."

"Because… I… I'd really like to go with you."

Laedron raised an eyebrow. "With us?"

She looked at him directly. "No. With *you*."

"Me? But why?" He leaned back and crossed his arms.

"You've watched out for me since my father died, you and your friends. It's as if you were there every time I was in danger, unwavering and brave. I don't know why, but I feel that going with you is the right choice."

Laedron shook his head. "The path we tread isn't a safe one, Val. You'll need to take time to decide for certain."

"I've made up my mind—"

"No, please. Think about what you're deciding and take some time. What you propose should not be done hastily."

She nodded. "All right, Lae. I will do what you say, but you shouldn't be surprised if my decision doesn't change. I cannot imagine a life here without my father."

"And if that's what you conclude after giving it some time, I won't argue with you. However, I want you to be sure. I know how the sentiments of home can bring you down once you've been gone for some time."

"Tell me of your home, Lae," she said, drawing her legs up and wrapping her arms around them. "Sorbia, isn't it?"

"Nothing to tell, really."

She gently swatted his hand. "That can't be true after what you've said. Your sentiments of home obviously run deep."

"You're right." Laedron shifted his weight. "My homeland is one of rolling grasslands and hills, fertile soil, and tall oaks and hickories. But that's not what makes it the place to which I am eager to return. To crave those things is for farmers, and stewards of the land we are not.

On the western coast lies a village called Reven's Landing, my home and the most serene place I've ever known. Gentle beaches, the warmth of the sun on your back most of the year, and all the comforts of our cottage draw me back there when I'm discouraged. I can still taste the redfish we had not long before I left. Those were easier times indeed, those times spent in my small fishing village."

"Sounds like a wonderful place, Lae. Your family?"

"They fled when the war started. The Morcaine mages'

academy was attacked, and Marac brought news that Ma had taken Laren, my sister, with her, but they didn't tell anyone where they were going. That was probably for the best; no one can seek you out if no one knows where you are."

"And your da?"

"That's a long story." Laedron rested his head on his hand.

"I'd like to learn of him if you don't mind."

"My da was the Bannor, a lower noble and administrator of sorts, to the king, appointed to Reven's Landing."

"Sort of like a mayor?"

"Somewhat, but he had been given more authority than you might see with a mayor. His name was Wardrick Telpist, and he passed away when I was still very young. If not for the portrait in our house, I would likely have forgotten his face. Ma always said I resembled him, but I couldn't see it. I always thought I favored her, and most people agreed."

"I never knew my mother," Valyrie said. "She died during childbirth, and Da was left to care for me. When I got old enough to understand, I pitied him for the sacrifices he was forced to make. He gave up everything—his ambitions, his career, and his friends—all so I might have a better life. He took the innkeeper job from my uncle so he could work and care for me at the same time. Things weren't always well between us, though. I took many of my blessings for granted, and I wasn't as kind as I should have been at times."

"I'm sure he looked past that, Val. Your father must have loved you above all other things in this world."

She nodded. "I know, but I have regrets."

"Ah, yes. Regret. I know it well, but I move forward. I find a way."

"How? You seem to find the path so easily."

"It's never easy, Val. Only quickly done, often as fast as the regrettable decision was made."

"That still doesn't answer my question."

"The *how* is different for everyone. When the thoughts crop up in my head, I remind myself why I'm doing this, who I'm doing it for. It gets me through it."

"My regret is that I never got a chance to tell him 'I'm sorry.'" Valyrie tightly clasped her hands in her lap, then rubbed them together.

Laedron nodded. "We rarely get the chances we want. I'm sure our parents understand, though. It's nice to hear an apology when you've been wronged, but they would forgive us, Val."

"I hope you're right."

"Why don't you tell me of your home?" Laedron asked.

"My home? You've seen it."

"No, I mean the details. The little things that an outsider might not know or see."

She searched her thoughts, then grinned. "I'm happy that Azura was a woman."

Laedron tilted his head in confusion. "What do you mean?"

"This country is a difficult place to live at times, and it favors males over females. The church, the militia, the merchant guilds— all of it is based upon patriarchal hierarchies. If Azura had been a man, we women would likely be forgotten as doers of menial housework and ensuring men always had full bellies."

"Ah, I see," Laedron said. "Nothing wrong with a full belly, but I see your point."

"Is Sorbia the same way?"

"What do you mean? Do we keep women as slaves?"

"Yes. How are they treated in your homeland?"

"We're…" Laedron paused, as if trying to find the right word to use. "I suppose you could call it *egalitarian*."

She gave him a broad smile, and Laedron asked, "What? It means—"

"I know what it means, Lae—equal, balanced. I like a man who knows his way with words. I am studying to be a lyricist, after all."

He swallowed hard, and she detected that familiar awkwardness and fumbling that he had displayed at their first meeting. "Of course. I… um… a lyricist?" he asked.

"Yes, of course. A composer of tales, a singer of songs." She raised her hand. "To sing of heroes loved and lost, to speak of things uncommon to lore, and to pen the tales to preserve for posterity."

"You've got a certain flair for it. Can't argue with you there."

She chuckled. "Of course, my father would hear nothing of it. He wanted me to be a seneschal, a keeper of books in some noble's house."

"Good money in that," Laedron said, at first with confidence, then his voice trailed off when she glared at him, "…or so I've heard."

"There's more to life than gold and silver. I want my riches to be in my words, my wealth to be in the tales I spin, and my

192

happiness to come from my travels and adventures in the wide world."

"You remind me of how I used to be years ago." Laedron crossed his feet and stretched out his legs. "So long ago, when things were different."

"Why did you change?"

"It didn't take long. When I arrived in Westmarch, the city to the east of my village, and started my training, I changed, little by little. Things that were once exciting seemed more dangerous than they previously had. That danger turned into anxiety, then into fear of what lay ahead on my path."

"You got over it, though, didn't you?" Valyrie asked.

"Not completely. I'm thankful for the fear, though. Fear lets you know you're still alive, the same way pain does. If I had been more brazen, I'd likely be dead by now—me and my friends."

"It took courage to do what you've done."

"Courage is easily confused with having the will to do what is necessary. A brave man without fear is simply too foolish to understand the consequences or outcomes. He is a danger to himself and to others."

"Whether courageous or strong of will, I'm glad that you held fast to the goal, Lae," she said, leaning closer. "Above all, I'm grateful that you've come here."

He dipped his head. "You are?"

She took his hand in hers again. "Yes, Lae. I..." She paused and looked away. *Take a chance or leave it alone?*

"Yes?" Laedron asked. "Please, continue."

A chance it is, then. "I have feelings for you, Lae. Feelings that

I've had since we first met."

"Really?" he asked.

She fought the urge to shake her head. *Men truly are blind to matters of the heart.* "Yes."

"I-I feel the same way."

"I hadn't noticed," she said with a snicker.

"What?"

"You couldn't have been any more obvious." She smiled.

He grinned, but then frowned.

"What's the matter? Aren't you happy?"

"I worry, Val. I… are you sure that you feel this way, or is it something else?"

"I'm sure, Laedron. I wouldn't have said it otherwise."

He nodded, but he still seemed to have something on his mind.

"Don't hide from me. What's bothering you?"

"I don't quite know how to put it." He pulled his hand from hers.

"Then speak plainly. You're not going to offend me."

"All right." He took a deep breath. "I only want to make sure that your interest in me isn't because your father passed."

"No, Lae. I've felt this way for some time, and I know that you have."

His face showed his confusion. "Then, why? Why tell me these things now?"

"Because you almost died, for one. The first thing that went through my mind was what might have been. I asked myself, 'Had I talked to him, would things have ended differently?' I told myself that I wouldn't let things pass me by any longer. If I ever got the chance, I'd do something about my feelings." She sighed and reached for his hand. "When they saved you from dying, I decided that I wouldn't let the opportunity pass again."

"I don't know what to say."

"There's nothing left to say. We've said all there is." She slid off her chair and onto the edge of the bed, then leaned forward. Running her fingers through his hair, she said, "Words shall keep us apart no longer."

"I—"

She raised a finger to his lips. "Relax." She lowered her hand, then closed her eyes. She tried to take her own advice, but she could feel her heartbeat drumming in her chest. Electrifying chills tingled her fingertips while the heat of a bonfire burned deep within her heart.

Inching closer and closer, she finally felt her lips connect with his, and the kiss told her volumes about Laedron—of his restraint, his respect for her, and of his desire. That simple kiss said more of the connection they clearly felt for one another, and she was convinced that, despite having kissed others, what she felt was unlike any other she had experienced. *Is this love? It can be nothing else.*

She couldn't help but let out a quiet giggle when she opened her eyes and saw Laedron's eyes still closed and the expression on his face indicative of the pleasure of the moment. She cleared her throat.

Opening his eyes, he gave her a wide grin. "That was amazing."

She took a deep breath, a smile and a tear coming at the same time.

"What's wrong, Val? Do you feel that we've made a mistake?" Laedron asked. He reached up and wiped away her tear.

"No, Lae," she said, lifting her face to the ceiling. "I never thought that I'd be happy again—that I *could* be happy. 'Tis a tear of joy."

Laedron wrapped his arms around her. "It's all right. I've felt that way many times, but things get better."

She returned the embrace. "Do you think you can walk?"

"I don't know, but I'd like to try," he said, sliding one leg off the bed.

"If we can make it to the common room, I have a fine soup simmering." She took his arm to help him walk. Upon reaching the long dining table, she helped him to a seat, then went after the stew. "I hope you like rabbit."

"One of my favorites," Laedron said with a smile.

❧ Chapter Sixteen ❧

A Palace Fit for Soldiers

Driven to the point of exhaustion, the horses slowed, apparently unable, or unwilling, to press on at the same speed. Night had fallen, and Marac looked up at the endless sea of stars in the cloudless sky. "Peaceful. Only fitting for a night such as this."

"A night when we return with hundreds of injured soldiers?" Jurgen asked.

"At least we've saved some, Jurgen. That's got to count for something."

"Of course, but I fear the negotiations we shall face with the Sorbians. What if they demand our surrender? To think, our holy places occupied by foreign troops, our people living under the heel

197

of an occupying army."

"You think he'll demand it?"

"I don't know," Jurgen said. "Anything can happen. He could demand anything, regardless of our acts of kindness and professions of peace."

"Whatever the outcome, I'm certain that it will be for the best."

"Truly?"

"At least no one else will die needlessly in the war. At least the lives of the people will be spared. That was our only concern from the onset."

"I only hope that you are right."

* * *

Once inside the city, Jurgen led the long procession of wagons to the Vicariate Palace.

Marac dismounted, gave the reins to a stable hand, and said, "You have our thanks."

Marac and Brice helped Jurgen and the other priests unload the injured soldiers from the wagons.

"Where are they going to stay?" Marac asked.

"Only the palace would be large enough to house them all." Jurgen started walking. "I must rouse the steward and have him prepare lodgings for these men."

Brice nodded. "What about us? What do we need to do?"

"Check on our sorcerer friend. He'll likely be awake by now." Jurgen turned to climb the palace steps.

"Well, back to the headquarters, I suppose," Brice said.

Marac touched his arm. "Not so quick."

"Why not?"

"Laedron... he could be upset." Marac stared down at the cobblestones.

"Upset? About what?"

"The spell. Jurgen using the soulstone."

"Nonsense. He'll be as pleased as I was. Who could complain about being alive?"

"You don't know Laedron as well as I do," Marac said, shaking his head.

"That's silly, Marac. Come on, and don't worry about that."

Reluctantly, Marac followed him through the streets on the way to the Shimmering Dawn. *How is he happy all the time? It seems like nothing gets Brice down. Maybe he knows that if Laedron's mad, it'll be me taking the brunt of it. Or perhaps he really believes what he says.*

Brice walked in first, and Marac paused before entering the headquarters building. *How bad will this be? Might as well get the tongue-lashing over with.*

Marac overheard Laedron ask, "How did it go?"

"Good, I guess," Brice replied. "Jurgen summoned all the priests in the city and brought—"

"All of them?"

"Yes, from what I could tell. They healed the soldiers and brought them back to the city. Duke Fenric was there, too, and he was alive."

Marac crept the rest of the way into the room, trying his best not to be spotted, but he gave himself away when he noticed

Laedron's complexion and hair. "You're back to normal? But how?"

"Don't play stupid, Marac. You know exactly how. Jurgen performed the spell at your request."

"No, have you not seen your reflection in a mirror? The gray tips, the wrinkles… they're gone!"

Laedron glanced at Valyrie, then back at Marac before struggling to stand. "What do you mean?" He took a metal plate in his hand, angled it with the light, and peered into it. "Creator! How can this be?"

"Did you not notice these things?" Marac asked.

"I wasn't that concerned with my appearance when I awoke." Laedron tilted the plate and his head, looking at his reflection at different angles. "We need to find out why this is so."

Marac relaxed slightly, glad that Laedron didn't seem to be angry with him. "And how do you suggest we do that, Lae?"

"By finding someone who knows. Perhaps Victor?"

"Victor?" Valyrie asked.

"Victor Altruis, the Shimmering Dawn mage of Westmarch. If anyone's left who would know, he'd be the one."

Marac nodded. "Certainly, but only after our mission is complete here. Jurgen may need us yet."

"Then we must go," Laedron said, returning the plate to the table.

Valyrie shook her head and took Laedron by the arm. "You're in no condition to go anywhere. You can't."

"I'll be fine," Laedron said, patting her hand. When they exchanged a smile, Marac knew precisely what feelings lay behind it. *Perhaps we should've left you two alone longer. Looks like the caretaker's smitten with my boy.*

"Let's be off, then," Marac said, interrupting the moment. *Though it's nice to see, we can't wait around all night for them to stop staring at each other.*

* * *

They reached the Ancient Quarter and heard a commotion from the consulship building. Entering the consul chamber, Laedron stood in awe of its splendor. *How many men and how long would it take to build something like this? Surely years and hundreds of workers.*

Jurgen had apparently called the meeting, and the consuls sat silent, staring up at him from the gallery. Few seemed to perceive Laedron and the others enter, but Laedron noticed the blood stains on most of them.

"Ah, you've joined us," Jurgen said. "Might I present my friends, Laedron Telpist, Marac Reven, Brice Warren, and Valyrie Pembry. Their hard work has helped to bring about the end of Andolis Drakar."

Sporadic applause came from the gallery, but it was clear that none of them were in the mood to hand out medals or high praise, and for him, the clapping seemed to be almost a slap in the face compared to the trouble he and his friends had gone through in dealing with such a terrible threat.

"Might I speak to the assembly?" Laedron asked.

Jurgen extended his open hand to the floor. "Laedron is a

Sorbian," Jurgen said, garnering a few hisses from the audience, "but he would like to speak with you."

"I have heard that you went to save the soldiers you could," Laedron said, walking to Jurgen's side, "and you have done the right thing. What have you decided to do, Vicar Jurgen?"

"Nothing as yet," he replied. "We can surrender or seek a truce, but we can do neither until Duke Fenric has recovered completely."

"Surrender? You're considering that even now?" a vicar asked, standing in the gallery. He was a younger man, older than Laedron, but not as aged as the other vicars as the average went. "They'll lay waste to our capital, to our honored traditions!"

Laedron waited for the gallery to grow quiet. "Andolis Drakar has done more damage than the Sorbian army could ever hope to do. No, your honored traditions and your capital have been besmirched by treachery and lies, and you were led by the nose to this day."

"Get him out!" the same vicar shouted, his face red with anger. "He comes to our chamber to insult us? After what we've been through?"

"He comes to our chamber to show us the truth, Vicar Alduin," Jurgen said, putting his hand on Laedron's shoulder. "Is it not true that we have been duped into the Zyvdredis' plans? Used to fight a war that wasn't ours? The Sorbians have been wronged by Andolis's actions, and we were victims, too. We can only hope our good deed will be repaid in kind."

"Why can't there be a truce? Sorbia returns to their shores, and we sign a treaty of peace?" Alduin asked.

Laedron folded his arms. "It won't be easy. Since Gustav Drakar orchestrated an attack on the Sorbian capital, this war will not be easily undone. Gustav Drakar, a man elevated to the rank of deacon by your church, murdered the crown prince of Sorbia, Prince Zorin, and the rest of the mages present at the Morcaine academy that day. This war is as much a father's wrath as anything else, the revenge of King Xavier of Sorbia for your mistakes. "Laedron pointed at the gallery. "You are responsible for this war. Indirectly, perhaps, but responsible nonetheless."

"Lies!" Alduin shouted. "How can you prove any of this?"

"I was there, Your Grace," Laedron replied with a sneer. "Men in the uniform of your militia guards were with Gustav, indiscriminately killing sorcerers. Their blood is on your hands, for you empowered him to do what he has done."

"Calm yourselves, Consuls." Jurgen waved his hand. "This forum exists for discussion, not for disorder and chaos. Let us speak calmly."

"The Sorbians declared war," Alduin said, clearly not as sure as he had been. "We would never begin a war—"

"That is beside the point. What *you* would do and what Andolis and Gustav *have* done are two different things. Forane was also in on their plans to conspire against the peace and commit murder. Justice has been brought to all of them," Laedron said. "If given the chance to surrender to Duke Fenric, I would suggest that you take the opportunity and all do your best to keep the populace calm when the Sorbian army arrives. If Vicar Jurgen agrees, I will speak with Duke Fenric personally to request an honorable peace, but you should prepare yourself for the possibility that he might not accept that."

"Then, you must do your best," Alduin said. "Our Falacoran allies just may have purchased us a fair peace with their lives."

Alduin returned to his seat. Laedron didn't get the impression that Alduin's mind had been changed though, simply that he was biding his time.

After a long pause, Jurgen said, "I think we should allow my friend to speak to Fenric in the coming days. Inform the people of the presence of the soldiers here and tell them that the war is on hold, at least for now. Advise them to remain in their homes or shops and to travel as little as possible on the streets until the armies have gone. We need not have any encounters—accidental or otherwise—with the Sorbian troops while they are here. We stand adjourned until the morrow."

Jurgen led Laedron and the rest of the group out a smaller back exit. "Though I feel we haven't heard the last from Vicar Alduin, you said what needed to be said."

Laedron shrugged. "I merely told the truth."

"I know, but the rest of the consulship might have a difficult time believing it."

"Why do they act in such a way? As if the war could have been good for them?"

Jurgen stopped. "When Andolis and Gustav first came to the capital, they pushed everyone to higher aspirations. Long ago, the church occupied a dominant position in the eastern world. It was by the will of the consuls that kings were crowned, that people stood in awe of our sacred cathedrals, and that priests held true respect and authority in society.

"The days of imperialism are long gone, but the taste of that validation beckoned. Being tired of merely tending the flock, the vicars saw in the Drakars a new beginning, a return to the old ways. Even if just for a passing moment, I entertained the thought of going back to the way things used to be so long ago."

"But tending to the flock, as you put it, is the church's job," Valyrie said.

Jurgen nodded and started down the street again. "Yes, of course. This war is a testament to what is possible through avarice, want, and a disregard of one's true purpose."

* * *

Turning the corner after Jurgen minutes later, Laedron glanced at the ruined steeple topping the Shimmering Dawn headquarters. Once inside, they gathered around the long table in the common room with Piers, and Jurgen said, "Now that we have a moment, I'd like to hear about Laedron's fight with Andolis. I've heard what Marac and Brice had to say, but I want to hear your side of it."

"We found him on the rooftop of the highest tower, holding his staff in the air and chanting."

Marac went into Laedron's bedroom, and returned to place the staff on the table. "Here it is. Andolis's staff."

Jurgen leaned forward, his brow furrowed. "Strange, but magnificent."

Laedron nodded. "Andolis intended to burn the city and make his escape. He said he would set a fire that would last a hundred years, likely by using the essence of the souls trapped in these stones to fuel his magic."

"You've done us a great service, young sorcerer. A great service indeed." Jurgen took Laedron's hand. "I shall personally ensure your order will be reinstated to its former glory, and you will be rewarded handsomely for your efforts here."

"I thank you for your generosity." Piers smiled. "We'll no longer be forced to live in the shadows."

"No, but keep your skills sharp, and educate those who come after you," Jurgen said. "Your order may be called upon to save us from ourselves another time, and I can only pray that day will never come."

"So long as vicars have a taste for those old, imperial ways, I fear you'll have problems, Jurgen," Laedron said.

"Perhaps, but why do you say it in such a way?"

"Forane admitted to helping the Drakars and told us they were Zyvdredi agents. She traded her loyalty for soulstones, those onyx gems containing the life energies of their victims. She wanted to be immortal."

Jurgen frowned. "She was willing to let countless people die so that she could live eternally? It is a shame to see one so devoted give in to the lure of a font of youth."

"Those stones along either edge of the staff are the same as the ones we found on the mages, the ones who killed militia men." Laedron took a deep breath. "The same as the one you used to save me."

Jurgen averted his eyes. "Yes. I did it at the demand of a man to see his friend returned to his side. I hope this doesn't anger you,

Sorcerer."

"'Tis a strange feeling and a hard argument, and it's something we all shall have to live with from this day forward." Laedron stared at the staff. "One of the stones of that staff could house the spirit of the late Daris the Second."

"It could be this one," Brice said, presenting the black onyx ring Andolis had worn. "Maybe to keep him separate from the others?"

"Creator..." Jurgen tapped his lip with a finger and eyed the stones. "Perhaps there is a way to free him?"

"Surely there must be, but I don't know how." Laedron shrugged. "The Zyvdredi were meticulous in designing spells. They never created a spell without a counterpart that could undo its effects."

"We can't approach a Zyvdredi with this information, that's for certain," Jurgen said. "There may be another way, though; we could contact the Uxidin."

Laedron nodded. "They are equally aged and gifted with magic. Perhaps they could answer the question of why I look the way I do now. But how can we find them?"

"I shall think of a way. In the meantime, I must seek a peace with the Sorbians and fix all the things the Drakars have done." Jurgen paused, taking a long look at Laedron. "Marac was right; we owe much to you, all of you."

"We've come a long way on a hard road," Laedron said. "We can only be thankful that the war may come to a close, and few have died as a result. I hope we can soon return to our homes with our heads held high."

Jurgen stood. "Yes, that you can. Remain here until I call for you, for you may be the key to securing peace with the Sorbians. The theocracy has some difficult steps before it."

❧ Chapter Seventeen ❧

The Wrath of a Father

The passage of days came with little news from the outside world. Marac and Brice—and sometimes Valyrie, much to Laedron's disapproval—practiced in the courtyard with blades to keep their readiness high. When not spending time with Valyrie, Laedron studied Ismerelda's spellbooks.

Following their outings, Piers and Caleb brought some reports of the happenings of the city. Above all other news, the fact that Duke Fenric had been saved—and, thus, could be a clear route to a lasting peace—gave Laedron some hope. *The people have suffered so much at the hands of the Drakars, on all sides of this conflict. I am proud to be a Sorbian this day.*

Laedron began experiencing sleepless nights. As the days passed, he was only able to sleep for a few hours at most. With the war ending and the Drakars defeated, he couldn't place the reason for his losing sleep. He felt more relaxed than he'd felt in a long time, quite possibly more than he had since before he left Reven's Landing, yet his sleep remained irregular.

"Your girlfriend surprises me," Marac said, entering Laedron's room.

Laedron looked up from the text he had been reading. "She's not—"

"Oh, don't give me that. I've seen the way you two watch each. I even spied a late night kiss in the garden if my eyes don't deceive."

"I'm in no mood for taunting."

Marac sat next to Laedron on the bed. "I haven't come to taunt you. Actually, I'm proud to see you've finally found someone."

Laedron closed the book and laid it aside. "I'm afraid to bring her with us, Marac."

"Is that what this moping about is for?"

"Moping? I call it concern."

"She's old enough to make her own choices, Lae."

Laedron shook his head. "The next leg of our trip could be dangerous. I've spoken to Caleb about the Uxidin, and he told me the only ones he's ever heard of live deep in the forests of Lasoron, along with all the other things only legends describe."

"What sorts of things?"

"Beasts, monsters… anything you might imagine in an ancient forest rarely traversed. The things that live well away from the realms of men."

"You're not getting scared of ghost tales, are you?"

"I just want her to be safe," Laedron said with a sigh. "I can't imagine the pain I would feel if she died because we allowed her to come with us."

"Like I said, she's old enough to make her own decisions and go where she likes. Tell her of the risks, but let her decide. She's lost her father, but that doesn't mean she needs another one."

"If I didn't know any better, I'd think you were trying to insult me," Laedron said.

"I only speak plainly. Embrace her, love her, do all the things that you're supposed to do at her side, but don't rule her, Lae. No matter how fine your intentions, you'll push her away."

"You really think so?"

"I know so, my friend. She's willful and stubborn. I can see that in her, just as I've seen it in you. She'll fight you every leg of the way unless you let her determine her own path."

"Thanks, Marac."

"Anytime," he replied, then he closed the door behind him when he left.

Laedron opened the book and flipped to the page he had been studying before Marac had interrupted him. He repeated Marac's words over and over in his mind. *It's not my decision to make. Marac's right. When the time comes, Valyrie, for better or worse, will have to choose for herself.*

He placed the book in his backpack, then thought of Ismerelda. *How your life must have been filled with intrigue and adventure to possess books such as these. And now, I shall never know how you came to own them or why you took such an interest in Zyvdredi magic to keep such a sizable collection.* He buckled the clasp on the leather bag and went out to the common room.

Just as he arrived, Laedron heard a knock on the door, and he went to answer it. "Ah, Vicar Jurgen, you've come to visit us at long last? It's been nearly a week."

Jurgen stepped inside. "Yes, I've come to summon you and bring some news. I've spoken with Duke Fenric, but he has been rather difficult to deal with."

"Come in, then. Care for anything to drink?"

"No, I'm well, thank you," Jurgen replied, taking a seat at the table. When everyone had joined him, he took a deep breath, then said, "Duke Fenric has recovered from his injuries and should be ready to speak with you, Laedron."

"Has he said anything?" Laedron asked. "About peace or the war?"

"Not to us, no. We've given him some distance and time to think about things, and we... well, we thought that might be best for one of his countrymen to speak with him first."

"Then it shall be done. By the time the night falls, I hope we can be done with this war."

Jurgen nodded. "Good. If you can secure the peace favorably for all sides, the consuls and your king should be pleased."

"We shall see. Have you come up with anything regarding the ring and the staff? Anything about the Uxidin?" Laedron asked.

"No, but I've made you an appointment with Demetrius Hale, the chief amongst the Arcanists."

Marac asked, "You're not coming along?"

"I cannot. I must return to the consulship once we have

finished here. Tomorrow evening, I shall return, and you can inform me of your next step."

"Arcanists? The navigators?" Laedron asked, remembering how they had discussed the order before arriving in Azura.

"Yes, they are an important group in Azura and have been for a long time," Jurgen said. "Beyond being able to navigate the Sea of Pillars, the Arcanists have kept detailed records throughout history, and they are patrons of art and science. Merchants, scholars, and seafarers make up their ranks."

"Even the university is administered by them," Valyrie said.

"Yes, that is true." Jurgen gave her a smile. "If it hadn't been for them, much of what we know now about alchemy, architecture, and the natural world would likely have been lost through the ages. Time has not always passed kindly for the theocracy."

"Where is the meeting?" Laedron asked.

"At his home. He can be found in the row houses across from the university, number four."

Valyrie nodded. "I know the way. When?"

"Tomorrow at lunch. He always takes lunch at his home at or around noon." Jurgen stood. "Perhaps he will have some answers. For now, I should take Laedron with me to meet with Fenric."

* * *

The steps leading up to the front doors of the Vicariate Palace remained in disrepair. Climbing the stairs, Laedron observed two pools of blood around the large crater where he'd fallen, one stain his and the other that of Master Greathis. His skin tingled as if the place itself reminded his body of the pain, and he walked quicker to put distance between himself and that spot which had caused him so much agony.

In the main hall, Duke Fenric sat with a group of his soldiers. A priest offered them food and drink. Fenric must not have trusted the man or his charity because he simply ignored the offerings.

The first thing Laedron noticed about the duke was the impressive signet ring which bore the crest of the Sorbian royal family. The duke's armor glimmered even in the dim light of the palace halls, and it had hardly a scrape or scratch from the previous day's engagement. His face, goatee, and hair were all perfectly groomed.

"Duke Fenric," Laedron said, bowing.

"And who are you, young man? Another priest coming to placate me?"

"Your servant, my lord. Your subject."

"My subject? Your dulcet words will garner you no more favor with me than speaking plainly," Fenric said with a sneer.

"I do speak plainly, Sire. I am Laedron Telpist of Reven's Landing."

"Telpist... a name that I have heard before, yet I cannot place. Reven's Landing, you say?"

"Yes, my duke. My father Wardrick Telpist was appointed as Bannor of that village by your brother, the king."

"No need to avert your gaze, then. My countrymen should look me in the eye when speaking."

"My apologies. I had gone so long in the guise of a Heraldan that their customs have become natural to me." Laedron looked up at Fenric's face. "I have come to talk of peace with you, my lord. These priests, being of weak will and filled with want for a time since passed, had elevated a charlatan to their highest office. The man persuaded them into a false conviction, then launched an attack against us in secret to provoke this war."

"What matter or concern is that of mine? Mistakes on their part do not facilitate a change of heart on mine. My nephew, your crown prince, lies dead at the hands of these miscreants, and my brother, your king, has ordered me to capture this country. Nothing has changed."

"My lord, I beg to differ," Laedron said, glancing at Fenric's soldiers. "You have few men left, too few, in my mind, to continue. Thus, now is the best time to consider alternatives."

"We can send word for more men. Surely, you know that we have many more men willing to fight—and die, if need be—for his majesty, King Xavier. A vengeful father is slow to forgive."

"Such a move is needless. His majesty has taken revenge upon the wrongdoers already, by my hand and those of my friends."

"Yours?"

"We serve the Shimmering Dawn, my lord. We have completed our mission against Gustav Drakar, and we have done away with Andolis, more commonly known as Tristan the Fourth. This priest, Jurgen, has helped us every step of the way because he believes in justice, not power or prestige."

"What of the Falacorans?"

Jurgen stepped forward and said, "If we declare a truce, the Falacorans will be forced to follow. They would have little choice."

"Little choice? They possess armies, ships, and the will to continue the fight, Priest."

Jurgen shook his head. "If we declare peace, I assure you that the Falacorans will obey the terms. They accede to our diplomatic actions in all things, especially those we create, and they would lack a case for war if they did not. The entire world would condemn them for continuing to fight without cause."

"Then you can promise that the Falacoran fleet will leave the Wayfarer's Strait and stop harassing our merchant vessels?" Fenric asked.

Laedron hadn't considered the impact of the war on the grander scale. *A Falacoran battle fleet in the Wayfarer's Strait? This war has taken on a wide-reaching scale. For him to even mention their presence must mean they are causing havoc on the open sea.*

"Yes, we will swear by it," Jurgen said, offering his hand. "If you say the word, I will dispatch the fastest ship I can find to carry word to Wintermere, then on to Talamere."

Wintermere and Talamere. A great port and the capital of Falacore.

Fenric took Jurgen's hand in an embrace. "Good. Then, I shall return to Balfan and depart these lands. Give me a day's time to return to my ships, and the blockade shall end. Your ship will pass unimpeded."

"Thank you for your kindness," Jurgen said with a bow.

Fenric narrowed his eyes. "Strange…"

"Yes?"

"I have never had a priest bow to me before. They usually expect it the other way around."

"No, my lord. I bow because you have given my people a

great boon this day. The gift of life and peace." Jurgen gestured to the door. "We can arrange wagons—"

"No need. My men can march. I, however, will require a horse. The sooner I can get word to my fleet, the sooner we can put an end to this madness."

"Take one of the geldings from the palace stables." Jurgen pointed over his shoulder. "Below those stairs and to the left."

"I hope we are never forced to meet again under such circumstances," Fenric said, approaching the door.

"So long as I live, I shall prevent it."

Once Fenric and his men left, Jurgen turned to Laedron. "You never cease to impress me, Sorcerer."

"Thank you, Vicar."

"If you'll excuse me, I shall speak to the consulship and inform them of this good news. I appreciate all you have done for us."

Laedron watched Jurgen leave. *The first of our goodbyes.* They'd had their arguments and confrontations, but Laedron remembered some good times with Jurgen. He also knew that he would probably never see Jurgen again, as their roads were unlikely to cross in the foreseeable future. *We're from two different worlds. He'll remain in his, and one day soon, I hope to return to mine.*

ঙ Chapter Eighteen ৶

Revelry and Reverie

Arriving back at the Shimmering Dawn headquarters, Laedron took a long look at the fountain out front, the golden chalice Meklan Draive had mentioned when he began the journey in Westmarch. The structure, a dilapidated church, housed the few men who remained of the order in Azura. It stood as a testament to strife and troubles in a time of madness and ancient grudges, a time of both triumph and defeat.

The journey had brought him a world away from his home, and he'd had the distinct privilege of seeing the best and worst of his fellows—the depths of Marac's grief and the heights of his bravery, the transformation of Brice from a mere tailor to a picker of locks and seeker of adventure. The journey had changed Laedron, too. No longer did he concern himself with learning lesser magic to appease a teacher. Magic had become a tool of survival, and he wielded it well. Ismerelda had passed her legacy on to him, and he had taken up the banner of her teachings and carried it forward against the Zyvdredi. In a way, he felt a part of a war still waged, one in which he hadn't realized he was a combatant. He knew that war, the ageless fight between the Uxidin and Zyvdredi, would carry on long after he lay down his scepter.

Some part of him didn't want the war to be over, for an end to the fighting meant an end to their adventures. *Perhaps the end need not come so soon. Maybe adventure lay before us still.*

The streets had seemed kinder on his return to the headquarters. They no longer appeared as hostile as when he had first arrived or any of the times he had gone out into the city before the peace settlement. Smiling, Laedron entered the building and dipped his head to Marac and Brice sitting at the common table.

"What's that smile all about? Have you done it?" Marac asked.

Laedron nodded. "It is done. Fenric has departed with an offering of peace, and the war shall soon be at an end."

"Finally," Brice said. "Now, we can go home."

"Yes." Laedron sat at the end of the table. "You could go home, or you could come with me."

"Where are you going?"

"Wherever the Arcanists send us. I must find out more about these stones, and only the Uxidin can provide the answers."

"Another trip," Brice said woefully.

Marac gave Brice a gentle slap across the arm. "Another adventure."

"Oh, yes. Right."

Laedron glanced at the hall entry and noticed Valyrie leaning against a post and listening in on their conversation. "When we've finished with that, we can return home."

"I've made up my mind," Valyrie said, joining them at the table.

"And what have you decided?" Laedron asked.

"I'm coming with you. There's nothing left for me here."

"It would be difficult for you to return. Are you sure you want to leave?"

"Yes, I'm sure. I've never traveled beyond this city, and I'll likely never see the outside world if I stay here." Her eyes turned downward. "I have too many memories of this place to stay, to watch you leave and not be at your side."

Laedron nodded. "If that is what you want, then so it shall be."

"So, what do we do now?" Marac sighed, seemingly bored with sitting around the headquarters. "Wait until tomorrow?"

"A night out ought to do us some good," Laedron replied, giving Marac a grin.

Marac met his smile with wide eyes. "A night out? Laedron Telpist is saying we go out for a bit of enjoyment?"

"Why not? Our mission is finished here, and we have nothing to do but wait. I thought you'd be pleased—"

"I am, just a bit surprised that you would suggest it."

"Good, then it's settled. Know any places, Val?" Laedron asked.

She bobbed her head.

"Let's all get cleaned up, then."

* * *

Laedron read the sign hanging above the door. *Hubbard House*. Going inside, he felt a rush of warm air, the heat caused by both the number of people within and the fireplace in the corner. From the stage resonated the sound of music, a harmonious mix of flute, tambourine, and lute. The performers, two men and a woman, were dressed in costumes, and the crowd seemed to be enjoying the performance, a contradiction to most places Laedron had visited. Overall, the tavern gave off a jovial ambience, but the owners of the establishment clearly expected a measure of restraint amongst its patrons.

"I like it, but Marac may be uncomfortable here," Laedron said, elbowing Marac in the ribs.

Marac shook his head. "I think I'll be fine. A fine meal and a mug of ale will please me more than a night of wild escapades."

"Something better than that stew we've been eating," Brice said, rubbing his belly. "That stuff's awful."

"Worse than awful." Marac turned to Laedron and Valyrie. "Maybe you two would like some privacy?"

"What? Don't be silly." Laedron folded his arms. "Privacy? For what? There's no need."

"Actually, I think there is indeed a need." Marac took Brice by the arm and led him away. "See you two after dinner."

"Ridiculous," Laedron said. "He insists on making a big show out of everything."

Valyrie put her hand on his. "Let's just try to enjoy ourselves, all right?"

Glancing at their joined hands, Laedron gave her a nod. "Something to eat?"

"Sounds delightful."

Laedron helped her to her seat, a custom his mother had always told him would be viewed favorably by women. Sitting at her side, he gestured at a serving woman to get her attention.

"Welcome to Hubbard House," the woman said with a slight bow. "What, pray tell, can I get for you two?"

"Wine?" Laedron asked, glancing at Valyrie and receiving an approving nod. "Yes, wine. What is the meal tonight?"

"Minted lamb and grilled leeks."

His mouth watered at the mention of lamb. "Two, please."

"Of course, and I shall have your wine out shortly."

When they were alone again, Laedron gazed into Valyrie's eyes. "Are you certain that you wish to leave with us?"

"Oh, Lae, of course. Why do you keep worrying over it?"

"I don't want to see you make the wrong choice."

"The wrong choice? No, I'm making the right decision."

"If you're sure, I'm sure," he said.

Valyrie gave him a grin in return. "I'm certain about something else, too."

"Thank you." Laedron smiled with appreciation at the serving woman's return, took a goblet of wine, and sipped it. "Yes? What's that?"

"I'd like to learn of magic."

"Really?" Laedron asked, raising his eyebrows.

She nodded. "I find it interesting. For a long time, I had only read of spellcraft in my books. When you came, I saw it, and then I wanted to perform it myself."

He remembered something his mother had told him. "Sorcerers aren't born, they're made. Some have an affinity for performing magic, but the door is open to anyone who will pass through." He paused. "We can try, but I must warn you that students usually begin much younger."

"What, am I too old to learn new tricks?" she asked.

Laedron smiled. "No, of course not. It's just easier to get accustomed to the effects when you're young—the headaches, the tiredness."

"Don't worry. I'll try my hardest."

"Try your hardest?" Laedron asked, remembering what Ismerelda had told him what seemed so long ago. "I see we'll have to work on your lack of confidence."

She had a puzzled expression. "Lack of confidence?"

"Nothing. Just something my teacher told me when I started my training. She thought my indecision was a lack of belief in my own abilities." Laedron paused. "Ismerelda was right. I was indecisive and unsure, but not anymore—not after what we've been through. She told me that I would have to learn to trust myself along the way, and Gustav and Andolis Drakar have done more to teach me about faith in myself than anyone or anything else."

The serving woman returned with platters piled high with roast lamb and grilled leeks, and Laedron thanked her before she walked away. Laedron could tell Valyrie had become as hungry as he was because she ate quickly and spoke little. *The sludge served in the Shimmering Dawn must have had the same effect on her that it did me.*

"Sorry," she said, clearly embarrassed by her haste. She patted her lips with a linen cloth.

"No need to be." Laedron continued happily through his meal, trying to make her feel comfortable by eating without a strict adherence to etiquette.

Finishing, she pushed her plate away. "I need a rest after a feast like that."

"Yes, it was quite filling."

She took a sip of her wine, and the musicians finished the song they had been playing. "Looks like they'll be taking a break for a while."

"Did you care for the tune?"

"Yes. It's a local favorite. It would normally have a lyricist accompanying the music, but it seems they don't have the luxury of a singer."

"Would you care to try?"

"What, sing?" She shook her head. "Oh, no, I couldn't."

"I thought you were preparing to be a lyricist?"

"Yes, but I couldn't. Not here and now."

"Why not?"

"I always preferred the writing part over the singing part, to be honest. I could never muster the courage to sing in front of a crowd."

"Have you ever tried?" Laedron asked.

"Well, yes, I tried a few times. Lost my nerve just before the performance every time. She wrapped her arms around her waist. "So much has passed that it hardly seems important anymore."

"Nothing is more important than keeping what we hold dear alive." He put his finger under her chin, turning her face to his. "I'd like to hear it. I truly would."

She swallowed the rest of her wine, nodded slowly, and pulled a scrap of paper from her pocket. "All right. If you want."

Valyrie stood and walked toward the stage, then gave Laedron a glance before approaching the band. Following a brief conversation, the lute player seemed to have convinced the others to participate because they nodded approvingly. She walked with them to the stage, then stood in front of the band. Looking out over the crowd, she wavered and appeared nervous, so Laedron gave her a nod of encouragement.

She glanced over her shoulder at the band, and they started playing. Laedron became fascinated at the tune, which began with a somber prelude, but evolved into spirited melody when she sang.

Laedron sat awestruck by the flawlessness of her voice, every note sang with perfect tone and inflection. The passion behind her words sent chills racing down his spine, a sensation he rarely felt with music, a feeling not unlike the one he had experienced when they had kissed. The sweet melody completed the picture of her true inner beauty, and his desire for her gentle embrace heightened.

When the song ended, a silence filled the room before the patrons gave her an ovation. Clapping his hands, Laedron rose to honor her singing, and she returned to the table, her cheeks flush and her eyes wet. The applause ceased only when she gave them a bow and took her seat.

"Quite a performance," Laedron said, scooting closer to her. "You have a wonderful, no, a magnificent singing voice."

"Thank you." She hid her face, seemingly out of shyness.

"What's wrong, Val? Did you make a mistake? If you did, I don't think anyone noticed."

"No, it's not that."

Laedron took her hand, trying to do something to help. "What is it, then?"

"The validation. I never thought it could feel so good." She brushed her hand across her cheek.

He knew the feeling. It was the same sensation he felt the first time someone called him *sorcerer*, and it was akin to the excitement that had stirred within him when he defeated Gustav. He raised her hand to his face and gently kissed the back of it.

"What's that for?" she asked.

"Appreciation." He glanced at the band when they began another song, then gazed at her again. "Would you care to dance?"

Caught up in the moment, Laedron had forgotten that he didn't know much about dancing. In fact, he didn't know the first thing about it, and the only time he'd ever done it before was when his ma or sister asked. Then, he wondered how well Valyrie could dance. *I bet she's experienced. Maybe she doesn't want to.*

She nodded, and Laedron swallowed deeply. He rose and escorted her to an open area of the floor. Thankfully, the band played a song with a moderately slow tempo. He drew her close to his body and placed his hand on her hip. She rested her head on his shoulder. He held her hand close to his heart and swayed with the rhythm.

Closing his eyes, he inhaled her scent, detecting the hint of perfume on her skin. *Jasmine? No matter. It's not important.* Blocking out everything except the music and her touch, Laedron felt as if they had escaped all of Bloodmyr in favor of their own nook of the universe, a place where time stood still and no one from the outside could enter. He couldn't remember the last time that he had been so relaxed, and he didn't want it to end.

When the song ended, he opened his eyes. "That was nice."

"Very nice," she said, taking half a step back and smiling.

He walked to their table, still grasping her hand, and the serving woman refilled their goblets. They sipped wine quietly for a few moments before Marac came over.

"Enjoying yourselves?" Marac asked, his words slurred slightly.

Laedron nodded. "I can see you're having fun. Where's Brice?"

"Left a while ago. Said he had something to take care of."

"Left? Just like that?" Laedron asked.

"Yeah." Marac let out a hiccup. "Sorry."

"Looks like we'd better get you back."

"No need to leave early on my part, my friend. I think I'll head on back, but don't trouble yourselves."

"You sure?"

Marac slapped him on the shoulder. "Absolutely. I've found my way back before with far more than this to drink. I'll be fine."

Laedron smiled when Marac turned away and weaved

toward the door. "Looks like he's lost his tolerance for fine liquor."

"Seems like you haven't," Valyrie said.

He furrowed his brow and stared at his half-empty goblet of wine. *How many have I had? Two-and-a-half now and no effect? No sign of inebriation?* "How do you feel, Val?"

"Oh, quite well, thank you," she said, giving him a smile that he attributed, at least in part, to the alcohol.

Laedron offered his hand after dropping a few coins on the table. "Want to get out of here?"

Taking his hand, Valyrie stood, stumbled over her chair, and balanced herself. "Sorry, stood up too fast."

"It's perfectly all right."

Exiting into the street, Laedron kept her hand wrapped under his arm and escorted her along the road back to the Shimmering Dawn. Although Valyrie was clearly intoxicated, she had consumed less wine than he had, and he felt no ill effects whatsoever. In fact, despite the late hour, he still felt well-rested and fresh.

When they arrived at the bedraggled church, Valyrie's hand slipped down his arm and clasped his hand. He gave her some resistance when she entered his room, but she pulled him the rest of the way through the door before closing it. Once inside, Laedron felt his back against the wall and her kiss on his lips. Then, he noticed her fingers slowly running through his hair and caressing the side of his face. Her other hand stroked his shoulder then slid down the side of his body.

The drink has gotten to her, taken control, he thought when her hand reached his waistband. "No, not like this."

"What do you mean?" she asked, the wine adding an unusual accent to her speech. He could tell she wanted him, but he feared that the alcohol might have heightened her lust instead of her affection.

"Just… not like this."

She backed away, looking ashamed. "You don't desire me?"

"Nothing like that." Laedron shook his head, walked over to the bed, and sat on the edge. "If *it* happens, I want it to be something special for both of us, something we'll remember in the morning and for the rest of our lives. I don't want to be too hasty."

She sat next to him. "It's all right, Lae. Really, it's—"

"No." He took her hand in his and kissed it. "I care for you, and I don't want what we have to be ruined by a night of carelessness; I don't ever want regret coming to mind when you look my way. Not ever."

She nodded, then pressed her hands against his chest, causing him to lie back until his head hit the pillow. His eyes fixed on the ceiling, he felt Valyrie crawl up alongside, then she rested her head above his heart.

"If you'll do nothing else, hold me close, Sorcerer."

He lay with his arm wrapped about her shoulders, holding her tight. Unable to judge the time, he decided to stay until he felt tired and could fall asleep, but the feeling never came.

⤙ Chapter Nineteen ⤚

Old Stories

Valyrie stirred at his side when the dawn light beamed into her face. The stained glass subdued the light, but it was clearly enough to rouse her from her sleep. Rubbing her eyes, she arched her back and stretched her limbs. Then, her eyes met his, and shock filled them.

"What… what happened?" she asked.

Laedron grinned. "Nothing to be ashamed of, for we've only slumbered here. You wanted more. Well, the wine took control once we returned, to be perfectly honest."

"You must think I'm a fool." She sat up and straightened her clothes.

Laedron leaned over and put his arm around her. "Not at all. I would never think that about you. Drunk, perhaps, but not a fool."

231

Her cheeks flushed. "This is so embarrassing."

He turned her to face him. "There's no reason to feel humiliated. I..." *Say something. I can't say how I truly feel. What if it pushes her away? Could it push her away?*

"Yes, Lae?"

"I..." *Just say it already.* "It may seem silly to you, since we haven't known one another for long, but... I care for you deeply, Val. There's something about you I find impossible to resist, and though I haven't felt this feeling before, it's unmistakable."

His anxiety rising, he watched her sit in silence until he could take no more. "Please, you must say something."

She blinked rapidly, then smiled. "I feel the same for you."

He sighed in relief. "I'm glad. It makes it easier to bear."

She gave him a concerned look. "Anything besides that on your mind?"

"I didn't sleep much last night. In fact, I haven't slept at all."

"Anxious about my being next to you all night?"

"No, not at all," he said, caressing her hand. "It's something else."

"You can tell me, Lae. Anything at all."

"I don't know what to say, really. I've been awake all night, yet I'm not tired in the least. In fact, I feel more refreshed and rested than ever. The wine, too. It had no effect. I drank nearly three goblets, and nothing."

Confusion riddled her face. "I wonder... wait." She looked past him, and when Laedron turned, he saw the Farrah Harridan book on the nightstand. Snatching it up, she flipped through the book. Then she said, "Here it is. This part is entitled 'Rituals of

Wizardry.'"

The ceremony called for an ancient essence. Once it had been acquired, the recipient was taken to a grove of standing stones, and the ritual was done. Imbuing one of their own with the essence, the druids proclaimed that, from that moment hence, he would be a wizard, one with the magic. He would take on the qualities of magic itself; he would be restless, impervious to toxins, and needing little sustenance. Flowing through him like water in the river, magic would embody his existence. Only one step remained for his full transformation, the final ritual bestowed upon them by their father's father — the Font.

"How can this be?" Laedron asked. "I've had no rituals performed upon me in dark, druidic circles."

"Jurgen did something to you to stop your death," Valyrie said. "He used one of the soulstones, and we don't know who, or what, was contained there."

"Does it say how long this is supposed to last?"

"The book doesn't give a frame of time. It could be permanent."

Laedron collapsed onto the bed. "Permanent?" He let out a growl.

"We should go to the Arcanists and see what they can tell us."

"No, we must find Jurgen."

"He'll return to us this evening. Knowing Demetrius Hale, we won't get many more opportunities to speak with him."

"All right." He stood. "If you think it's worth it."

When Laedron entered the common room, Marac and Brice were sitting at the table. They both smiled when Valyrie stepped out behind him.

She was clearly upset at their cocky grins because she said, "I'll get ready," and ran into her room, slamming the door behind her.

Laedron shook his head and sat beside Marac. "It's not what you think."

"A pity," Marac replied. "I should have expected as much, though."

"Must we talk about this?"

"No, not if you have something else to discuss." Marac looked over at Brice and laughed.

"Jurgen's made me into a wizard."

Brice and Marac exchanged odd looks.

"What?" Marac asked.

"With the spell, the one you asked him to cast, he put something inside me, the essence of whoever, or whatever, was in that stone."

"And how did you come to this conclusion?"

Laedron clasped his hands on the table. "The book Valyrie has describes the ritual. The wording differs, but it sounds eerily familiar."

"I'm so sorry, Lae," Marac said, his head drooping.

"Nothing can be done about it now, not unless we find out more from the Arcanists."

"Do you think they'll have an answer?"

"Unlikely, but maybe they can point us in the right direction." Laedron stood with Valyrie's return. "Ready?"

Marac and Brice followed him out, and Laedron turned to Valyrie. "Can you show us the way?"

She nodded.

* * *

Arriving at the row houses across from the university grounds, Laedron breathed in the scent of fresh cut grass. The sounds of birds chirping and young people talking were thick in the air. *It's as if the war never touched the lives of the people around this district. How lucky they are.*

Valyrie stopped before a red brick building marked with the number four cast in gold. "This is it," she said, climbing the cement steps to the front door.

Laedron joined her on the landing and knocked. A few moments later, the door opened to reveal a man clad in red and black, apparently the garments of a Heraldan university scholar. The tunic was stitched in such a way that the clothes had a repetitive diamond pattern throughout, the center of each diamond adorned with a small black embroidered Azura's Star.

"Demetrius Hale, I presume?" Laedron asked.

The man removed the cob pipe from his mouth. "Jurgen's friends?"

"We've come to seek answers from you."

Demetrius chuckled heartily. "I shall endeavor to help you, but a true scholar knows only that he truly knows nothing. Won't you come in?"

Undaunted by the man's peculiar statement, Laedron followed him inside. The entry parlor immediately reminded Laedron of Ismerelda's house in Westmarch—the decadent furniture, the rich floor coverings, and the pleasant scent. Laedron reckoned that the man was wealthy, a senior member of the powerful Arcanist guild.

In a wide, open room past the parlor, Demetrius took a seat in a plush leather chair behind a massive oaken desk. Papers occupied the entire surface of the desk, but they all seemed to have a place. Nothing was strewn or scattered, and most everything was arranged in perfect stacks.

"Won't you tell me more of your dilemma?" Demetrius asked, pulling a fiery stick from the hearth and lighting his pipe from it. "I must have driven Jurgen to madness with my questions, but he could answer none of them."

Laedron sat across from him. "We seek information on the Uxidin. We need to locate and speak to them about a sensitive matter."

"What matter is that?"

Laedron didn't want Jurgen to get in trouble for saving his life, so he said, "Gustav and Andolis were Zyvdredi."

"Yes, quite an unfortunate happening. Glad the church got that one sorted out before it was too late."

"Yes, well, Andolis trapped someone in this onyx ring," Laedron said, gesturing to Brice. "Since the Uxidin are the most gifted magicians in the world, we seek one to tell us what can be done."

Demetrius narrowed his eyes. "Trapped someone inside a ring? That's preposterous."

"I cannot say if it's true, for I do not know," Laedron replied. "Perhaps you could take a look at it."

Taking the ring from Brice, Demetrius produced a loupe and peered through it. "Interesting. Yes, very interesting indeed."

"You see something?"

"Glints of energy are sparking through the crystal formations. That's what gives it the unnatural glow." Demetrius tilted his seeing lens, examining the gem on each side. "Tiny symbols."

Laedron leaned over the desk. "Symbols?"

"Yes," Demetrius said, handing over the ring and his lens. "If you'll look closely at the edges, you should see small runic characters scribed along the perimeter."

"I see them." Laedron squinted through the lens, awestruck by the meticulous precision of the foreign lettering, then returned the seeing glass and pocketed the ring.

"I've never seen anything like them." Demetrius took another puff from his pipe. "Far too small and precise to be made with any set of tools I know or any jeweler I know for that matter. Do you know who is purportedly trapped within this stone?"

"We have suspicion that it's Daris the Second."

"Daris the Grand Vicar?" The man's eyes grew wide with surprise.

"One and the same," Laedron replied. "If we're to free him or learn more of this, we must find an Uxidin. That is, unless you know of someone else."

"No, unfortunately. The trapping of souls in gems is a thing of legend, an evil practice performed by the Necromancers of old."

"Then, do you know where we can find an Uxidin?"

Demetrius scratched his chin with the mouthpiece of his pipe. "No, but I know someone who might. If he cannot, there are few who could."

"Who?"

"His name is Cedric Tamden, but I can't say how much help he might be," Demetrius said. "He has studied the Uxidin and Zyvdredi cultures for longer than I've known him, and he even possesses a few of their texts."

"Where can we find him?"

Demetrius grimaced. "At the center of the university grounds is our ancient library. Deep in the lower levels, Cedric hoards his texts and artifacts, and few ever go down to visit him."

"He doesn't teach classes?" Valyrie asked.

"No, and you shall require my permission to reach the lower levels." Demetrius took a quill and began scrawling on a scroll. "Be careful down there, by the way."

Laedron raised an eyebrow. "Is it dangerous?"

"The library is the oldest structure in the city besides some of the shrines in the Ancient Quarter. When the city planners constructed the Heraldan Channel, this area became a swampland, and the library tower sank into the ground. It continued sinking for years, and eventually, the first floor became the lowest level in a series of flooded basements.

"The consulship had little concern over the issue in the early years of the church, but we Arcanists convinced them when we got tired of waiting. We threatened to halt all transportation to Azuroth, and that got their attention. It took quite some time to get the water out, but now, the lower levels are dry as a bone. Of course, the structure is damaged from years of neglect, so tread carefully."

"Thank you," Laedron said, taking the scroll. "When would be the best time to go?"

"He rises early and works long hours, constantly in pursuit of the location of something he calls The Bloodmyr Tome, a record of the times before Azura, before most written records. You should be able to find him there now." Demetrius relit his pipe and puffed it a few times. "Best of luck."

Laedron led the way out, across the street, and onto the university grounds. He easily picked out the library building. It had an archaic design which differed significantly from the other university buildings. The walls were built of smooth stone, which had darkened over the centuries, and dimples and cracks indicated many years of weathering. Nearing the tower, he could see moss clinging to it, and he noticed that the door set into the front of the structure seemed much newer than the rest of it.

The marble faces of the other buildings appeared younger and more modern, and he attributed the presence of high-quality stone to the rise of the Arcanist guild over the centuries. *They began with this simple limestone tower, improved upon it, and added buildings as they grew in wealth and power.* He eyed the magnificent structure beyond the library. *That is probably the latest addition, the richest of them all.*

"A brand new door on a place like this?" Marac asked, apparently noticing the same thing Laedron had.

"Likely to replace one several stories beneath the ground." Laedron glanced at him. "Demetrius did say that the building has sunk over time. The first door is well beneath our feet." Laedron opened the door, and Brice closed it behind them.

A man looked up from a tome and asked, "Might I help you?"

"Yes," Laedron replied, approaching him with the scroll in hand. "Master Hale has sent us to speak with Cedric Tamden."

"What?" The librarian snatched the paper from Laedron's hand. "Truly?"

"Yes, we need his help."

"Good luck with that. He said he's not to be disturbed... ah, he always says he's not to be disturbed. Grumpy old codger, that Tamden."

"Can we see him?"

The librarian shrugged. "If you want, I care not. You have permission, so go right ahead. The door in the back." He pointed over his shoulder.

After giving the man a nod, Laedron went to the door and opened it. The door heaved a sigh, and Laedron looked back at the librarian.

"Oh, worry not. It does that if it's been closed long enough."

Entering the passage, Laedron led the descent down a set of stairs. "Hale said the final level, didn't he?"

Valyrie nodded.

He followed the stone steps, spiraling downward until he reached a dark landing and could proceed no further. The only exit was a solid oaken door, and presumably behind it he would find Cedric Tamden. With the creak of wood, the door opened at Laedron's push.

Inside, he saw the back of a man crouched in the middle of the room, his tunic deep red and adorned with designs identical to the one that Demetrius Hale had been wearing. Strands of gray hair draped over his tunic in the back, and the man whispered quietly to himself.

"Cedr—"

"I told you I wasn't to be disturbed!" the man snarled without turning. "I can't abide these constant interruptions."

"Master Tamden." Laedron stepped into the room. "We've come to ask some questions. Master Hale sent us."

"Hale? He's too busy with his school and the guild to worry about my research." Cedric looked over his shoulder. "Why would he send you?"

"We seek answers, and he thought you might be able to help."

"Me? Ridiculous," Cedric replied, turning away again. "No one cares about my research. No one."

"I need your help. Something terrible has happened."

"Terrible? Perhaps you should speak plainly, young man."

Laedron crept forward and pulled the onyx ring out of his pocket. "We believe we carry the essence of Daris the Second, his soul trapped within this ring."

Cedric stood and turned to face him. "Daris? Then, the stories are true, and it may yet exist."

"What may yet exist?" Laedron asked.

"The Bloodmyr Tome."

"A book?"

"*The* book. The ancient book of knowledge held secret by the Uxidin, an artifact and quite possibly a holy text. Some say it is a historical record, but I have come upon information that speaks to the contrary."

"What do you think it is?"

"A book of miracles. An ancient spellbook, young man, a tome of magic to rival any others seen before or since. Most importantly, an outline of the ancient rituals of the Uxidin, the history behind their direct link to the Creator, and much, much more."

"You would want such a book?" Valyrie asked. "The Arcanists don't deal in magic."

Cedric scoffed. "I only wish to possess it for its significance. Such a piece would be a prized addition to the guild's assortment of rare and wondrous artifacts."

Brice stepped forward with a puzzled expression. "What does this have to do with the ring?"

"The ring? Everything, of course. The stealing of men's essences is central to several of the rituals."

"How do you know all this?" Laedron crossed his arms. "Are you just venturing guesses?"

"Guesses?" Cedric pointed at the strewn papers on the floor. "These texts are my life's study. Uxidin writings, Zyvdredi ponderings, and even a few documents written by early Arcanists. Some of them speak of capturing life force and using it, but I didn't know how until you showed me this ring."

"Do you know where we could find an Uxidin?"

Cedric laughed. "Find one? If I did, do you think I would have been lingering in this basement for years?"

Laedron, insulted by the man's laughter, turned his back and stepped away.

Valyrie asked, "Have you ever heard of Farrah Harridan?"

"Harridan? No, I should think not. Who is that?"

"A writer of tales," she said.

Cedric shook his head. "Tales? I have no time for tales, girl. Works of fiction will do little more than waste my time, time that would be better spent in studious research."

"Fiction may hold the answers you seek, but you must indulge yourself to find them." She produced her book, flipped to a marked page, and handed it over. "Read for yourself."

Cedric nonchalantly scanned the pages, then seemed to focus on the words, whispering them as he read. After flipping through a few pages, he looked up. "Creator! Do you know what this means?"

"Yes." Brice smiled. "This is The Bloodmyr Tome."

Cedric sighed. "No, fool boy. The Bloodmyr Tome wouldn't be written in some common Midlander dialect. However, one thing remains."

"And that is?" Laedron asked.

"Whoever wrote this text had access to one of two things: an Uxidin or The Bloodmyr Tome itself." Cedric returned the book. "No one could describe so many of the ancient secrets in such detail without a guide."

"It cannot be coincidence?"

"Coincidence? Impossible." Cedric clasped his hands. "This person, this Farrah Harridan, has written a translation of the original tome or spoken at length with an Uxidin. To find the answers you seek, you must first find the writer of this book."

"Which task would be more difficult? We have no idea where

to find an Uxidin or this writer."

"I know that she was Lasoronian," Valyrie said. "I've read the books, and she constantly references her home, the south of Lasoron. At least it's something to go on, but I'm afraid she hasn't been heard from for quite some time. She may be dead."

Cedric rubbed his chin, then raised his index finger. "Might I ask something of you?"

Laedron shrugged. "And what is that?"

"If you should find the tome, I could convince Demetrius to purchase it. Such an artifact could be worth a vast fortune of gold." Cedric smiled. "That is, if you find it and care to part with it."

Brice extended his open palm. "When you say a fortune, just how much—"

"We'll think about it, but don't hold your breath waiting," Laedron interrupted, giving Brice a harsh glance.

"Of course, of course. I only wanted to mention it, to plant the seed, so to speak." Cedric walked to the oaken door. "If you have nothing else, I shall see you out."

"Thank you for your time," Laedron said, walking past Cedric and into the spiral staircase. "Best of luck with your studies."

"And you, too, young man. All the best indeed."

❧ Chapter Twenty ❧

The Next Leg of the Journey

On the way back to the Shimmering Dawn headquarters, Laedron considered the possible existence of The Bloodmyr Tome. He'd never heard of such a thing before, but given all the things that had come to pass, he wasn't prepared to dismiss the possibility outright. On the contrary, he presumed that such a book could and probably did exist. *Farrah Harridan. How does she fit into this? Is she merely someone who came across a loose-tongued Uxidin, or has she found the tome and used it for her fantastical stories?*

"We'd better discuss the trip," Laedron said, when they were all in the common room.

Once everyone sat around the table, Laedron stood at the end and said, "Any thoughts as to what—" The door flew open, startling Laedron until he saw Jurgen come through. "Ah, you're back."

"Of course," Jurgen replied, coming closer. "I told you that I would return this evening. Have you learned anything from the Arcanists?"

"Before we go over that, I must tell you something. Whatever you did to save my life has done something to me. It's changed me."

Worry crossed Jurgen's face. "Changed you?"

"I can't sleep, yet I feel refreshed and eager. What spell—miracle—did you perform on me?"

"The restoration miracle," Jurgen replied with a shrug. "It is designed to repair all of your wounds and remove anything hindering you."

"That would explain why the wine had no effect," Laedron said, glancing at Valyrie. He cleared his throat when she looked away. "No matter. I can't sleep at all."

"I apologize, but the injury was too severe to treat without the stone." Jurgen took a deep breath. "The stone seemed to make the miracle easier to perform, too. Almost effortless, in fact."

Laedron eyed him for a moment, thinking about Ismerelda's scepter and the ruby set in its end. *I find spells easier to cast with that rod, too. Does that gem also contain the essence of someone? Something? Ah, I can't even say what's wrong with me, let alone determine what that ruby may possess.*

"Is something bothering you?" Jurgen asked.

"No. Let's move on. You asked about the meeting with the Arcanists?" Receiving a nod from Jurgen, Laedron continued, "Demetrius Hale was little help, but he did send us to speak to

246

Cedric Tamden, a reclusive man spending far too much time in the library cellar."

"I see. What did Cedric have to say?"

"He seems to be convinced that we must find one Farrah Harridan, the author of an untitled book. Valyrie thinks the woman is somewhere in the south of Lasoron."

"What do you think, Laedron?" Jurgen asked.

Laedron paused, then swallowed deeply. "I can see no other possibility. We seek either an Uxidin or the tome. If we pursue Harridan, we have a name and a starting point, but if we go out looking for an Uxidin, we have neither."

"Better to go after a peer than a legend, eh?"

"What do you mean by that?"

"Oh, I have heard of Mistress Harridan, and I know of her works. The church has hunted these books to the point of extinction over the past several decades since we first heard of them, and we suspect that she's a sorceress."

Valyrie tilted her head. "Several decades? I thought they were far older than that."

"The style of writing is older than most contemporary works, but I recall their first appearance in our libraries," Jurgen said. "I would say they first started showing up about twenty or thirty years ago."

"And you suspect she's a sorceress?" Laedron asked.

"Yes. Her words carry a consistent affinity for magic, and she has twisted prophesy and scripture to better fit a mage's world view."

Laedron shook his head. "Cedric Tamden seems to think

otherwise. After reading through the book, he was convinced that she's seen or heard something to inspire her work. Whatever that is, we need to find it."

"Then you will seek her out, Sorcerer?"

"If she's still alive. If not, I hope we're not left walking in circles."

"I wish you luck, but I hope you will stay for a while yet."

"Stay?" Laedron shrugged. "We have nothing left to do here. You haven't started any more trouble, have you?"

"No, nothing like that. The consulship and I merely wish to thank you for everything you have done for us."

"You're welcome."

"It's not quite that simple, my young friend. The consulship has instructed me to summon you for an assembly two days hence."

"Two days? I'd much rather get underway sooner than that."

Marac came alongside and swatted Laedron. "Oh, come on, Lae. I know you're not one for praise, but take a little recognition when you deserve it, won't you?"

"The sooner we can find out what's wrong with me, the better."

"I'm sure you'll be all right." Marac turned to Jurgen. "Go ahead and make the arrangements, my good man. We'll be there."

Jurgen left, and Laedron gave Marac a scornful glare. "We have little time for ceremonies. I must know what's happening to me."

"We can't go without a plan," Marac replied. "At the least, they'll probably pay us something for our trouble. We can't go without supplies, either, Lae."

"Very well." Laedron took a seat at the head of the table. "Let us discuss our next step, then."

"If we're to go to Lasoron, we must decide where." Valyrie retrieved a map from a nearby bookcase and spread it across the table. "In the south, there is but one major city—Nessadene. It lies on the coast of the Sea of Pillars. Aldrissa is a small logging village just west of the city, but it's unlikely that a writer as skilled as Harridan would be there."

Laedron smiled, remembering his little fishing town of Reven's Landing and the fact that he, his mother, and his sister—all gifted mages—lived there. "Of course, no one of any importance could be in a place like that."

Valyrie glanced at him, seeming to notice the insult she'd cast. "Forgive me—"

"No, think nothing of it," Laedron said. "You're probably right. After all, nothing world changing ever happened to my family while we were there. I would doubt something as mystical as The Bloodmyr Tome, or an Uxidin, for that matter, would be in a logging village. Even Ismerelda hid herself in a sizable city."

"How will we travel?" Marac asked.

"The same way we got to Azura. Along the roads."

Valyrie crossed her arms and leaned back in her seat. "There is another way."

"If you mean by magic, it's dangerous." Laedron shook his head. "No, it must be by land."

"Going by land presents several problems," Marac said.

"What sorts of problems?" Laedron asked.

"Well, for one, highwaymen. Battles tend to draw unseemly sorts from all over to profit on the dead and travelers."

"And the war," Brice said.

Laedron rolled his eyes. "The Sorbians aren't going to attack again. Why would they?"

"Not the Sorbians. The Falacorans. Jurgen is sending a ship, but the message has much further to travel."

"He's right," Marac said, nodding. "Armies could still be moving along the roads, and word might not have reached them yet. We could be mistaken for enemy scouts."

Laedron threw up his hands. "Then how?"

"By sea," Valyrie said. "We could acquire passage on a ship."

"A ship would take us away from the direction we're going, and I thought only the Arcanists could sail the Sea of Pillars. You did say Nessadene lay on its coast, right?" Laedron leaned forward over the map, then struck the marker with his finger. "The northeastern end of the Sea of Pillars, right there."

"Yes, but that's what I'm suggesting." She traced the map with her fingertip. "We could convince the Arcanists to ferry us across the Sea of Pillars. We'd save days—maybe even a week—compared to the other options."

Laedron nodded. "The sooner, the better, and since Marac's volunteered us for this ceremony, we need every bit of time we can muster."

"You'll hold that against me?" Marac asked.

"No, no. I don't look forward to being paraded up and down the streets, but I'll let it go this time. The potential rewards would do much to further our task."

"All right." Valyrie rested her arms on the table. "We'll speak to Jurgen about getting passage then?"

"Yes." Laedron glanced at each of them. "What supplies do you think we'll need?"

"If we go by ship, we'll have little need for food," Brice said. "Some, but not much. That pretty much goes for any other supplies, too; if we're not to be in the wilderness, I don't see us needing much."

"Right, but I don't want to go empty-handed." Marac took a sip from his cup. "We'll need some basic things to tide us over until we learn the city, and travelers without supplies make easy targets for greedy merchants."

Laedron smiled. "Agreed. Let us get our things together and take care of any other business we have so that we're ready to leave as soon as possible."

"All right," Brice said, standing. "I'll return later."

Laedron said, "Wait. What have you to do?"

"I have to see someone one last time before I go. I'll be back. Trust me." Brice left without another word.

Laedron raised an eyebrow, then gazed at Marac. "Have you any idea what he has in mind?"

"No. I just hope he doesn't get himself in trouble—" He stopped when Laedron glared at him. "Sorry. I won't pick on him anymore."

"Have you anything to do, Val?" Laedron asked.

She stood. "I'd like to see my teachers one last time, to tell them farewell. And a few friends." She stood and went out the main door.

"Looks like it's just us, old friend," Laedron said.

Marac grinned. "A terrible proposition."

Laedron chuckled. "Perhaps, but it gives us a little time to talk, a luxury we haven't had lately. Things have gotten so complicated."

"Complicated? I'm no master of language, but I'd bet there's a word far stronger than *complicated* to describe our lives recently." Marac paused. "Tell me about this girl of yours."

"Nothing to tell."

"Nothing to tell? Come on, Lae."

"I think I'm in love, Marac."

Marac laughed. "Sorry, my friend. I'm only surprised to hear those words cross your lips at long last. She's quite a catch, isn't she?"

"Quite. We haven't known each other for long, but I feel something when I'm around her. Is that strange? To feel in love after so short a time?"

"You're asking me?" Marac asked. "Well, I guess you are, aren't you? No, not in my mind. A week or two is plenty of time to get the feeling, but now, you have to own it."

"Own it?"

"Yeah, you have to own it. Take the heart out of it and see if you line up with her." Marac scooted closer. "You have to look at it from the outside. Can you see yourself living with her for the rest of your life? Getting into fights and making it out with your skin?"

"Oh, we won't fight. I could never fight with—"

"You will. Take it from me. You'll fight, and you'll be bitter. There'll be times that you can't stand to be around her, but you have to decide beforehand if you think you can make it. No, you have to know that you can repair the breaches as they come."

"I just never see us fighting. Not ever."

"You'd better at least think about it. I don't mean to spoil things or get you down, but these things happen. Everybody fights sometimes. Laren and I have argued. My parents fight and bicker, but they make amends. That's what it is to be together."

"You and Laren?"

Marac sighed. "Yeah, after we suspended the wedding plans. She still saw me after that, and she'd always climb up and down my back about the drinking and my night life. We made up each time, though. We know that we're meant for each other."

"You're making me rethink this whole thing, Marac."

"That's a good thing."

"Is it?"

"I only mean to say that you have to know. When you know, you'll *know*, but don't do anything too hasty before you're sure. Take things slow. Get to know her well before pursuing anything permanent."

"I've never seen this side of you before, Marac. I have to admit that it's kind of nice."

"There's more to me than drunken wildness and chasing women I don't care about. You should know that, Laedron Telpist."

"Of course that's not all I think of you. I only mean to say that it's a pleasant difference from what I've witnessed lately."

Marac nodded. "We've been through a lot. The war, fighting with priests who turned out to be Zyvdredi sorcerers, and the heartache. Every day that passes, I worry that I'll never see Laren again."

"You'll see her. I'm sure of it."

"I hope so."

"Enough of this talk for now," Laedron said. "Why don't we go for a walk?"

"A walk?"

"Yes, a walk. Have you forgotten how?"

Marac stood. "I only wonder why."

"With everything that's happened, we've never been able to take in the sights. The city bears many places to see, and we may not have a chance to visit here again."

"All right. It could be nice."

"That's the spirit," Laedron said, opening the door.

Marac followed him outside. "Where do you want to go?"

"We've seen most of the Ancient Quarter, and I'd rather go somewhere a bit more secular, to tell you the truth."

"Secular?"

"To get away from the religious themes for a time." Laedron started walking. "The city's covered with symbols of Azura, but there must be somewhere that doesn't exist as a tribute to her."

"We *are* in the capital of the Heraldan Theocracy. It may be difficult to find what you seek."

"The university wasn't bad, only a few Azuran Stars here and there. How about the seaside?"

"The city doesn't extend all the way to the sea, but the channel runs along the north end. Want to try there?"

"It's worth taking a look." Laedron turned onto a boulevard

leading north.

They crested the last hilltop before the Heraldan Channel, and Laedron could see a number of masts rising above the roofs lining the water. "Seems the blockade's been lifted."

"How can you tell?"

Laedron pointed at the masts in the distance. "The flags. I recognize the Cael'Brilland banner, but not the others. I do know they don't belong to the theocracy, though."

"Well, you know what they say."

"What's that?"

"Where there's a Cael'brillander, keep a watch on the keg." Marac laughed.

"Are you sure? I could have sworn I heard that before, but it was said about a Reven."

Marac poked him. "Ah, Lae... they'd be right about that, too."

✎ Chapter Twenty-One ✍

The Lives We Lead

Brice followed the boulevard to the Ancient Quarter, taking note of the spectacles he saw along the way. The people had already begun their peace celebrations, and the entire city seemed to boast a pleasant, happy aura. Jubilant relief showed in the faces of every man, woman, and child he passed. Every cart was full of goods and the merchants handed out baked rolls at no cost to anyone who wanted one, including Brice. When he reached the entrance to the Ancient Quarter, he tossed a couple of the rolls into a bush, unable to stuff any more into his stomach.

Arriving at the former residence of Vicar Forane, he spotted a militia guard standing post at the front door. "Have you seen Collette?"

"Who?" The guard swayed a bit, probably from an ache in his feet after standing guard for quite some time. "I don't know any

Collette."

"The servant girl who resided here," Brice said. "What has become of her?"

"Ah, yes. You may want to speak with Commander Wilkans outside the gate." The guard pointed at the portcullis behind Brice. "I remember mention of a girl, but I don't know where she went. I only know that she's not here."

Brice turned and walked to the nearby militia headquarters. After passing through the front entry, he ascended to the third floor and knocked on the heavy wooden door still bearing Master Greathis's name.

"Come in," a muffled voice said.

Opening the door, Brice glanced at the boxes and crates all over the room. "Master Wilkans?"

"Yes. Come, have a seat."

Brice sat in one of the two empty chairs in front of the desk. "Moving things around?"

"Master Greathis's things. I'm preparing them for shipment back to his relatives in Falacore."

"I won't waste your time, then. I seek Forane's servant girl. Her name is Collette."

"And what, pray tell, for? She's suffered greatly at Forane's hands, and I'm not inclined to let anyone trouble her any further."

"I want to thank her for what she's done. She was just as important as the rest of us in revealing Forane's plans and stopping the Drakars." Brice tried to think of something better because Wilkans looked unconvinced. "I won't cause her any suffering. I swear it."

"You're a friend of that sorcerer fellow, aren't you?" Wilkans asked, narrowing his eyes. "Yes, you were here just the other night helping us. Very well." Wilkans leaned forward and scribbled on a scrap of paper, then handed the paper to Brice. "Go on the boulevard west of the Ancient Quarter and take your third right. There you shall find House Steadfahl."

"House Steadfahl?"

"Aye, a manor house, and you will have trouble missing the sight of it. She comes from a wealthy, influential family. Pity that her father passed while she was imprisoned in Forane's house. Double the torture in my mind."

"Thank you," Brice said, rising and heading for the door.

* * *

Brice found the mansion with little difficulty. The house consisted of two wings attached by a great hall through the center which ran parallel to the street. Two massive chimneys stood at the far ends, and smoke billowed out from them. He stood at the wrought iron gate and tried to summon his courage. *It won't get any easier than right now. What's the worst she can do?*

The creaking of the gate set his nerves on edge, heightening his anxiety. He only hoped that he could reach the front door before anyone saw him from one of the second-story windows. Relieved at reaching the awning without any apparent notice of his arrival, Brice rapped on the door. He quickly groomed his hair, then spit in his hand and used it to wipe away any dirt he might have had on his face.

Brice threw his hands back down to his sides when the door opened. "Evening, sire. Might I speak with Collette of Steadfahl?"

The butler, his nose fixed permanently in the air, asked, "And what business have you with her?"

I've come all this way and gone through all this trouble to be stopped by a man wearing a tight suit and wielding a snobby accent? Brice considered whether he should be polite and ask again, or if he should demand her presence and state in a clear and loud voice that he wouldn't be insulted by the likes of a butler.

Before he could decide on how to respond, Collette appeared at the bannister above the butler and said, "Let him in. He's no trouble."

No trouble? I guess that's better than 'an unbearable pain.' The butler stood aside, and Brice entered the house.

Collette was dressed in all the finery of a young noble. She wore a dress made from silk or some equally fine material, gold and silver jewelry, and sparkling shoes that drew Brice's eye. "Miss Steadfahl—"

"After what has passed, call me Collette, but I don't know what to call you."

Thinking back, Brice realized that he'd never told her his name. "Brice Warren of Reven's Landing."

"That will be all, Percy." The butler bowed, and Collette descended the stairs. "Reven's Landing, you say? I can't say that I've ever heard of it."

"It's a small village in the west of Sorbia."

She smiled. "A week ago, revealing such would have landed you in a jail to rot."

"Then, I guess I'd better be glad it's not a week ago. I only came to thank you for what you did."

"You thanked me already."

"Yes, but we were in quite a hurry. I just wanted to tell you that before I leave, and I wanted you to know that we all— Sorbians, Heraldans, Falacorans, and all the rest—appreciate the favor you did for us."

"Think nothing of it. You did a service for me, so we're even."

"For you?"

"Yes, of course. You got me out of that house, out of the clutches of that terrible woman. I'm free again because of you and your friends."

"Then, we're even."

"What will you do now?" Collette asked.

"We must go to Lasoron."

"You just said that you're from Sorbia. Why Lasoron? Won't you return home?"

"One of our party has some unanswered questions, and he seems to think the answers are there."

"Then I wish you luck in your journey," she said, turning to the stairs. "I appreciate your stopping by."

"That's it?"

She looked back. "What do you mean?"

"No favor? Not even a kiss?" Brice stared at the floor. "I was always told that knights were supposed to get things like that."

She put her hands on her hips. "You're a knight?"

He bobbed his head, and she turned back to him. She ran her fingers through his hair, and he closed his eyes in anticipation of a kiss.

"Ouch!" He reeled from the slap.

"There. Now you have something to take with you on your journey."

"Did you have to hit me so hard?" He rubbed the side of his face.

"This is no fairy tale, and you're no knight in shining armor. You think I would go around kissing any man who fancied me? My father met his end for doing just that!"

"I'm sorry if I offended—"

"I appreciate what you've done for me, but assume nothing more."

"Then I will only say that I'm glad you didn't turn us over to Forane. Good day, miss." He turned and opened the door.

"Wait, Brice. I'm sorry. I was too harsh with you."

"I couldn't agree with you more."

She sighed. "I don't know how to feel. I miss my father, but he caused me insurmountable grief. That's not your fault, and you don't deserve my ire."

He didn't know exactly what to say in reply. So he waited for her to speak again.

"Here," she said, slipping an iron ring off her finger. "I bestow upon you this ring, a symbol of my favor."

He took it and gave her a deep bow. "M'lady."

"Be careful out in the wide world, Sir Brice. If you should find yourself in Azura again, pay me a visit and tell me of your travels."

"Of course." He smiled, then went through the door and closed it behind him.

This knight business is hard work, he mused, the sting of the slap still fresh on his cheek. *I couldn't resist seeing her one last time, though. Maybe we will meet again.*

* * *

Laedron and Marac entered the Shimmering Dawn headquarters, and Laedron noticed that the long table had been filled with a feast—a variety of fresh vegetables, meats, and desserts. Brice had returned sometime earlier, and he was busy indulging himself, along with Piers and Caleb.

"Are we invited?" Laedron asked.

Around a mouthful of food, Piers replied, "Dig in."

Marac sat and grabbed a cut of beef from a serving platter. "We have much to thank you for, Master Piers."

"No, no. We should be thanking you. If not for you, we would still be lurking in the shadows, biding our time until the army could reach us."

"That was your plan?"

"We suspected for quite some time that the Heraldans would be unable to summon the assistance of anyone other than the Falacorans." Piers popped a slice of tomato into his mouth. "It would have been bloody, but the Falacorans would have been forced to retreat."

Marac shrugged. "You sound rather confident of that."

"You think it would have gone another way?"

"I saw the battle to the north, and both sides were nearly annihilated. The Sorbian army would have had its hands full for years, and that's if they could set a siege."

"Perhaps, but we have no need to worry about such things now."

"Yes," Laedron said. "Fenric should be close to Morcaine by now with the terms of peace if he hasn't arrived already."

Brice looked up from his plate. "We can only hope."

"What did you go do, anyway?" Marac asked. "What in the heavens could you have to do here that doesn't involve the order?"

"I had to say goodbye to someone."

"Who?"

"A girl named Collette." Brice took a bite of mutton and chased it with some wine. "What? You think I'm incapable of doing something without your watchful eye?"

Marac glanced at Laedron, then said, "No, of course not."

"Good," Brice said, rising. "See you in the morning."

Having finished his meal, Laedron stood once Brice had left. "I'm going to get some rest, too, if I can."

"Goodnight, friend," Piers said.

* * *

An hour or more passed, and Laedron lay awake, staring at the ceiling. *Why can't I sleep? After two whole days of being awake, I don't tire? What sort of cruel joke is this?*

A knock on the door broke his train of thought. He sprang out of bed, opened the door, and saw Valyrie standing in the darkened hall outside.

"I was wondering if I could come see you for a while,"

Valyrie said.

He opened the door the rest of the way. "Certainly. Come in."

"I'm anxious about the journey," she said. "I've traveled with Da before, but never outside the country."

"It's nothing major," Laedron said, closing the door behind her. "I can see why you might be nervous. I was nervous when we left Sorbia. But the feeling will pass."

"I'm glad that you think so. The churning of my stomach says otherwise."

"It'll pass. Trust me."

She smiled. "You're having trouble sleeping again?"

"You can tell?" he asked, letting out a laugh.

"We could talk for a while if you want. Maybe that will help."

Laedron was willing to try anything, so he nodded. "Do you think the war—"

"I'd rather speak personally." She sat beside him. "We've all talked at length about the war and the Drakars. I would prefer a change."

"All right."

She folded her hands in her lap. "Tell me about Ismerelda."

"Ismerelda?"

"Surely you know of whom I speak."

"Yes, yes. Of course. She was an Uxidin and a gifted sorceress. Taught me much of what I know of magic."

"Could you describe her to me? I'd like to get a mental picture of her."

"Fair skin and slender, long golden hair, and a remarkable beauty. Centuries old, yet eternally youthful." He tried to

265

remember her the way he'd seen her in the boarding house in Morcaine. "She always had a close eye to detail, and she spoke, walked, and dressed as a noble would."

"Did you desire her?" Valyrie asked.

Laedron tried to swallow the massive lump in his throat. "What do you mean?"

"Plainly, did you want her?"

"I... well, I..." He had seen that look in another woman's eyes. It matched a gaze his mother had given him before, and it always resulted in silence and stuttering until Laedron finally came clean with the truth. "I did have an attraction, but it could not have been. Though she appeared young, she was far older than I was. Though I felt a physical attraction, I would never have pursued anything with her."

"Had she been younger, would you have considered it?"

Laedron shook his head. "Why speculate on things that do not matter?"

"I only ask to understand you better."

"Very well," Laedron said, sighing. "If she'd been younger, I still wouldn't have tried for her hand."

"Why?"

"For starters, we were too different, and knowing that she was Uxidin, our life together would have been riddled with confusion and hardships. Uxidin are immortal, Val; I would have grown old and died while she would have remained young and beautiful forever. A long, cruel torture for both of us. Now, will you tell me why you ask?"

"I worry."

266

"What about?"

"I've grown close to you, but strange things are happening to you. My book tells of strange rituals, and it's unsettling."

"What does your question have to do with that though?"

"Jurgen's spell restored your body—made you perfect, in fact —and you've not been able to sleep at all. What if the spell has done more than that?"

"Plainly, Val," Laedron said. "Tell me what truly concerns you."

"Just what you said. If his spell has made you immortal, then what concern would you have for me? How could we be together if you had to watch me grow old?"

"Nonsense. Your book never said I would live forever."

"Not all things are written in books," she said, a tear dripping from her eye. "I feel like everything and everyone I care about will be snatched away. Just like the story of Azura and Tristan, a forbidden love that was never to be, a love destroyed by immortality and that awful torment of which you spoke."

"It won't happen like that."

"How can you be so sure? You said it yourself. One of us ages; the other does not. A cruel torture?"

Laedron grabbed her by the shoulders. "We need not get ahead of ourselves. No need to worry yourself over questions to which we do not have the answers." His words apparently having little effect, she continued to sob until he said, "We'll find a way."

"What do you mean?" She wiped her face with her sleeve.

He thought about what Marac had said, especially the part about knowing for sure if it would work with a woman before committing to anything permanent. Looking into her face, Laedron saw the woman he loved. The fire behind her eyes gave him a glimpse of the fighting they would do in the years to come, but he didn't care because when he held her close, he knew that the tears flowing down her cheeks would wash away his mistakes. He knew that, regardless of what happened, he wanted to be near her for the rest of his days, as long or as short as they might be. Laedron resolved that he would always give it his all.

"Whatever may come, we shall find a way to get through it. This is no different."

She reached for him. He took her in a tight embrace and didn't let go until morning.

❧ Chapter Twenty-Two ❧

Order Restored

After another night without sleep, Laedron roused Valyrie from her slumber, and they joined the others in the common room.

"Good news," Jurgen said.

"Yes?"

"The consuls have come to the conclusion that we have been too harsh on our Shimmering Dawn chapter." Jurgen opened a scroll and read aloud, "Be it known to all that the Order of the Knights of the Shimmering Dawn, having shown bravery, courage, and loyalty to our prosperity and safety, shall be reinstated to the highest place of honor. Be it further recorded that the Heraldan chapter of the order shall henceforth enjoy the status of Most Holy, and it and its membership shall forevermore be protected by this declaration."

"That sounds good, I suppose," Brice said, then turned to

Laedron. "That's a good thing, right?"

Marac rolled his eyes, and Laedron chuckled and said, "Yes, that's a very good thing. It means Master Piers and your friend Caleb will be well taken care of in our absence."

Piers could hardly contain his excitement. "Thank you, Vicar Jurgen. You're very kind to have pressed them on our behalf."

"It was the only proper thing to do after the way you and yours have been treated," Jurgen replied, offering his hand. "Besides, I wasn't forced to press them too harshly. They are well aware of your good deeds and your dedication. One other thing." Jurgen glanced around at the common hall. "Beyond the status, possession of the Shimmering Dawn citadel is restored to your keeping, Master Piers."

"The citadel, too? Oh, this is wondrous news. I shall gather my men, and we'll be off as quick as a flash." Piers jogged toward the hall, then stopped and turned. "As for this place, the church may keep it. Make it a place of charity and community, for the betterment of the people."

Jurgen smiled as Piers left. "I'm thankful for you, Sorcerer."

"Thankful for me?" Laedron asked. "I've accomplished little compared to you."

"Without you, I would have abandoned this land to the iron grip of the Drakars. The war would have lasted years, and the theocracy would likely have been destroyed completely. You and your friends instilled in me the will to do what is right. For that, and for you, I am thankful."

What a strange position I find myself in, Laedron thought. *I have helped to save the same church that not long ago would have seen me dead.*

"You're welcome," Laedron said, giving Jurgen a grin.

Jurgen approached the door. "Ready yourselves for the morrow, my friends. We shall revel in your triumph and honor you. Oh, and one other thing." Jurgen tossed a small leather sack, and Laedron caught it. "Visit a tailor and tell him you need something to wear for the ceremony. Keep the difference for whatever else you may need." Then, he left.

Piers returned with a crate in his arms and a pack on his back. "Care to come with us?"

Laedron nodded. "Of course. Let us get our things."

* * *

Piers led Caleb and his men through the streets, and Laedron had never seen him in a more pleasant mood. Every street corner they passed seemed to instill more confidence in Piers until they arrived at a massive stone structure topped by a silver metallic dome.

"This is it," Piers said. "Our old headquarters, our headquarters once again at long last."

Along the exterior, carvings of the mark of the Order of the Shimmering Dawn were prominently displayed. Two huge oaken doors stood at the entrance, and they had been left standing open. Entering the great hall, Laedron passed a number of militia soldiers. Beyond the troops, he noticed exquisitely vibrant tapestries, which matched the thick runner laid along the center of the floor. He tried to recall if even the Westmarch keep, the primary headquarters of the order, could match the splendor of the place.

"They left it intact. No, they even made a few repairs," Piers said, glancing around. He set down his crate and pointed. "Remember the crack at the top of that column? It's gone."

Caleb nodded. "Seems they've fixed the holes in the dome, too. Not a beam of light coming through."

"I wonder..." Piers ran to the back. Laedron and the others struggled to keep up.

Piers flung a door wide, and Laedron peered over his shoulder. With gleaming armor and weapon stands abounding, the room clearly housed the order's arms.

Entering the room, Piers exhibited a wide grin. "We shall be able to restore ourselves to our former glory and equip our members properly. Today is a great day indeed."

"You'll be more careful this time, won't you?" Laedron asked.

"What are you inferring?"

"Only that a traitor got in, that's all. Are you forgetting Lester?"

Piers's eyes shifted shamefully. "Taking in Lester and some of the others we wouldn't have normally was a matter of necessity. With many of our men jailed or slain, we had to replenish our numbers. Aside from that, yes. We will take far better care in the future."

"Good. I would hate to see you undone by the likes of another like Lester. For men like that, only an appropriate amount of gold would stand between you and a knife in your back."

"Point taken," Piers said, "but let us not swim in the mistakes of the past."

Laedron nodded. "Very well. Are we invited to stay until we leave?"

Piers tilted his head. "Of course. I would never deny my brothers in arms. The residences are on the second and third floors, and you have your pick of living spaces until you leave. We won't begin recruiting for days yet, and we'll be sending news abroad for traveling knights."

"Traveling knights?" Marac asked.

"The Heraldan chapter prefers a good mix of nationalities in our number. It keeps us from being dominated too heavily in favor of one religion or political standing, and the Dawn Knights must remain loyal to themselves above all others."

"I think the place is in good hands," Laedron said, patting Piers on the shoulder. "You've seen the order through some rough times, and I can see you leading your chapter through the flames of the hells, no matter how hot."

"Thank you, Sorcerer." Piers looked past them when more men entered from the main door. "If you'll excuse me, we have things to attend."

Laedron watched Piers go over to the newcomers, and said, "Let's visit our new lodgings. Then we should go visit a tailor like Jurgen recommended."

"What sort of clothes do you think he'll prefer us to wear?" Brice asked.

Laedron shrugged, then opened the leather pouch Jurgen had given him. His jaw dropped when he saw the contents: two coins stamped with the Azuran Star and the words, "Platinum One," repeated around the perimeter.

"What's in there?" Marac asked.

Laedron slowly shook his head. In Sorbia, minted coins made of platinum were a myth, a fable told to young children to flood their minds with amazement and awe. Rumors abounded that the Sorbian treasury possessed such coins, and no one other than the king could be allowed to enter that forbidden chamber. To Laedron, platinum coins lay at the base of any nation's wealth, and they were never used in trading.

Taking the coin from the pouch, Laedron held it up for their inspection.

"Well, that answers that," Marac said. "Either he doesn't expect much from us or you can get some nice clothing for a silver piece in these parts."

"No." Laedron held the coin closer to Marac's eye. "Platinum."

Brice gasped, then he and Valyrie crowded close around Laedron's hand.

"He gave us a whole platinum to get clothes?" Marac asked.

Laedron pulled out the other coin. "Two."

"Two!" Brice yelled, hardly able to contain himself. For a moment, Laedron thought Brice might faint from the sudden excitement.

Piers glanced back at them, apparently alerted by Brice's loudness, and Laedron hid the coins back in the pouch. *I can't trust even Piers to know that we now possess two whole platinum coins, regardless of our relationship.*

"Quiet, you," Laedron whispered, glaring at Brice. "We don't want anyone finding out that we're carrying two platinum pieces. Do you know how much these are worth?"

"Of course. They're worth two platinums." Marac nudged Laedron and laughed.

Laedron rolled his eyes, and Marac said, "Oh, Lae, you should've seen your face. You were awfully serious."

"And for good reason. Never mind." Laedron tucked the pouch into his waistband. "Let's find a tailor. Know of any, Val?"

"For that kind of money? Only the Best."

"Yes, but where?"

"Only the Best."

Laedron blinked his eyes rapidly. "Yes, but *where*?"

"That's the name of the place. Only the Best *is* where."

He sighed. "All right. Take us there, then."

* * *

Well, she didn't lie. Laedron studied the ornate placard in front of the tailor's shop. Judging by the people walking in and out of the establishment, he reckoned that the business had earned its namesake because only those with deep pockets utilized the service.

Upon entering, they were immediately eyed by a man behind the counter. The portly man's walk was more of a waddle as he approached, his fat finger outstretched at them. "If you're looking for a privy, we have none for the public. Best see your way out the way you came."

"Is this how you treat all of your customers?" Laedron asked.

275

The man scoffed and tried to keep his measuring tape from falling off his shoulder. "I have no time for games, young fellow. Can you not see that I am busy? Now, see your way out."

"I was told that you were the finest tailor in Azura. I suppose we'll have to bring our platinum elsewhere."

"Platinum?" The man shook his head, looking at their clothing. "The likes of you with a platinum? I think not. Quit wasting my time."

Laedron produced the coin. "I suppose you lost out on a sale, my good man. Let's go."

"Wait, wait, wait! Don't be so hasty," the tailor said, waving his hands. "I'm busy, but I can take orders. Come, come." He returned to the counter.

Laedron grinned, then relaxed his face when the man turned around.

"So, my good people..." The tailor opened a ledger. "By when would you require your clothing?"

"Tonight," Laedron replied.

"Impossible."

"Impossible? Then we must find somewhere else to go."

"Wait, please. Let me explain."

Laedron folded his arms. "If you're too busy, then we must seek our wares at another shop. No amount of explaining will change that."

"I'm busy with alterations. Don't you see?" The tailor gestured at the numerous mannequins standing around the room. "There shall be a ceremony tomorrow, and all of my customers are vying to get their best suits altered in a hurry."

"What sort of ceremony?"

"Why, the consulship has announced an end to the war, and they have released this paper here. They've gotten the whole city in an uproar."

The man slid a poster across the counter, and Laedron read it aloud.

To All Citizens of Azura,

Your Holy Consulship Commands your Respect at a Ceremony to Honor Heroes and Celebrate the Peace. Respond Ye to your Steward with Haste and Reserve your Place.

The Azuran Star with vines and flowers appeared below the inscription, and the bottom of the poster contained details of the ceremony and the following feast.

"Then, you had better get your needle and thread ready, friend," Laedron said, returning the poster. "We are the heroes of which this notice speaks."

"You?" the man asked, his chubby face filled with surprise.

"Yes. Think of it, if you will. All of Azura was present to witness… what's your name?"

"Manfred. Manfred Shoffe… well, Manny is fine."

"All of Azura was present to witness Manny Shoffe's fine garments draping the backs of the heroes who saved us in our darkest of times," Laedron said, gesturing grandly for effect. Manny clasped his hands and peered upward as if seeing the possibilities.

When he could see a stack of gold sovereigns behind the tailor's eyes, Laedron asked, "You think you're busy now? Imagine the patronage you might receive after such a claim."

"All right, all right," Manny said, snatching the tape from his shoulder. "I'll fix you up fine. I don't have time to make anything from scratch, but you're all lean enough to fit some of my back stock."

"Back stock? Old fashions?" Laedron asked.

"No, no. They're in style, but not entirely custom. I'm sure they'll be quite fetching."

"How much is all of this going to cost?"

"The four of you? You did hold up a platinum—"

"And we saved the city, you understand."

Manny frowned as if the thought of a discount was abhorrent. "Fine, fine. Three-quarters a platinum, then. Seventy-five sovereigns, which means I'll give you twenty-five back."

"Seventy-five?"

Manny gave him a firm look. "That barely accounts for the materials and my hours of labor. Seventy-five is far cheaper than the regular rate."

"Fine, fine. Here you are." Laedron handed over the platinum coin and received the difference. The gold gleamed nearly as bright as the platinum, and he remembered the days when even the sight of a gold coin would pique his interest in the one possessing it. Holding twenty-five gold coins and still having another platinum in his pouch, he was richer than he ever had been, even with splitting the entire purse four ways. Opening the pouch, Laedron dropped the coins into it with a pleasant jingle.

"Who's first, then?" Manny asked.

Laedron raised his hand. "I'll go first."

"Very well." Manny turned to the back of the shop. "Larson!"

A boy came running up the aisle. "Yes?"

"Fetch my wife, boy. Tell her the shopping can wait. And my daughter if she's there. We'll need everyone we can muster to get these orders finished on time."

"Yes, sire," the boy replied, then ran out the front door.

Manny turned back to Laedron. "Come along, and we'll see if we can find you something suitable."

* * *

After toiling with Manny for an hour, Laedron returned to the front parlor of the shop, wearing the fine coat and pants the tailor had fitted for him. He had never worn crimson, but the dark red vest accented the black coat and the white silk shirt.

"You clean up nicely, Laedron Telpist." Marac stood. "I suppose I should go next."

"While I'm fitting him, change back into your other clothes carefully," Manny said, pointing at Laedron. "I'll need to alter the clothes, and my marks were made with great precision."

By the time Laedron finished changing clothes, Marac had been fitted and Brice was already in the back with Manny. "That was quick."

"You like it?" Marac asked.

Looking at the light blue vest and the tan overcoat, Laedron smiled. "Very nice."

"He had this one already done. Said a nobleman requested it, then cancelled the order at the last minute." Marac stretched out his arms. "It's a little snug, but it fits well."

279

"That it does," Laedron said, then turned when the curtain flew open to reveal Brice.

Brice shook his head and paced through the parlor. "I don't like it."

"What's wrong with it?" Manny chased after him, still trying to take a measurement of the sleeve. "Will you hold still?"

"I've made a pair of pants or two in my time," Brice replied, kicking his legs. "These will never fit."

"Trust me, would you? If you would just hold on, I will show you."

Brice sighed, freezing in place. Manny manipulated the pants around the waist, then tugged at the back around the knee. "Any better?"

"Yes, but how did—"

"Secrets of the trade. I can't give everything away, can I?" Manny pinned the pants. "Now, get changed so I might get started on her dress."

Brice disappeared behind the curtain, and Manny put his hands on his hips. "What colors do you prefer, miss?"

"Violet and pink, if you're able. I've always favored those," Valyrie said.

Manny glanced at the ceiling and tapped his chin with a finger. "It could take some time, but we'll find a way. The rest of you have a little wait on your hands."

"We'll remain here," Laedron replied. "She sat peacefully through our fittings, so we shall wait through hers."

"If you wish, but I'd at least recommend sending someone across to the tea house. Get me a pitcher all my own." Manny handed Brice a silver piece as he came out from behind the changing curtain. "Dresses can take much longer to get perfect."

Laedron nodded and looked at Brice. "Do you mind?"

"No, I could go for something to drink about now."

Valyrie followed Manny to the back, and Laedron and Marac sat on the tufted bench which ran along the front of the shop. Returning shortly with a pitcher of tea and some mugs, Brice took a seat with them.

* * *

Normally, Laedron would have become uncomfortable and drained from waiting so long, but Jurgen's spell apparently held strong because Laedron felt fresh and eager regardless of how much time passed. Marac had fallen asleep, and Brice, having plenty of open bench on his side, had lain down and stretched out.

Manny came out and slid the curtain to the side, revealing Valyrie wearing a deep purple dress with soft pink trim. Speechless, Laedron leaned forward, taking in her beauty. Though she lacked a crown atop her head, he likened her appearance to that of a princess. The dress fit perfectly, accentuating every curve and the lines of her body.

She did a quick twirl. "What do you think?"

"Amazing," Brice said.

Marac roused from his slumber and stared at her with wide eyes. "Beautiful."

Laedron stood and took her hands in his. "I think it's wonderful. Breathtaking."

She simpered, apparently embarrassed by their reactions. "Thank you."

"I'm surprised it fit so well. I'd planned to give that one to my daughter as a gift, but I have plenty of time to make another like it." Manny tugged at the sides of the dress. "You're very close to her size, close enough not to require any sweeping alterations, at any rate."

"You've certainly earned your keep," Laedron said, giving Manny a grin. "I can see that your shop lives up to its name."

"Thank you." Manny turned to Valyrie and gestured to the back room. "Lay it across the table when you've changed, and I'll finish everything up by nightfall."

"We'll send someone around to pick them up after dark, then."

Once Valyrie returned, Laedron led the way into the street. "Have we anything else to do?"

Marac shook his head. "A good meal tonight and plenty of rest for tomorrow, I'd say. Beyond that, I can think of nothing."

Laedron smiled even though he knew that the next morning would come after another sleepless night. *It could be worse. Combined with an inability to sleep, I could be fatigued all the time. At the very least, I feel wonderful, despite the fact that I feel unnatural.*

Arriving at the Shimmering Dawn, Laedron glimpsed a full table and said, "Looks as if the quality of the food has increased with the quality of the lodgings."

Along with the others, Valyrie gave him a nod and said, "I'll be in my room. Much to do in preparation for tomorrow."

"Agreed," Brice said. "I'll see you two a little later."

"Where are you going now?" Laedron asked.

Brice tugged on his hair. "I saw a barber on the way back, and my hair's getting long enough to irritate me. I'll return shortly."

Left alone with Marac, Laedron grinned. "Well, I suppose it's just us again."

"Just like old times," Marac replied.

"Do you think things will ever get back to normal?"

"To normal? Sure," Marac said, opening the door to his room. "The same? Not in a hundred years. I hope this war woke the church up to what can happen if they're careless."

"So long as Jurgen's there, I have faith that they'll do well." Laedron closed the door once he was in Marac's quarters.

"You believe in him, eh?"

"Of all the priests I've met, though there haven't been many, I think Jurgen's the best of the breed. Kind, well-meaning, and wise."

"The other vicars, weren't they well-intentioned?"

"Not really, not in the same way. They meant well only for their own country, their own prosperity. Jurgen's view is more centered on helping everyone and living in peace."

"If that's the case, I agree with him. I could live the rest of my days without seeing another battlefield." Marac took off his belt and leaned the sword in the corner. "I hope I won't need that for quite some time to come. In fact, if I never had to wield that weapon in anger again, I could die a happy man."

"You mean the fight at the palace?"

"That too, but the battle to the north was far more vicious, far larger in scale. I don't regret joining the Shimmering Dawn now, no matter how much I've mourned Mikal."

"Did you see anyone we knew?"

"Only Fenric. The others' faces blended to a blur. Too many to remember each one." Marac shook his head. "So many of them died while I watched. It was horrible."

"There's little that I can say to make it any easier to bear."

"You don't have to say anything, Lae. We've stopped it before it could claim anyone else."

"I never thanked you for what you did for me, for bringing me back."

"I had to." Marac folded his arms and sat on the edge of the bed. "I couldn't bear it, Lae. I had to do something. I couldn't sit there and watch you die."

"What are you saying?"

Marac cleared his throat. "I threatened Jurgen. I told him we wouldn't help anymore unless he brought you back. Now, you're… I don't even know what to call it, and Jurgen is filled with regret."

"I'm sure he'll be fine, Marac." Laedron sat beside him. "Though the act itself is questionable, I would have no hesitation in saving any of you the same way."

"And go against the Creator? The Fates?"

"If the Creator would look down upon me for saving you, then the Creator is someone in whom I would not want to believe. The Creator is life and mercy. I can't believe that a god symbolic of all of those things would be angered with someone trying to prevent the destruction of life."

"Yes, but we're not gods. Life remains in the hands of the divine, not us."

"Does it?"

Marac gave him a confused look, and Laedron added, "If we possess the tools and ability to stop it, does it still remain in the hands of the divine? Or are we to disregard the things we know so as not to irritate deities who cannot keep secrets?"

"Cannot keep secrets? What do you mean?"

"The source of magic." Laedron stood and began pacing. "Magic was taught to the Uxidin by the Creator. Then, when Midlanders came to these shores, the Uxidin shared that knowledge with the early settlers. If the Creator didn't want us to know, She should never have given us the gift of spells."

"So, returning the dead to life and making immortals is a wonderful thing? I suppose you could cure the entire world of death before you're done."

"No, that's not what I mean. Everything must be done in moderation, for things taken to excess throw off the balance."

"I don't know if I can agree with you, Lae. Who gets to decide who lives and who dies, then?"

"No one, Marac. We don't decide the Fates, but we can change what we are empowered to change. Given the chance, would you not take the opportunity to live forever?"

"What sort of question is that? No, I wouldn't choose that, and I'm sorry if that's what Jurgen's spell has done to you."

"You look forward to growing old? To dying?"

"It's the way of things. If the Creator made us, we are destined to pass away, one way or another. Using your reasoning, the Creator would have made us all immortal if that was the original intent."

"But we've been given a way around it by Her hand—magic."

"Please, Lae, forget this line of thinking." Marac stood and grabbed Laedron's shoulder. "I want no part of it."

Laedron, seeing the fright in Marac's eyes, gave him a grin. "Very well, friend. I'll leave it alone."

"Now," Marac said, with a relieved sigh. "Why don't we see if we can find some supplies for our trip? The gold alone should be plenty to get what we need."

Laedron nodded. "Lead the way."

❧ Chapter Twenty-Three ❧

Honor and Glory

Another sleepless night passed, but Laedron was forced to spend it alone. Valyrie, apparently wanting her privacy that night, had remained in her room the rest of the evening, coming out only to get food from the main hall, then returning as quickly as she had emerged. He and Marac had found and purchased supplies for their trip, then had separated the provisions into backpacks of equal weight. Afterward, Marac volunteered to retrieve their clothes for the ceremony, and Laedron decided to see if he could sleep.

Laedron got up from the bed and assumed that his sleep would never return, having spent an hour or more staring at the ceiling. With that in mind, he went over to the desk and pulled out one of his Zyvdredi tomes. *Might as well make the best use of my time. If I'm not going to sleep ever again, there's no telling how much I could learn compared to others.*

After reading the book and practicing a few of the incantations, Laedron stood, walked over to the window, and peered across the city. *How long had it taken to read that book?* Without impatience, tiring, or the light of the day outside, he had little concept of time. The constant rested feeling had diluted his ability to measure the time it took to perform the simple act of reading a book.

Returning to the desk, he eyed the other spellbooks. *Does time matter to me anymore? Am I truly immortal? Perhaps, but perhaps not.* Like a starving man with a newfound bounty, Laedron devoured the material, reading book after book and taking time to practice each spell—except the big, spectacular ones. By the time the dawn's rays pierced the window, he had finished reading every spell in his tomes.

"Creator," he whispered, noticing the light of the morning. Every bit of what he had read through the night was fresh in his mind, and he even believed he might be able to locate the tome and page of each spell without considerable trouble. *What's happening to me? The speed at which I read has been dramatically increased, and I can recall all of it without a second thought?*

A knock on the door broke his concentration.

"We'd better start getting ready for the day's events," Marac said, handing Laedron the garments Manny had fitted for him.

"Thank you." Laedron took the clothes. "Be ready in a flash."

A flash, he mused, closing the door. *By what would I judge it?* He undressed and put on the clothes, taking time in front of the mirror to ensure everything was in its place. Then he joined Marac and Brice in the hallway.

"Has Valyrie come out yet?" Laedron asked, straightening the back of his collar.

"Not since last night."

"Jurgen?"

"He hasn't sent for us yet, but I imagine it'll be soon. Every window along this road bears a banner or decoration of some kind. Clearly, they're preparing for a parade."

"Oh, what have you gotten us into, Marac?"

Marac smiled. "Me? You're the one who wanted to come to this city and do all these heroic acts. I only went along with you."

"You're blaming it on me?" Laedron asked.

"Would you two cut it out?" Brice folded his arms. "Being honored isn't anybody's *fault*. It's a good thing."

"If you say so, Thimble." Marac started down the stairs. "I'm going to wait for the messenger."

Laedron felt a rumble in his belly. *Apparently, Jurgen didn't block my anxiety with his miracle.* The sensation was not that of hunger, but of nervousness. Ignoring it, he went over and gently knocked on Valyrie's door.

He received a muffled, "Just a minute more," from the other side.

After fighting with the back of his collar for a while, Laedron heard the door open, and Valyrie stepped out wearing the violet dress. He couldn't believe his eyes. At some point unbeknownst to him, she must have gone to the market and acquired makeup. Her skin was pale with powder, her lips appeared full and bright red, and her cheeks had a blush to them. The moderate application had resulted in sharpening her beauty like a master's stroke upon the easel.

Happily, Laedron came alongside her and lifted his arm. "You look very beautiful, Val."

She slipped her hand underneath, resting her fingertips on his bicep. She smiled, holding on tighter as they descended the stairs. Piers, Caleb, and their men met them at the bottom of the stairs.

Marac gestured, and when Laedron approached, he saw that the white and gold coach from the palace was parked outside by the curb. A driver sat on the top bench and four militiamen stood on step-sides at every corner, and all of them were dressed in fine garments to match the occasion.

An attendant opened the side door of the coach, then lowered the step aid. Laedron helped Valyrie inside before getting in himself. Proceeding through the streets, the coach maintained a slow pace, and Laedron waved at the people gathered along the roadsides.

"I never expected this." Laedron then remembered the rather nasty conversation he'd had with the consulship. "I suppose I had better apologize to the consuls for my harsh criticism."

"You owe them no such thing for telling the truth." Marac leaned forward, pointing his finger at Laedron. "They owe *us*."

Nodding, Laedron leaned back in the seat, and Valyrie took his hand. The farther they went, the more crowded the streets became until the coach rolled to a stop outside the consulship chamber. The same attendant opened the side door and helped each of them down. When Laedron emerged from the cab, he could hear nothing over the loud cheers and whistles of the thousands gathered in the square.

Two lines of militia soldiers stood on either side of a deep red carpet that ran under the massive archway and into the chamber beyond. As Laedron and his party passed, each pair of militiamen presented their spears and held them high.

Entering the chamber itself, Laedron glanced at the gallery of consuls, all of them wearing their gaudy ceremonial garb. Jurgen waved and gestured for Laedron to approach.

Standing in the center of the ringed chamber, Jurgen spread his arms wide and said, "Our saviors. Today is a joyous day indeed." He wrapped his arm around Laedron's shoulders. "We have much to thank them for, and this ceremony shall be the first way we show our gratitude. The second way is in the form of this bag." Jurgen waved his hand at two guards, one of them carrying a leather backpack.

When the guard came forward, Jurgen said, "This is your payment for a job well done, my friends."

Laedron took the sack and smiled. "Thank you. We appreciate your generosity."

"We appreciate *you*, my friend." Jurgen turned to the consuls. "And I, as your Grand Vicar—"

The world seemed to slow to a halt, and Laedron couldn't help but smile. *The culmination of Jurgen's life. He made it.*

"—recognize these as heroes of our church. May a feast be held this day in their honor at the Vicariate Palace and throughout the city of Azura." Jurgen turned to Laedron. "Come, you will walk at my side."

Laedron followed Jurgen up a staircase to the Grand Vicar's

platform, then out onto the open walkway leading to the palace. A roar of applause came from the thousands gathered on either side of the platform. Jurgen kept the stride slow, the speed of his step in keeping with that of a parade, and when they arrived in the great hall of the Vicariate Palace, nobility from all over the city, perhaps the whole country, judging by the number, were gathered to welcome them. A series of long tables ran the length of the hall, every surface completely obscured by platters of delectable food.

Jurgen led them through the packed room. Like a ship cutting through the waves, Jurgen caused the gathered nobles to make way at their passing. Taking his seat, Jurgen gestured for Laedron and his friends to rest upon the plush chairs.

"The servants will be along shortly with food," Jurgen said, leaning toward Laedron.

"Congratulations are in order for you." Laedron gave him a grin. "The consulship deemed you competent to rule it would seem."

"Not to rule. To serve."

For the first time in my life, I have faith that the church will do good things. Laedron nodded at the serving woman as she placed a plate in front of him. *With Jurgen at the helm, I can't see them doing anything foolish.*

Exchanging smiles with Valyrie, Laedron nibbled at his food. He found it difficult to eat, and his friends apparently felt the same way because they all ate carefully. He felt the constant glare of eyes upon him, the nobles watching every move, every subtle gesture. *Now I know why royals look so weary. It's not out of boredom; it's to keep anyone from guessing what they might be thinking.*

Part of the way through the meal, Laedron detected the sound of music coming from somewhere in the crowd. The tune picked up, and the nobles parted like wheat in the breeze to reveal a band of musicians and dancers.

"For your entertainment, my lords and ladies!" the lute player shouted, strumming.

With his emphatic thrum of the melody, the dancers became animated. Though the waltz was tasteful and elegant, Laedron could tell that his friends were disinterested with the performance. He kept from bursting with laughter when he thought, *What do you expect, Marac? We're fortunate to see dancing at a church function in the first place!*

More people joined in with the dancing, but Laedron hesitated when he thought about asking Valyrie to dance. His enjoyment of dancing notwithstanding, Laedron thought it would be better if he didn't embarrass himself—or her—with blundering around in front of the entirety of high Heraldan society.

* * *

When the party had died down and he didn't feel as many eyes upon him, Laedron leaned over to Jurgen and said, "Might we ask a favor of you?"

"Of course. Anything."

"We require transportation to Nessadene. Would you mind asking Master Hale if we could pass on one of his ships?"

"I don't see him having a problem with such a proposition." Jurgen gestured for a page and whispered something to boy who

293

came forward.

The page disappeared into the sea of guests. When he returned moments later, he had Demetrius Hale in tow. "Master Hale, Your Holiness."

"Master Hale," Jurgen said, "we have need of your services."

"Whatever Your Holiness commands." Demetrius dipped his head, his hand over his heart.

"Can you arrange for my friends to travel by one of your ships to Nessadene?"

"Why, yes, Sire. We would have little problem arranging that. When?"

"In the morning, or as soon as you can manage," Laedron said.

"We have nothing going that way within the week, but we have spare ships." Demetrius tapped his fingers together, seemingly deep in thought. "The Galerunner. We can make it ready to leave before midday."

"Would that be acceptable?" Jurgen asked.

Laedron nodded. "Yes, that will do."

"Then it's settled." Jurgen stood, raising his goblet and tapping it with a spoon. Eventually, the room grew silent. "Let us have a toast to our friends before they depart. May their journeys be safe and carry them home to gentler times."

"Thank you," Laedron said, standing and taking a sip of his wine. Valyrie and the others rose, as well. "I could live the rest of my life gladly to never see such times as these again."

Jurgen patted him on the back. "Well said."

"Only the truth of the matter." Laedron glanced at his friends, then back at Jurgen. "May the Creator keep you safe."

* * *

Once he had returned to the Shimmering Dawn headquarters and his friends had split off into their respective rooms, Laedron was alone in his quarters once again. No quiet knock ever came upon his door, and he realized that he would be left by himself. *Does she find me repulsive?* he wondered.

Might as well get after it, then. Perhaps I can experiment a bit tonight with a new spell. But what kind, and would it work? Am I capable of creating something from nothingness? He licked his lips and stared at the blank sheet of paper.

Taking a lesson from every other invention he'd encountered, Laedron examined his tomes closely and looked for spells that might combine together in a pleasing manner. *I want to create something different altogether. Something never considered, at least as far as I know.* He scrawled notes, drawing concentric circles out from a common focal point. Then, he drew a line from the center point outward, intersecting his other lines.

I know a spell for every kind of energy, for every offensive purpose. He recalled all of Ismerelda's teachings in an attempt to compare the things he had learned against new ideas, new possibilities. Then he thought about the attack at the academy and how so many had died in the assault with no way to escape. *Escape. A means of avoidance or retreat.*

He began writing in his own spellbook. *In times of immediate danger, a sorcerer must be prepared for any possibility. Even when a mage finds himself trapped with no obvious means of egress, he must find a way out. Thus, I propose to study such a means by use of magic.*

Below the entry, he drew three circles . Then, he scribbled a black dot in the center of each one, and gazed at them for some time. Connecting the dots with a line, he put his head in his hands and considered the shapes.

An idea jumped into his head, and Laedron flipped open the tomes and searched any similar or related spells. With four books laid out before him, he glanced at the pages, then began writing again.

First, the subject must be made incorporeal. The lack of physical substance would make escape far easier. Second, the location to which one escapes must be well known and familiar—and probably nearby. Third, travel between the points should be instantaneous.

He stopped. *Instantaneous. Instant travel? From one place to another?*

Using a logical flow, he combined words of power of similar spells until he had produced a formulaic representation of the effect he desired. He stood in the center of the room and presented his rod. He focused upon himself and concentrated on the spell, but then, he stopped.

"What in the hells am I doing?" he asked aloud. He had been about to cast a new and unproven spell on himself, with the possibilities unknown and potentially destructive.

Spotting an empty candlestick on his nightstand, he focused on it instead. The candlestick sparkled with energy as he chanted, then it disappeared and reappeared a few feet away, hovering in the air. It plummeted to the floor with the clank of silver against stone. He crouched and examined the candlestick. He found no noticeable differences in it.

He concentrated on the candlestick once more and repeated the spell, focusing on the great hall at the bottom of the stairs. With a flick of his wrist, the candlestick disappeared in a sparkle of white light. He quickly descended the stairs and found the candleholder a few feet from the spot he had tried to send it.

Now, to test it for distance. He closed his eyes and pictured the common room of the former Shimmering Dawn headquarters. Casting the spell again, Laedron watched the glints of light on the silver until the candleholder vanished.

He took to the streets. After running for some time, he stopped in front of the old chapel. His heartbeat slowed, and he couldn't feel the burn in his muscles. In fact, he felt well rested even though he had just finished a run across the city. *What other surprises shall I face from this rejuvenation spell?*

Laedron entered the chapel and searched the common hall. The coals of the fireplace had grown cold without someone tending them, and the place seemed more deplorable without people and activity. He located the candlestick beneath the dining table and closely inspected it.

Finding the candlestick to be pristine, he sighed. *The moment of truth.* He knew that he had to cast the spell on himself, and it had to work to be useful for escape. After all, moving a candlestick across an entire city would give cheap thrills to a crowd, but the performance had little utilitarian value. He had to know if the spell could carry people across such distances.

He took a deep breath to steel his resolve and firmly grasped the scepter. Closing his eyes, he recited the incantation, waving his rod to and fro and imagining the great hall of the Shimmering Dawn across the city. *It must be somewhere I've seen before, somewhere I'm familiar with.* Though he didn't know if it would help, he tried to center his concentration on a spot above the ground. He would be more than a little upset if he appeared in the hall with half of his body in the stone floor or a wall. Once he was confident, he flicked his wrist.

The world was suddenly replaced by a torrent of swirling color, but he could see the buildings along the route flash as he passed. His entire body felt as though it was being yanked in ten different directions, and he thought his head might spin off at any moment. He caught a glimpse of the morning light before he vomited the contents of his stomach onto a beautiful rug, then his body heaved uncontrollably. Eventually, he lay on the floor, not even caring if his face was in the vomit, and he savored the cool stone against his cheek. The flashing colors still clouding his vision confused him and made it impossible to tell if he had arrived in the real world or somewhere else entirely, and he couldn't recognize the walls or the floor. *Maker… where am I? What have I done?*

❧ Chapter Twenty-Four ❧

Upon the Sea of Pillars

"Lae! What in the heavens are you doing?"

Laedron couldn't respond since his body was still busy convulsing and trying to expel food that was no longer there to expel.

Marac crouched next to him, putting a hand on Laedron's shoulder. "Lae, are you all right?"

"What was that?" Valyrie asked.

"I don't know," Marac replied. "There was a flash of light, and he just... appeared."

"Appeared?" Stepping over the vomit, Valyrie fell to her knees on the other side of Laedron. "Lae? Can you hear me?"

"I... made it." When he heard his own voice, Laedron likened it to a handful of gravel being ground into power.

"Made it? What in the hells is that supposed to mean?" Marac, with Valyrie's help, rolled Laedron onto his back. "What have you done?"

"A new spell."

"New spell? What kind of spell?"

Laedron turned his head and spat the foulness out of his mouth. Brice handed him a mug, and he took a swig. He used the first mouthful to rinse his mouth and spit, then he swallowed the next few.

"I call it 'instant escape.'"

Marac furrowed his brow. "Instant escape, eh? Looks more like 'instant regurgitation.'"

After taking another sip from the cup, Laedron felt his belly rumble, then he vomited again, doing his best to avoid hitting Valyrie or Marac. Afterward, he lay flat on the floor, staring up at the ceiling. "Looks like I've overdone it this time."

"That's an understatement," Marac said, reaching to lift him.

"No, no." Laedron waved his hand and wriggled away from Marac. "Not yet. Can't get up."

"Well, I hope you're pleased with yourself, Lae." Marac folded his arms and stood. "We're supposed to be leaving today, and you go and do something like this?"

"He's been restless," Valyrie said. "Completely unable to sleep. We can't fault him for trying to find something constructive to do with his time. Oh, Lae, I should've stayed with you."

Perhaps she hasn't grown cold to me.

Brice shook his head. "Yes, he's found a new way to summon

up two days' worth of meals and decorate the floors with them."

"This is no time for jokes." Laedron turned onto his side in anticipation of more heaving, but the dizzy feeling was beginning to subside. "Oh, my head!"

"Do you think you'll be fit to travel by midday?" Marac asked.

Laedron started to nod, but thought better of moving his head again. "I hope so."

After lying on the floor for several minutes, he pressed his palms to the floor and raised himself to his knees. The dizziness had subsided, and he was left with a light-headed sensation. "Such is the way with progress. I'll have to adjust the spell."

"You intend on trying this again?" Marac threw up his hands. "What if you suffer the same effects? Or worse?"

"I'm a sorcerer, Marac. This is the sort of thing sorcerers do."

"I can't see how anyone could find this attractive," Marac replied, glancing at the pool of vomit.

"We study magic and learn its secrets. The spells that I can perform now had to be learned and studied, and I cannot accept that what exists now is the only possibility. New magic remains uncovered, just as I've demonstrated."

Marac sighed. "Would you at least tell someone before you attempt something like this again?"

Looking at Marac, Laedron felt some measure of guilt for having performed the spell without telling them. *But they were asleep. I didn't want to disturb anyone.* He nodded, accepting the fact that his friends deserved to know his intentions. "Very well. I promise."

"Good." Marac helped him to his feet. "Let's get you cleaned up. Care for anything to eat?"

Laedron held up his hand, imagining what effect food might have on his upset stomach. "No, not just now. Perhaps in a while."

"Upstairs, then. A change of clothes and a wash would do you some good," Marac said.

* * *

By the time the sun stood directly overhead, Laedron had taken a bath, changed his clothes, and eaten a light meal—soup and some greens. Hearing a coach stop outside, Laedron and the others went to the open doorway to see who had arrived.

The black cab had a solitary Azuran Star on the door. After a moment, Demetrius Hale hopped down from the back. Laedron dipped his head. "Master Hale, I had no idea you would be personally seeing us off."

"Of course. I'll go with you to the docks to ensure you have no problems getting aboard your ship."

"Then, if you don't mind, we'll gather our things." Laedron ascended the stairs, gathered his things, and met the others by the cab. The coachman loaded their belongings into the trunk.

Laedron spotted Piers and Caleb on the front steps. "Thank you for your hospitality," Laedron said, shaking their hands. "Without you, we would not have been able to complete our mission here."

"Without *you*, we would still be milling around in the dark." Piers handed Laedron a small leather pouch. "Take this with our thanks. May it help you on your journey."

"What is it?"

"A bit of money we were able to save up. It's not much, but perhaps it shall be enough."

Laedron eyed the pouch, then tried to hand it back. "We cannot take this. The order needs—"

"You've given our chapter everything that we need, Sorcerer. Now, take this charity as a symbol of our appreciation."

Laedron nodded, then returned to the cab and climbed inside. He gave the Shimmering Dawn headquarters one last glance as the coach lurched into motion, then he prayed that the Creator would protect them in the days to come.

"Didn't you want to say anything to Caleb?" Laedron asked, glancing at Brice.

"Already did. We had a long talk this morning." Brice waved to Caleb through the window. "I hope things go well for them here."

"They will," Marac said. "I'm sure of it."

Laedron nodded. "With the Zyvdredi threat gone, they should be free and clear. What step they take next will dictate their future, but we've done all that we can for them."

"You've done more than you had to," Hale said. "More than I would have ever expected you to do."

"Why do you say that?" Laedron asked.

"A Sorbian Sorcerer? Coming all this way to free us from an unknown enemy? The theocracy would have lost the war, and you easily could have left us to the path of destruction. Instead, you came and did away with Andolis."

"No, we couldn't have sat idly by. Scores of our countrymen would have been killed, many more than we've already lost. My presence here is self-interest as much as anything else."

"We can be glad that your self-interest has matched up well with our mutual interests, then," Demetrius said, smiling.

* * *

The coach rolled to a halt near the docks, and Laedron caught a glimpse of the ship that would carry them to Nessadene, the largest city in the south of Lasoron. Laedron read the name painted on the side of the vessel. *The Galerunner.* Opening the door, the coachman extended his hand for each of them as they departed the cab, then stacked their bags on the pier.

"You've been a great help, Master Hale. We appreciate this special favor," Laedron said.

"And you, too. The ship's sound and shall carry you swiftly to your destination." Demetrius produced a pipe and chewed on the end, presumably due to a lack of fire to light it. "May Azura, the Creator, or the Fates, whichever you believe in, take you safely there."

Laedron raised an eyebrow. "A scholar such as yourself doesn't know to whom or what sorcerers pay their respects? The Creator, of course."

"The Creator, then. Customs and culture were always lost on me, my young friend. I apologize."

"No need. Farewell," Laedron replied, picking up his bag. Glancing back at the street by which they had come, Laedron thought of Jurgen and the trials and tribulations of their journey together. *Perhaps he couldn't bring himself to say goodbye this last time.* Then he glimpsed the white horses drawing a white coach coming over the hill above the docks, and his heart warmed.

The Grand Vicar's carriage stopped next to him, and Jurgen stepped down from the cab and embraced Laedron.

"I thought you wouldn't make it," Laedron said.

Jurgen grinned. "I wouldn't miss it for the world. And I have one last thing to give you."

"What else could you give me that you haven't already?"

Jurgen returned to his carriage, retrieved a scroll, and handed it to Laedron. "A ledger."

"A ledger? What's this for?"

"I spent quite a while this morning sorting through all of our old records. This ledger indicates the place from which the Farrah Harridan books originated, an address in Lasoron that may prove useful." Jurgen grinned. "It's yours. Farewell, my friend."

"Farewell." Laedron turned away and ascended the gangplank, giving Jurgen one last wave.

Valyrie hugged Jurgen before joining Laedron on the ship. Once they had all boarded, the crew pulled up the footbridge and untied the vessel from the dock.

A young man sporting the uniform of an Arcanist scholar approached. "Greetings. I am Bannelt, day navigator of this ship. Being that the vessel and the water upon which we sail belong to the Arcanists, I would be the one you should see for any question or concern."

"Day navigator?" Marac asked.

Bannelt nodded. "We have a day navigator and a night navigator, for we cannot watch the sea all day and night without rest."

Seems I would have been fit for that job, Laedron mused, thinking of his sleepless nights over the past week. "You're the captain and the day navigator? You seem rather young for those tasks."

"And I might point out that you seem a bit young, the lot of you, to be our blessed saviors." The young man grinned with a certain arrogance. "I would have thought that my peers wouldn't discriminate based merely upon my age, and especially not without seeing me in action."

"Point taken," Marac said, nudging Laedron.

"I meant no offense, and I apologize. I only mean to say that every ship's captain that we've met thus far has been well along in years."

"Perhaps that is a necessity on the open sea," Bannelt said, gesturing for them to follow when he turned. "On the Sea of Pillars, you only need be gifted in the navigation symbols which guide the way. The helmsman is my second-in-command, and he is skilled in the handling of the ship and crew."

Laedron glanced at the large wheel on the bridge, the man behind it carefully piloting the boat on its departure from the dock. "I'm intrigued to hear more about these symbols."

"I can reveal little about them, unfortunately."

"That's something I wanted to ask you about. Why must the Arcanists be so secretive? Why the special navigational code?"

"To protect the ruins of Azuroth and the security of the

theocracy. Things have not always been as they are now. In the centuries and millennium past, the Sea of Pillars served as a natural barrier to rampaging barbarian hordes and the intrigue of foreign nations. After the Great War, it served to protect the early settlers from many threats from the east, and we maintain these secrets so that the gains it offers will not be jeopardized."

"So, the Arcanists agree with Azura's use of magic?" Laedron asked when Bannelt stopped near the forecastle door.

"Not necessarily, no, but we must use that which exists to our advantage. Knowledge, science, technology, and yes, even magically created seas, can be exploited for our security and benefit." Bannelt opened the door. "We are faithful to the church, and we hold knowledge and science above any mystical meddling."

"Meddling? A true sorcerer is just as methodical and scholarly as any of the Arcanists I've met. What was that you said about judging people prematurely?"

"My apologies. I meant no harm with my comments. My only purpose was to explain our differences."

"The symbols, what are they?" Brice asked, apparently trying to keep the exchange friendly.

Bannelt glanced at Brice. "According to all the records we possess, the pillars came about with symbols across each face, and the patterns were unique to each one, for the most part."

Laedron furrowed his brow. "For the most part?"

"The patterns indicate our location in the sea, and it took years to find them and assign them a meaning."

"You don't know what they actually say?"

"No, but the patterns are indicative of the pillar you're viewing, and you use that information to determine where you are and what your next turn will be. During our training, we memorize the ones we'll need to know for a given route, and unless we are retrained or reassigned, we run that route our entire lives. All Arcanists must serve their time aboard the ships before moving on to bigger and better things. Some never move past navigation, and some like it that way."

Laedron stepped through the door behind Bannelt, observing the comfortable, albeit cramped, living space. "These are our quarters?"

"Yes. The ship doesn't allow for plush staterooms or fine dining halls due to its size, but I'm sure you'll find them suitable for a couple of days."

Laedron nodded, and Bannelt left. They each selected a bunk, but Laedron piled his belongings on the mattress instead of stowing them underneath. *It's not as if I need a place to rest.*

"I think I'll take a look around the ship," Laedron said. "I have some more questions for our host, as well." Exiting the forecastle, Laedron made his way aft where the bridge stood high above the water.

With a spyglass in hand, Bannelt said, "Begin your turn now. Two points to the port."

Without hesitation, the helmsman rapidly turned the steering wheel, and Laedron felt the tilt of the vessel beneath his feet. He joined Bannelt on the bridge deck. The spires and silver and gold banners of Azura grew smaller in the distance as they exited the channel and entered the Sea of Pillars. In the vastness of the sea, pillars shone in the afternoon light, looking like the spear points of an entire army aimed toward the heavens.

"Might I have a word?" Laedron asked.

"You'll have to wait. Another turn ahead," Bannelt replied. A few moments later, he added, "Starboard, five points. Quickly now."

Laedron was forced to grab the wooden railing to keep his balance during the turn. "Is the whole trip to be like this?"

"No, we have few turns as sharp as that." Bannelt called to the helmsman, "Straight and steady on until I tell you otherwise," then turned back to Laedron. "Your questions?"

"This sea is a mystery to me. Could small ships not traverse without being destroyed?"

"No. Even rafts would have great trouble making it more than a few miles."

"Why is that?"

"The pillars you see aren't the only ones. Come. Look here." Bannelt came alongside Laedron and leaned over the rail. "You can see the points below the waves if you look closely."

Laedron spotted sharp points revealed by the occasional trough. "Creator! How many spikes lie below the waves?"

"More than you could ever count. Enough to impale an entire army of undead," Bannelt said.

Laedron recalled the story Ismerelda had told him about Vrolosh's army and how it had been destroyed when Azura called the spikes up from the earth. The deluge she had cast afterward had apparently concealed the shorter projections. "And you know how to miss them all?"

Bannelt sighed. "As I told you, we're highly trained for our routes. If it were easy, everyone would travel the Sea of Pillars. It took the original Arcanists a long time to document the pillars and the safe passes through the water."

Nodding, Laedron said, "Truly remarkable. I can see we're in good hands."

"The best, if I might say so."

"How long do you think it will take to reach Nessadene?" Laedron asked.

"Tomorrow night. No later."

Not wanting to irritate the captain with a barrage of questions, Laedron simply nodded in reply. *I wouldn't want to distract him and cause us to crash into one of those spikes.* "I'll leave you to it, Master Bannelt."

"Thank you." Bannelt returned to the helmsman's side. "Oh, and one other thing. Meals aren't served aboard the ship; you acquire your food from the stores on your own schedule."

"The food isn't rationed?"

"No need. We spend so little time at sea that we would reach land well before starving or even becoming uncomfortably hungry."

Laedron returned to the forecastle, and upon opening the door, he felt a sharp pain in his hand.

Then, he heard a gasp, and Brice said, "Lae! I'm sorry!"

The blood poured from Laedron's palm like a dam that had given way to a reservoir, and he spotted a bloody blade in Brice's hand and a clean one in Marac's.

"What in the hells?" Laedron shouted.

Valyrie took Laedron by the arm and pressed on his hand with a cloth. "They were practicing—"

"Practicing? You've nearly sliced off my hand!" Laedron writhed in pain, and the cloth that Valyrie had pressed against his skin quickly became saturated.

"I'm sorry, Lae," Brice said again. "I didn't mean to."

"What were you doing practicing in here? You couldn't go out on the deck? In the open?"

"He was showing me a move. I'm—"

"Silence." Laedron shook his head, then moaned from the excruciating pain.

Valyrie snatched away the cloth, replacing it with a fresh one. "What's this?"

The flow of blood had stopped completely, and only a red smear besmirched the clean rag. Laedron examined either side of his hand in astonishment.

"Must not have been that deep," Brice said, crouching beside Laedron.

Laedron gasped, "How can this be?"

"Like I said, it wasn't deep, right?"

"No, it went down to the bone." Valyrie took hold of Laedron's wrist and turned his hand. "Now, nothing. Not even a scratch."

Marac pursed his lips. "The spell Jurgen cast. It must be."

Glancing at Marac, Laedron's jaw dropped. "I can't sleep, I never tire, and now I cannot be injured?"

"I don't know," Marac said, "but I think we should work quickly to find out once we reach Lasoron. I hope this Farrah

Harridan person can tell us something."

Valyrie shrugged. "I hope that we can find her at all."

* * *

The remainder of that day and the next passed without incident, and evening set over the sea for the second time. Laedron pondered the possibilities and mysteries of the spell that had been placed on him, unable to come to a conclusion about its full impact on his body and his life. He experienced the gamut of thoughts and emotions attributed to the changes he had seen, his gladness for being saved from death and his abhorrence to the undesirable side effects, his newfound abilities along with his inhuman faults, and the unknown with the realized.

❦ Chapter Twenty-Five ❧

Nessadene at Nightfall

T he last one," Bannelt said, pointing at the pillar passing the starboard side. "Straight on from here, we'll make the port of Nessadene."

"Good. I'm eager to get there," Laedron replied

Bannelt nodded. "I see that. My day's ended, and the night watch will be on to take you into the harbor. Best of luck."

"And to you. Thank you for your courtesy."

Valyrie walked across the deck. "How are you feeling?"

"Well. Better than I could ever expect at this late hour."

She leaned on the railing. "Do you think we'll find Farrah Harridan?"

"We can do nothing but try, I'm afraid. She's our only lead." Laedron ducked his head. "Do you find me repulsive?"

"What? No! Why do you ask that?"

"I've noticed you keeping your distance of late. You stopped visiting me at night, so I began to wonder if I had done or said something to offend you."

"No." She sighed. "I didn't want to torment you."

"Torment me? After what we've shared, how could you ever think that you were tormenting me?"

"I know that you haven't been sleeping."

"And what does that have to do with it?"

"In some small way, I thought that you might be upset at me for sleeping so well while you lay awake, unable to do that simple human act. I didn't want you to feel any worse."

He shook his head. "That wouldn't have upset me, Val. None of this is your fault. It's no one's fault. It's happened, and we must find out what to do about it."

"I agree, but I'm afraid of what lies ahead," she said, taking his hand in hers. "I've heard that the streets of Nessadene can be difficult for those inexperienced with the city."

"Whatever happens, I'll protect you. You need not worry about your safety."

"No, now's not the time for that. We must simply say that we'll watch out for each other."

"You doubt my abilities?"

"No, and don't be too sure, Lae," she said, resting her head against his shoulder. "We all know that you're a gifted sorcerer, but you have to learn to rely on us more than you do."

He lifted her chin. "The battles with the Drakars should have taught me that, but it took you reminding me for it to truly settle in."

"What happened with them? With Gustav and Andolis?"

Turning away, he said, "No matter now. All of that is in the past."

"I'd like to know."

314

"Why?"

"To better understand you. To know what you went through to get here."

"All right, if you must." He cleared his throat and took hold of the railing with either hand. "I found Gustav in the Pilgrim's Rest cathedral after he captured Marac and Mikal. I fought with him from his inner sanctum, up the stairs, and in front of the congregation. He was powerful, far stronger with magic than I ever imagined, but I survived."

"How did you defeat him?"

"I caused a massive chandelier to fall, crushing him, and I took my teacher's scepter back that day."

"And Andolis?"

"I never defeated him."

She looked confused. "But, he is dead?"

"The killing stroke belongs to Marac. Andolis had beaten me completely, bested me in magic on every exchange. If Marac hadn't been there, I would have died, and your city would be burning still."

"If your friend hadn't been there, you would have failed," she said, giving him a smile.

"You're right." He took her hands and gently squeezed them, then he looked across the sea and spotted the glow of light on the horizon. "One day soon, I hope that we'll be free of these troubles, that we can live our lives normally, like everyone else."

"With me at your side?"

Laedron swallowed deeply. "I hope that will be the case."

"You have no need to hope for it." She kissed him. "Hope is

only necessary when either heart is unwilling."

"Be that as it may, we have much left before us and many questions unanswered. I don't want us to act in haste, for we could face any manner of danger in the days ahead."

She nodded. "Very well. After."

Watching her walk away, Laedron sensed her disappointment and couldn't let that be the last word of the evening. "I don't want to hurt you, on purpose or otherwise."

"You won't," she said, turning back. "You can't."

Can't I? What if the only answer to my current condition is my death?

More of the crew walked onto the bridge after Valyrie returned to the forecastle. Without a word, they kept the ship on a steady course toward that ominous glow in the distant sky. *Nessadene.* He had been told that it was a large, magnificent city, and he would soon walk its streets and mingle with its populace.

As the city inched closer, Laedron spotted the tallest of its towers. He found it interesting that all of the buildings seemed to be of a square or rectangular design. Whereas all the places he'd visited before had a mixture of angular and round designs, he couldn't spot the first cylindrical structure. *Odd. Not even the lighthouse is circular at the base.*

Laedron stared out across the harbor, the glowing light from the city reflected off the gentle water. One chapter of his life had ended, spurring another to begin just as sudden as the last.

What sort of adventures will we see in these lands? And what dangers? Would Ismerelda and Ma be proud of all that I've accomplished, or would they be disgusted at what I've become?

Next in the Series:

THE IMMORTALS
OF
MYRDWYER

Book III

⚜ CONNECT WITH THE AUTHOR ⚜

You can easily reach author Brian Kittrell by the various methods described below.

On Twitter:
> @Brian_Kittrell
> http://www.twitter.com/Brian_Kittrell

On Facebook:
> http://www.facebook.com/author.BrianKittrell

On the Web:
> http://www.latenitebooks.com

On YouTube (author interviews, discussions, and more):
> http://www.youtube.com/user/LateNiteBooksDotCom

Through eMail:
> brian@latenitebooks.com

Through the Mail:
> *Late Nite Books*
> *Attn: Brian Kittrell, author*
> *P.O. Box 321*
> *BRANDON, MS 39042*

CPSIA information can be obtained at www.ICGtesting.com
Printed in the USA
LVOW100712130113

315479LV00001B/13/P